Lost Angels

CREDITS

Written & Designed by: Matt Forbeck with
John Goff & Paul Beakley

Editing & Layout: Matt Forbeck & Hal Mangold

Cover Art: David Cherry　　**Logos:** Ron Spencer & Charles Ryan

Interior Art: Mike Chen, Tae "Terry" Kwan, Ashe Marler, Chris Musto,
Andy Park, Michael Phillipi, Erik Polak, Jacob Rosen,
Mike Sellers, Kevin Sharpe & Loston Wallace

Maps: Jeff Lahren　　**Cover Design:** Hal Mangold and Matt Tice

Special Thanks to: Barry Doyle, Martin Forbeck, Joyce Goff, Michelle & Caden Hensley,
Christy Hopler, Ann Kolinsky, Dave Seay, Matt Tice, Maureen Yates & John Zinser

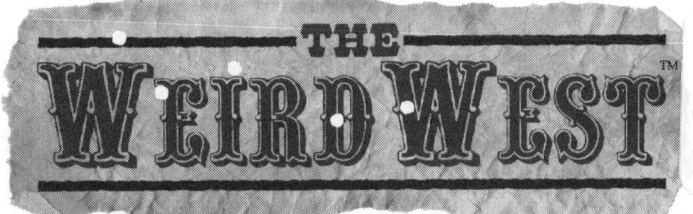

D1808133

Pinnacle Entertainment Group, Inc.
P.O. Box 10908
Blacksburg, VA 24062-0908
www.peginc.com or deadlands@aol.com
(800) 214-5645 (orders only)

Dedicated to:
Beloit Catholic High.

Deadlands created by Shane Lacy Hensley.

TABLE O' CONTENTS

POSSE
TERRITORY

Dear Allan:

Here's my final report from the City of Lost Angels, and I damn well hope you think it was worth my time--and the lives of the dozen operatives I lost accumulating it. This is a city under siege, and it's not safe here for anyone anymore, much less an operative of the Pinkerton National Detective Agency.

Don't bother pointing out that none of us technically work for Pinkerton's anymore. Even if the US Government's decided to "decline to renew our contract" and start up an "Agency" of its own, it's the same old song and dance. Either way, you're still calling the tune.

One of our operatives is a worker for the "End Times" as the locals call the city's only church-approved paper. That thing's a rag, the only redeeming value of which can be found when you're out of proper outhouse paper. I wouldn't insult even our most-deserving friends in the fourth estate by referring to it as a "newspaper." Grimme's people manage to make the people at the "Tombstone Epitaph" look great by comparison.

Anyhow, our friend took the time to actually typeset my notes and print up a number of copies for you to hand out to any Agency operatives unlucky enough to find themselves with an assignment in this messy little corner of Hell. He even managed to find some illustrations to toss into this pamphlet for those operatives who can't even handle the small words I write in.

Even if this thing might be pretty enough, the words its got in it aren't. Despite Grimme's efforts (or perhaps because of them), this place is a cesspool of the first order. Demons circle overhead, keeping watch over a city of starving souls trying to scratch out enough to keep their bellies from folding in on themselves.

That's right. The Reckoning's not much of a secret around these parts anymore, at least not to anyone paying attention, although its not quite as simple as that. (Is it ever?) I'm in total agreement with making this place a no-go zone for US citizens, and I can only hope the Rangers feel the same.

Anyhow, read this damned thing and pass it on to as many operatives as you can. If it keeps one more soul from getting lost in this Hell on Earth, then maybe it'll all be worth it.

Either way, I'm finally out of here, and if Hell wants this city, it can have it!

Adios!

Samuel Q. Hellman

Samuel Quincy Hellman, Badge #314

Agency Special Report #187: The City of Lost Angels

Alpha Clearance Only

Agency Special Report #187: Lost Angels, 1877

Top Secret   "Read It & Weep!"   Alpha Clearance Only

Chapter One: Welcome to Hell!

Call it the City of Lost Angels, call it the Celestial City, call it whatever you want. I don't care if you call it home. Lost Angels is the next-closest thing to Hell on Earth.

Things have never been great here, even before the Great Quake, but they've gotten worse since my last report on the region—a lot worse.

But I'm getting ahead of myself.

Please Allow Me to Introduce Myself

For those of you who don't know who I am, the name's Samuel Q. Hellman, badge #314. Friends call me Sam. You can call me sir.

Back when the US of A was hiring the Pinkertons to keep tabs on things for them throughout the western states and territories, I was the head of the Pinkerton National Detective Agency in California. Now that the government has seen fit to "divest" itself of that fine organization, I'm employed by the US government instead.

Of course, like all of you who are reading this, I'm now working for the Agency, the United States' brand-spanking-new intelligence organization. Under "intelligence," as you know, there are a lot of other subheadings, including squelching rumors of paranormal threats and executing any other objectives that might come down to us through the chain of command.

Basically, we're the nation's janitorial crew. Whenever there's a mess, we're sent in to clean it up and make sure that when we're gone no one knows we were even there, much less that there was a problem in the first place.

That's one Hell of a trick to pull off on a regular basis, but we manage. Nearly all of the Agency's agents are ex-Pinkertons. Hell, the big boss in Washington is Allan Pinkerton himself, so this apple isn't going to fall far from that old tree.

In any case, I'm in charge of California for the Agency, just like I was for the Pinkertons. And it's been one Hell of a job. I don't regret switching over to the Agency any more than I expect the rest of you do. The USA's my country, dammit, and even if I hadn't been asked to serve, I'd follow Allan into Hell itself.

But Allan, don't let that go to your head.

Why Revisit Lost Angels?

If you want to know all about what's left of California, this heap of rubble the natives lovingly call the Maze, dig through the old Pinkerton reports you've got until you find the one I did on this part of the world last year. If you don't have a copy, send Allan a personal request for one. He loves being bothered by field operatives about bits of trivia. Just ask him sometime.

Anyhow, once you get your hands on one of those reports, throw the damned thing out. It's not worth the paper it's printed on. Things out here change faster than the currents in the Maze, and that thing was already pretty darn useless by the time I was done writing it. Now it's only good for outhouse paper, if that.

So why am I returning to this subject one more time? Beats me. Why don't you ask Allan again.

Okay, Allan, I can practically hear your voice in my ear already. "Come now, Samuel. We're an intelligence agency. What good are we if we don't somehow gather that intelligence for people to use?"

Well, as those of you can call me Sam know, I'm a lot fonder of the other matters under the Agency's directive than I am of "gathering intelligence." But Allan, in his wisdom, had decided once again that I need to plant my behind in a chair and get to typing.

If that's sounds a bit snippy, it's meant to be. We've lost more operatives than I'd care to count while I knocked this thing out, and I've never been one to suffer that lightly.

Anyhow, how I feel doesn't change what needs to be done. Under Allan's direct orders, I'm closing down this region to any and all Agency operations. Simply put, it's too damned dangerous for us to waste any more personnel in this place, and we're not getting enough in return.

Sure, the city's lousy with ghost rock, but ever since Grimme handed down his Edict, that's become less important. Under his guidance, the people of the city have developed a deep-seated problem with representatives of any government—North or South—in their backyard. And they're not shy about showing it, often with a length of rope.

This is my last report from LA. After this, the city is closed, so if we're going to know anything about it, I've got to get it all down now.

Agency Special Report #187: Lost Angels, 1877

A Little History

When I was in school, I hated history. Why did I need to know about all those dead people when there was a great, big world out there, ready to be explored?

What I didn't know then is that the world's a dangerous place. The more you know about it, the better off you are.

With that in mind, I'm going to tell you a bit about Lost Angels. If you've heard some of this before, bear with me. It's not all common knowledge, so stick around while I catch up the slower kids in class.

The Great Quake

If you haven't heard about the Great Quake, you're in the wrong line of work. You're sure as Hell not going to have a whole lot of luck in "intelligence."

Anyhow, for the slow ones, the Big One hit in '68, and it knocked the better part of California into the sea. And I mean that bit about the "better part." The sandy beaches, the fertile valleys, the parts of the coast that you used to always think about when someone said "California," they all slipped under the waters.

All that was left in the Big Shake's wake were lots of cracked earth. The ocean rushed in to fill that all up pretty quick, and that left us with the series of water-filled channels that riddle the coastline today, a place called the Great Maze.

As you might expect, thousands of people died in the quake. But there were survivors.

Reverend Grimme

That's where the Reverend Ezekiah Grimme comes in.

Before the quake, Grimme was the pastor of a small church in the hills overlooking Los Angeles. From the few reports we've been able to gather, he wasn't much of a preacher. In fact, rumor has it he was a bit freer with some of the female members of his flock than was probably appropriate, but there's little way to prove any of that now.

Anyhow, when the quake hit, Grimme really came through for the folks in his congregation. When everything was falling down around everyone's ears—sometimes literally—he managed to gather together all the survivors he could find, and he led them to safety.

Of course, just because the people weren't in danger of sliding into the ocean where the rest of their neighbors had already taken up the lockers next to Davey Jones' didn't mean they were out of the woods yet. With all the devastation from the quake itself came floods, fires, and death.

It was almost like Armageddon in that little corner of the planet.

The worst problem these people faced was the fact that the disaster had destroyed all the crops and scared off all the game. The people that had managed to survive so far still had to contend with one other challenge: starvation.

Lots of folks died of hunger in those days, and there were even reports of cannibalism in the hardest-hit areas. Not where Grimme was, though.

The good reverend managed to lead his people to the only spot in the area in which game was plentiful and there was actually fresh water to drink. How he found it, I don't know, but he and his followers attribute it to the fact that during the quake he personally developed a direct line to God Himself.

Anyway, you can't argue with the results.

Agency Special Report #187: Lost Angels, 1877

You may have heard about the Men of the Grid before, but the ones running around these days don't have a whole lot to do with that first group. These were a bunch of cranks who decided that just because Grimme wanted circular streets he had to be crazy. (There are plenty of reasons why you might think Grimme's crazy, but this is an awfully stupid one to pick at.)

Of course, chances are these folks couldn't give a damn if the streets ran right up the sides of the buildings. This was just an old-fashioned power struggle of the kind we've seen ever since people first put two huts next to each other.

Anyhow, like many of the people who've challenged Grimme's authority in the past, these Men of the Grid disappeared under mysterious circumstances. As a nine-year-old incident, I doubt there's much to investigate there, but that's not where the story ends.

There's a new group of idiots calling themselves the Men of the Grid these days. Instead of arguing about which ways the streets should go though, these madmen just blow the damn things up. Buildings too. Apparently a group of them even got caught trying to blow up the Cathedral of Lost Angels, but that's a whole, other story. I'll get to that later.

Founder Grimme

It wasn't long after Grimme led his people to their promised land that he told them that he'd had a vision of a vast Celestial City (as he called it) built on the edge of Prosperity Bay, the very place he'd brought them to after the quake. At this point, after all he'd done for them, these people were ready to crown him king. Not a single one of them left to try his luck elsewhere. Nope, they all stayed behind to help build the city, transforming the shattered land into "a glorious haven for all those seeking shelter with the Lord."

As the story goes, before things got too far along, Grimme drew up plans for the city that he claimed he had been able to reproduce from his dream. Like most planned cities, the streets were orderly and regularly spaced, unlike the older cities Back East, the ones that just grew from nothing into something. The strange thing about this city though, was that the streets were laid out like a gigantic wheel.

This was actually when the first rift happened in Grimme's faithful, creating the original Men of the Grid.

Citizen Grimme

In the years after the founding of the city, Grimme set himself up as the benevolent father of his Lost Angels, the shepherd to the grateful flock. And he's fleeced them good, you can count on that.

With contributions to his Church of Lost Angels—an organization of which Grimme is the supreme head of, recognizing no other power but that of the Lord Himself—Grimme managed not only to build himself a city, crowned by a cathedral, but also one Hell of a house. Grimme Manor sits right at the one o'clock position of the Golden Circle, right in the heart of the city. It's the most lavish place west of the Mississippi, which—considering the number of people starving in this place—turns my stomach. His followers seem to think he deserves it well enough though.

Apparently he also deserves the luxury Maze runner he rides around the bay at all hours. The *Charon*, as he calls it, ferries him back and forth from the city to Rock Island, the island prison in the middle of the bay. I don't know what he's doing out there all the time, but it can't be any damned good.

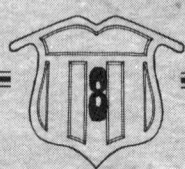

Chapter Two:

Ready for Armageddon

81

Anyhow, if you want to know more about Grimme personally, pick up his autobiography: *Serving Your Fellow Man*. Of course, it's 300 pages of church propaganda, but if you can stomach it long enough to churn your way through it, you can learn a lot about how the man's mind works.

Either way, it's not Grimme himself who's all that important. It's what he's done. More to the point, it's what he's done over the last few months that's set the entire Weird West (as our friends at the *Tombstone Epitaph* like to call this wild land we work in) afire (figuratively).

The Beginning of the End Times

Again, though, it's not that simple. Let's step back a few months to Bloody Sunday. You probably read about it in all the papers, and if you're lucky you might have read my preliminary report on that incident.

Now that I've had a good while to poke my nose into what happened that dismal Sabbath, I can pretty much confirm what I wrote in that earlier report: I have no idea what in Hell went on there that day.

Okay, that's not exactly true. We do know that the incident (as Allan likes us to call these inscrutable situations we find ourselves investigating) happened at the height of morning services, right as Grimme was wrapping up one of his thundering sermons on the evils of sin and the wrath of God that awaits the unfaithful. (Say what you will about the man, he can preach!) At that moment, a dozen or more creatures burst into the church and starting dismembering the 2,000-plus faithful crowded into the pews.

As the saying goes, no two stories are the same, but from what I've been able to puzzle out, it appears that these creatures were actually demons, servants of Lucifer himself! Could it be that it's actually Satan behind the Reckoning?

If so, Grimme fought on the side of the angels that day. The one thing everyone agrees on is that the good reverend stood toe to toe with the leader of these creatures and laid into it with nothing but his Bible and his bare hands.

And he won.

Grimme's Crusade

Of course, that wasn't the end of it. Once the bodies of the less-than-lucky faithful were carted out of the cathedral, Grimme went on the warpath. He was positive the rail barons had been behind this direct attack on his people and his city (not to mention himself).

By Grimme's way of thinking (according to his sermons at least, which get reprinted in the *Lost Angels Times*, or the *End Times* as that church-sponsored rag is known around town), the rail barons were finally closing in on the prize: Lost Angels itself. One of them had decided to launch a preemptive strike at Grimme, hoping to demoralize the Lost Angels, leaving the town open to be taken by one of the railroads.

In other words, the Great Rail Wars had finally spilled over into the City of Lost Angels.

To combat this incursion, Grimme decided to send missionaries out into the rest of the West, spreading his word and encouraging resistance against the rail lines as they slowly crawled their way toward his Celestial City.

This was the start of Grimme's crusade.

Agency Special Report #187: Lost Angels, 1877

Helltown

If you've been paying much attention to the world around you, you might have already run into some of Grimme's missionaries by now. You can find them at train stations, stage stops, and even street corners in nearly every major city in the West.

In their meanderings, they also make periodic stops in smaller towns, spreading the message of Grimme's brand of Christianity as they go, like some kind of religious Johnny Appleseeds. Most folks don't pay much attention to them, but they get some converts in every town, and so their following grows.

At least that's how it was going until Helltown.

Helltown's a dying little boomtown in western Nevada, and you wouldn't think anyone would ever give a damn about the place since the nearby mines played out. For some reason, though, Grimme got it into his head that he was going to build himself a chapel in this out-of-the-way spot. He sent a column of over 100 "laborers" in to set to work.

I say "laborers" because that's not the way our government saw it. According to reports from Agent Nevada Smith (now with the Agency as well), Grimme's craftsmen were actually soldiers on the warpath, looking to make a dent in the Great Rail Wars.

General Joshua Chamberlain sent off a well-armed column of Union Blue forces directly into Helltown to run Grimme off.

From there, things get a bit fuzzy.

According to reports from the townspeople, there was one Hell of a fight, with the Union Blue forces driving out the heavily armed "craftsmen." (Apparently they were gunsmiths.) Chamberlain easily won the day, but his victory was short-lived.

In the middle of that night, something came into town and killed every last member of that Union Blue force but one. The lone survivor was left a gibbering idiot who can only repeat a single phrase over and over: "The eyes. The eyes."

Of course, the townspeople saw nothing.

In the aftermath, the Ghost (who Allan had already made head of the Agency's Western Bureau) stepped up and took command of Union Blue's forces, folding them into the Agency's. So now we're apparently in the rail-building business as well.

Stepping up the Crusade

Once word of what happened at Helltown got back to Grimme, he immediately claimed that the wrath of God had cleansed from the face of the Earth those who would take arms against the Church of Lost Angels. He also dropped any pretense of not being at all-out war with the rail barons heading toward his Celestial City.

Basically, he called for a holy war, and the people of Lost Angels gave it to him.

More accurately, the members of the rapidly expanding Church of Lost Angels got behind him. As you might imagine, there were plenty of folks in Lost Angels who had little or no interest in going to war with six of the most powerful organizations on the continent, including—in effect—the governments of both the USA and CSA.

But that didn't give Grimme much pause. He immediately assembled an army of his faithful and sent them out to start tearing holes in the rail barons' plans for getting to the Maze in one piece. The bulk of Grimme's troops are his Guardian Angels, but they're hardly the most impressive portion of his forces.

Agency Special Report #187: Lost Angels, 1877

Top Secret   "Read It & Weep!"   Alpha Clearance Only

The Army of God

While I've not been able to get any pictures of this, Grimme claims to have actually inducted fallen angels into his army. You read that right: fallen angels.

Some of our operatives have actually been able to get into Grimme's army, and they've managed to confirm these reports. Grimme's got what look like honest-to-God, grimy-winged angels leading his troops.

In his sermons, Grimme claims that his Bloody Sunday victory earned him the right to call on those of God's shocktroops that had fallen from His grace. In exchange for serving Grimme, these creatures have a chance to redeem themselves in the Savior's eyes, winning back the right to return to Heaven.

Honestly, I find this hard to believe, but I've seen what look like massive birds circling over the Cathedral of Lost Angels from time to time. I'm not sure what a fallen angel's supposed to look like, but I've used my spyglass to look at these things. I can tell you one thing: They're sure as Hell not birds.

Now, I've seen a lot of things in my days out here in the Maze, some of which I'll be taking with me to my grave, but these things are something else entirely. As to what they really are, I'm afraid that some of our troops in Union Blue's employ are going to find out the hard way—and soon.

The Edict

To emphasize Grimme's new "if you're not with me, you're against me" stance, he did something I'd been dreading for months. He declared the City of Lost Angels to be an independent state, sovereign unto itself.

Grimme stated all of this in a document now known as the Edict, which he read from his pulpit on the Sunday after the incident at Helltown. The whole thing's full of fire and brimstone, but in the end it boils down to this.

Lost Angels' civil government (what little there was of it) was disbanded. The Church Court is now the only court in the land, the Guardian Angels are the city's only police force, and Grimme himself is the head of both the church and state.

All citizens of Lost Angels had to either immediately join the church or leave town. No exceptions were made.

Any visitors must pass a checkpoint upon entering town. There they are registered with the Guardian Angels and given papers of passage. Basically visitors have no rights at all under the new government and can enter the city only at the whim of Grimme and his representatives—in the form of the Guardian Angels.

All members of the church must carry registration papers on them at all times. If they are found without them, they're subject to arrest and incarceration. Also, as members of the church, they must follow all orders given to them by anyone in the church's hierarchy, including the Guardian Angels.

All members of the church are obligated to surrender 25% of their earnings to the church as a tithe.

This last one's a doozy.

Lost Angels is a sovereign city-state, recognizing the power of no other government over its boundaries, which extend up to 75 miles from the center of the Cathedral of Lost Angels. Any government which fails to recognize this new nation can immediately consider itself at war with the Lost Angels.

So now you know why the Agency's pulling out. Can the last one out shut off the lights?

Agency Special Report #187: Lost Angels, 1877

Top Secret   "Read It & Weep!"   Alpha Clearance Only

Chapter Three: Church & State

83

Of course, the Edict shocked a whole lot of people, not to mention the governments of both the United States and the Confederacy, which weren't about to go along with it. As the central shipping point in the Maze, most of the continent's ghost rock passed through the city at some point or another—not counting the stuff coming out of the Black Hills and the smaller strikes scattered about the West.

Over the past several years, both American governments had laid claim to the entire Maze, and they weren't about to let the jewel in that crown get away. Still, what could they do?

The fact is that while the North and South are still at war, neither side has the troops to spare for the kind of all-out assault it would take to unseat Grimme. Even if they did, getting that kind of force out to Lost Angels would be a challenge in and of itself. For now, Grimme sits in his den in Grimme Manor, scheming how to hold the power he's claimed is his. It's only a matter of time before this one comes to a head.

Civil Government Disbanded

You might think that breaking up the civil government would have thrown the city into chaos, but that wasn't the case at all. Grimme had obviously been planning this for months.

In effect, Grimme already had an alternate government in place. All he was really doing was dropping the pretense that anyone else in town had in kind of say in how the place was run.

Mayor Miller and the town council immediately surrendered their positions, which Grimme had practically given to them anyhow. They were instantly awarded senior positions in the new church government.

Make that read: bureaucracy. Grimme knew from the start that holding sway over so many people was going to take some paperwork, so he just asked the people already in place to switch over to the new church government or get booted out of the city. Over 90% of the people agreed.

The Law

Since Grimme handed down his Edict, the Great Maze is under no nation's jurisdiction. US Marshals, Texas Rangers, Agency operatives, and other unleashed law dogs have exactly zero authority in Grimme's sovereign nation.

However, that doesn't mean that these folks don't occasionally have business in LA. To paint himself the hero, Grimme allows traveling law men to register just like any other visitor. Because of their special status, however, they are assigned a partner from the Guardian Angels to work with them in their investigations within Grimme's domain.

The guest law dog has no authority of his own, and he must rely on his Angel partner in nearly all matter, up to and including permission to visit the outhouse. If the law man causes the Guardian Angel any problems at all or disobeys any orders given to him by any Guardian Angel, then he's forcibly ejected from the city—if he's lucky. Otherwise, he's just bought himself a one-way ticket to the Rock.

One thing I forgot to mention before is that only churchgoers are permitted to be armed within the city limits, yet another reason why most folks are happy to sign up with the church, at least in name. This applies to visiting law officials too, so if you end up there in the open, you've only got your wits to rely on.

Agency Special Report #187: Lost Angels, 1877

Dunston Checks Out

Of course, not everyone took the Edict lying down or ran out of town at the first threat from a Guardian Angel. The most notable of these folks was Sheriff Job "Hogleg" Dunston.

As the law officer who was duly elected by the people of Lost Angels—over Grimme's handpicked candidate, and much to the reverend's chagrin, I'm sure—Hog wasn't going anywhere. He felt like he'd gotten a mandate from the citizens themselves, and no pulpit-thumping preacher—not even one as powerful as Grimme—was going to kick him out without a fight.

Unfortunately, most of Hog's deputies didn't see it that way. They lit out of town like someone had stuffed a packet of lit firecrackers in their pockets. Only one man stayed behind, a faithful deputy by the name of Luther Crane.

Hog and Luther did their best to assure folks around town that Grimme's Edict was a load of horse apples, but they didn't have much luck. In fact, only three days after the announcement Luther was found dead in the middle of the Golden Circle, only yards away from the cathedral's front steps. Despite the fact that it's one of the busiest places in town, there were no witnesses.

After that, Hog took to sleeping in his office, locking all the doors at night and bedding down in one of the cells. By his thinking, it was the safest place to be.

However, Luther had left behind a wife and three kids, all of whom were immediately taken in by the church. Apparently the kids held the sheriff responsible for Luther's death, because Hog woke up one night to find they'd used their dad's keys to sneak into the jail.

According to Hog, he'd been handcuffed to the cell he'd been sleeping in. He was awakened by the kids' giggling, and when he looked up, they were in the process of setting the place on fire. Before the kids hightailed it out of there, they tossed the man a hacksaw, daring him to cut his own arm off before the fire consumed him.

Hog set to sawing right away, and he was lucky to get out of that place with his life. Did he have to amputate his hand? Let's just say he walked out of that tinderbox with a new bracelet and that his new nickname's not "Lefty."

Hog took the hint and left town soon after that. No charges were ever filed against the kids, but given the Guardian Angels' feelings about Hog, that's hardly surprising.

Church Scrip

One of the stranger side-effects of Grimme's Edict is that Confederate and Union dollars aren't considered legal tender within the city. Sure, most folks still honor them anyhow, but the church is now printing its own currency, known as church scrip or LA bucks.

Of course, no one outside of the City of Lost Angels accepts church scrip in a store, but there's often demand for it so people can buy ghost rock from the Rockies in Lost Angels with it. In any case, it's the only kind of currency the church accepts its tithes in—at least in theory. In practice, the Guardian Angels are happy to take their churchly taxes in just about any form they can find it. Often the taxes are taken in food, and it's rare that the entire amount makes it back to the church larder intact.

Church scrip comes on white paper with reddish ink. The ink doesn't always stay on the scrip too well if the bills get wet, so careful with them. The ink often leaves red stains on the hands of people who handle it regularly, which gave rise to its other nickname: blood money.

Church Morality

Grimme's Guardian Angels may be the city's arbiters of good taste as they see fit, but they do have a set of guidelines they're supposed to ensure the populace is sticking to. Grimme's code of morals runs throughout the city, and it crops up in daily life in several ways.

For one, every place of business is required to publicly display, on a large wooden plaque provided by the Church of Lost Angels, a list of the sins and biblical scriptures being broken by that business. The most common sign reads:

Now the works of the flesh are manifest, which are these:

Adultery, fornication, uncleanness, lasciviousness, idolatry, witchcraft, hatred, variance, emulations, wrath, strife, seditions, heresies, envyings, murders, drunkenness, revellings, and such like: of the which I tell you before, as I have also told you in time past, that they which do such things shall not inherit the kingdom of God.

— Galatians 5:19-21

A friendly reminder from your Guardian Angels.

That pretty much catches all of the possible offenses—or at least the most popular ones. Despite what you might think, in this "holy" city there's plenty of sin to go around and no lack of sinners eager to commit more. A lot of lip service is given to piety, but not much is practiced.

Smaller plaques inscribed with the Ten Commandments (Exodus 20:3-17) also appear a lot of the less troublesome establishments. These plaques don't appear to have affected profits—there's not really anywhere else to go after all—but everyone in town now knows the scriptures by heart now.

When the Guardian Angels pass moral judgment on some hapless soul, they always quote the relevant text or some other Bible passage like they're quoting a law book. It's kind of disconcerting at first, but it's almost funny when you realize that many of these people simply can't read and are just mimicking what they've heard in church. The misquotes some of them throw down are hilarious.

Of course, laughing at a Guardian Angel while he mangles scripture is a serious offense of its own. Most folks don't ever get away with it more than once.

The Walls Have Eyes

Even more insidious than the plaques is the requirement that every room of every building in town must be observable through conspicuous peepholes that let through to the outside of the building. The only exceptions are interior rooms and those not on the ground floor. These still must have easily usable peepholes elsewhere in the structure. Each peephole has a locking cover, and only the Guardians have the keys, so no private peeking is allowed.

After you spend more than a few hours in Lost Angels, you just ignore the damned holes. Even though they're everywhere, the Angels can't watch them all at once. The fact is, though, that when the Angels aren't around, anyone can use the peepholes. It makes it damned hard to get any kind of privacy, much less have a sensitive conversation. Still, people seem to get by.

Any attempt to block a peephole or redirect them one with a mirror is met with sudden and swift retribution from the Guardian Angels—once they find out. Most Guardians aren't the sharpest knives in the drawer, but even they can tell when a hole's been covered.

Surprisingly, none of the brothels have been shut down because of what might have been seen through those peepholes. I understand that some Angels actually line up to get a peek into one of these establishments. This doesn't say a whole lot about the piety of these people, but apparently clean living isn't a job requirement for the Guardians. I hear some of them even supplement their meager salaries by charging other locals for the privilege.

The Wages of Sin

Finally, Grimme bribes his flock to watch one another's behavior for immorality. Each report of immorality is rewarded with a free meal at the Guardian Angels headquarters, properly known as the Rectory. Children who report their parents' sins are rewarded with "better" parents from among the Guardian Angels and other Church-approved houses.

This has created a city in which no one can trust anyone else, even members of the church. After all, the charges don't have to be true for them to stick. Lots of times, people file preemptive charges to keep themselves safe.

Sins & Suffering

The punishment for immorality increases with the scope of the offense and how many times a particular person has been brought before the Church Court on immorality charges. Since anything that a Guardian Angel takes offense to can be considered a crime, anyone a Guardian wants to pick on can quickly rack up a stack of charges. For lesser offenses, the Guardian Angels on the scene can hand down the punishment.

A first offense for a minor moral offense, such as lying or covetousness, earns an embarrassing announcement at Grimme's sermon on the following Sunday, followed by ostracization by even your closest friends. After all, no one wants to risk angering the Guardian Angels by being caught with you. After the first charge, you're basically damaged goods.

A second offense, or a more extreme moral offense like committing adultery or taking the Lord's name in vain, warrants a public flogging on the steps of the Cathedral of Lost Angels. The whipping post in the front of the circle gets a lot of use these days.

A third offense, or a really immoral act such as feeding the poor or publicly questioning Grimme's doctrine means a trip to the Church Court. This is truly bad news.

Joining the Church

If Grimme's got the only club in town—there are others, actually, like the Men of the Grid, but I'll get to them in good time—how do you get in? You march straight over to the Rectory and sign up.

The Rectory is a tall, wedge-shaped building located just north of nine o'clock on the Golden Circle, distant enough from Grimme Manor. Maybe he doesn't care for the screams from the folks waiting for their time in front of the Church Court. God's voice in the city's got to sleep sometime.

Anyhow, it's an impressive building, matched only by Grimme's home and the cathedral itself.

The Dotted Line

To register, all you've got to do is come down in person and pledge your soul to Grimme and his church. To do this, you have to sign a contract with the church, promising to uphold the tenets of the church and obey the Reverend Grimme's teachings in all things. If you fail to do so, you surrender your immortal soul—and that's not even in the fine print.

Of course, lots of folks just laugh all that of and put their John Hancocks on the dotted line. I'd estimate that anywhere from 30% to 50% of Grimme's people are only paying lip service to him, but as long as he's running the show in town, they'll continue to do so. In a town like this in which parents sell out their children before their kids can do the same to them, not many believe in anything they can't eat, and a soul doesn't qualify.

Honorifics

Church members call themselves brothers and sisters, even on the streets, so they're easy to identify in even a casual conversation. If Allan was a member of the church, for instance, we'd call him Brother Allan most of the time. In formal circumstances, he'd be Brother Pinkerton instead.

Lord save us all if we ever hear those words.

The damn titles can be pretty irritating after a while. Most folks don't bother with them, except in the presence of the Guardian Angels. In those situations, people are eager to identify themselves as tithe-paying members of the church, and they take every opportunity to make their situation clear.

Recruitment

Despite the stranglehold Grimme's got on the citizens of his town, he still invests a lot into his recruitment efforts. Every visitor is a potential convert, and he treats them that way—at least at first.

The Guardian Angels are usually polite to visitors until they disparage the church. Sooner or later after that point, the Guardians are going to quit kidding around and get down to the business of saving your soul whether you like it or not. Their methods range from intimidation to outright threats.

If you're careful with how you talk about the church and you do your best to avoid the Guardians, you've still only got about a week before the theocracy gets around to sending a Guardian Angel recruitment specialist to your place. Again, at first they just want to talk, to "suggest" you consider joining up with the church. You can expect another visit at least every other day until you join up, and as the days wear on, the Guardians become less and less willing to take "Get the Hell away from me, you brainless Bible-thumper!" for an answer.

Moving Up the Ladder

Once you're a member of the Church of Lost Angels, there's always room for advancement. Most folks simply stay quiet, attend services, and eat their free meal on Sunday. More ambitious—and perhaps power hungry—souls join up with the Guardian Angels.

Others of a less violent bent can join the church government. Grimme calls it the Lost Angels Theocracy, but no matter how you slice these paper-pushers, they're bureaucrats. They spend their days collating data and writing reports instead of doing something useful.

(Sounds a bit too familiar to me, Allan. If I wasn't leaving town, maybe I could ask them for a job.)

A favorite means of advancing in the church is to accuse a superior of immorality. If the accuser can get this to stick, she often moves right into her old boss' office. Of course, at that point, she's got to watch out treachery from those below her as well.

The Guardian Angels are well aware of the politics that dominate the theocracy, and they do their best to stay above it all. Unfortunately, the Guardians have to deal with politics in their own organization as well. It's rare for anyone to keep a position longer than three months. The most savage always rise to the top.

Church Staff

The current theocracy is headed up by Andrea Baird, a steel-haired woman who keeps her hair bound up in a bun tight enough to cut off the circulation to her brain. She keeps the theocracy running like a tight ship, even if it sometimes doesn't seem like she knows where it's going.

Direction is Grimme's domain though, not hers, and this is a woman who's content in her place. She's one of the original survivors Grimme hauled out of the Great Quake, and she's been his right-hand woman ever since the church began.

Once the city council was disbanded and Mayor Miller was stripped of his office, the theocracy moved right on into City Hall. A good number of the workers there didn't even have to move offices, as long as they signed on as members of the Church of Lost Angels within a few days of the handing down of the Edict. The transition of power—if it ever really was in the hands of someone other than Grimme—went extremely smoothly.

Spreading the Word

Grimme likes to lay it on thick, but for many years he was the only ordained minister in his entire flock. Now that he's decided to branch out into establishing other chapels across the West, he's discovered a need for more preachers to join the ranks of his followers. After all, he can't be everywhere at once.

There's only one reverend in Grimme's church, and he's not willing to share the title with anyone else. The other preachers in his organization are called deacons instead, although they have the same powers and responsibilities of a priest of a traditional faith.

For an aspiring despot, Grimme's pretty egalitarian with regards to who can preach in his name. Both men and women can serve as deacons in his church, although it tends to be the men who are sent out to do the missionary work.

Deacons are well-respected folks within the city's confines, but they don't always get the same amount of respect when they venture into the rest of the West. Most cowpokes spot these tinhorns and what they're about from a mile away. I've got a pet theory about these missionaries actually being advance scouts for Grimme's army, but it's difficult to prove.

The Guardian Angels

To join the Guardian Angels, all you've got to do is be a member in good standing of the Church of Lost Angels and have a taste for abusing power and those unfortunate enough to not have any. It doesn't hurt if you're something of a bruiser as well. In this city, there's no shortage of qualified applicants.

Guardian Angels usually prowl the streets in flights of five. In a city like Lost Angels, even the lawmen have to travel in groups to be safe. The city streets are usually pretty quiet, but when the shan hits the fan, things get ugly quickly.

Each flight of Guardians reports to in to a captain at the start and end of every shift. Above these men, there are only Grimme's two archangels: Michael Coulter and Gabriel Fannon.

You can always tell a Guardian's rank by the color of his robe. Regulars wear white, flight leaders wear brown, captains wear red, and the archangels wear gold. Also, I finally managed to confirm rumors of a black-robed Guardian.

The Angel of Death

The Guardian in black is known only as the Angel of Death. I've actually met the man on one occasion, but he's really not much of a conversationalist.

Despite this, it's clear that this guy's Hell in a black cloak. Whenever he shows up on a scene, all conversation stops. Other Guardian Angels show him nothing but respect. In fact, it's almost like they're afraid to talk directly to him.

I've even see the Archangels bow to the Angel of Death's requests. The only one who would seem to hold sway over this man is Grimme himself, and I'm not even entirely sure about that.

The Mourning Brigade

The Mourning Brigade is a special task force of Guardian Angels responsible for gathering up the dead bodies in town and making sure they get carted off to Jehosephat Valley, the local excuse for a boneyard, up in the nearby hills.

Grimme claims to be concerned about ensuring that the bodies are buried with the respect they deserve. Roughly translated, he doesn't want his starving populace chopping each other up for steaks. Not reporting a death immediately is a sure way to get yourself a date in front of the Church Court

The Rectory

This is the main headquarters of the Guardian Angels, and like I mentioned before, it sits right on the edge of the Golden Circle. The building houses the Guardians' offices, as well as holding cells for offenders awaiting their date in Church Court. Additionally, the top floor contains the Church Court itself.

The Rectory is the dominion of Clem Norbert, a petty bureaucrat that keeps the Guardians in line. He wears a red robe these days, having been promoted to the rank of captain shortly after the Bloody Sunday incident.

The Rectory also features one heck of a kitchen. This is where the meals are prepared for Sunday's after-services feasts, and its also where the Guardians meet every evening for dinner. The Guardians eat in three shifts to make sure that the city's not left undefended while they stuff their faces.

Meals here are also used to reward folks for ratting out their fellow citizens. In a city full of starving folks, that's some bounty.

Church Court

This is where you go if you've really annoyed Grimme or fallen afoul of one of his Guardian Angels. The holding cells for those accused of immorality are located in the basement of the Rectory, and prisoners are hauled up to the court's hall on the top floor in an elevator.

Unlike the ones you see sold in the Smith & Robards catalog, this elevator is run by hand, and the labor is provided by Guardian Angels that have committed some kind of minor infraction against the church.

The Church Court still uses medieval methods of trying a person's innocence. They test by ordeals of one kind or another, or by a person's knowledge of scripture. For more about how this works, see my last report. Overall, it's pretty gruesome.

The men who sit on the bench here are universally cruel bastards, and they come up with ordeals that would make even Grimme wince. Anyway, the verdict is almost always guilty. If a person's been brought before the court, he's got to be guilty, right?

There are only two sentences here: death or time on the Rock. Given the number of people who've actually made it off the Rock, I'd go with death. Worse yet, this is the highest court in the land. Only Grimme himself can overturn a conviction.

In other words, once you've been sent to Church Court, you're better off dead. Lots of prisoners come to this sad conclusion on their own, and suicides in the cells are extremely common.

The One That Got Away

Did I forget to mention that all other religions have been declared illegal within the confines of the city? Given the other parts of the Edict, it seemed pretty obvious.

Anyhow, being a worshiper of another faith is reason enough to be denied entry into the city. If you're discovered to actually be a member of another kind of clergy, you go straight to Church Court and from there directly to the Rock.

Most religious folk give LA a wide berth, but there's one priest that keeps showing up and preaching in the Golden Circle every week. The Guardians always haul him away, but he's always back next week. My guess is he's the same man—the only one—who actually passed every one of the court's trials last year.

Grimme's Army

Since Grimme began his open crusade against the rail barons and any government that refuses to recognize his new nation, he's brought his armed forces out into the open. At this point, there's no point in covering it up any more.

For years, some of the more excitable members of the Church of Lost Angels signed up with the Guardian Angels to launch raids against the rail barons at the reverend's behest. He always made sure to distance himself from these people as much as he could, even going so far as to have Colonel Ludlow Prather, formerly of the US Army, organize the force without the reverend's direct knowledge. This gave him plausible deniability should the church's connection with these terrorist ever have been revealed.

Few of these zealots were captured over the years, and they never could be forced to talk. After the Edict, though, Grimme dropped the pretense and converted these ragtag troops into a proper army.

Joining Up

All able-bodied churchgoers are encouraged to serve in the Army of Lost Angels for at least a two-year tour of duty. Many sign on for more.

New recruits in Grimme's army are trained at Camp Grimme, a place about two miles east of LA, in the hills just north of the Ghost Trail. Colonel Ludlow Prather runs the camp with an iron fist. It used to be you didn't have to be a member of the church to join Grimme's forces. With the Edict, that changed.

The training is pretty rigorous, but the recruits are fed regularly. In the Maze, this kind of benefit is a big draw.

Avenging Angels

Grimme's top troops are known as the Avenging Angels. Considering how lousy most of his soldiers are, you wouldn't expect these folks to be anything to worry about, but they can hold their own with just about anyone.

Supported by the strange creatures Grimme claims are fallen angels that God's inducted into his service, the Avenging Angels do a damn good job of leading their scrawny recruits into battles, and they win at least as often as they lose. Overall, this is a force to be reckoned with, no matter which side God's really on.

Chapter Four: The Lost Angels

85

Talk about unwashed masses, Lost Angels has sure got them. For one, it's the transportation and shipping center for the rest of the Maze, which means that well over half of the nation's ghost rock passes through here at one point or another.

There's a lot of money to be made here if you know what you're doing or you're just plain lucky. (Most folks, it seems, just plan on being lucky.) That's where the masses come from.

As for the "unwashed" part, fresh water's a precious thing around these parts, and it don't come cheap. Most people would rather spend their hard-earned cash on a meal than a bath. You wouldn't believe the price of perfume or cologne around here either.

State of the City

This city's a pit, and I'll be glad to see the last of it. Despite the church's efforts, the place is full of thieves, con artists, and murderers. That's what happens when you've got millions of dollars flowing through a place in which the only excuse for the law is a gang of corrupt, poorly trained thugs.

I'd call them religious zealots, but most of the Guardian Angels in town don't qualify. The ones who care that much about Grimme's message are on the front lines of his crusade. The rest of them just stir this cesspool until whatever filth they're looking for floats to the top.

Entering the City

Ever since Bloody Sunday, the City of Lost Angels has become a truly foul place to live. The skies are always dark and hazy, but it never seems to rain. The trees and plants are dying from some strange kind of blight that turns them black, and still people of all races, religions, ages, and classes come here in droves. It's just another case of greed overwhelming good sense.

There are really only two ways into the city: by land or sea. If you're coming in by land, you're probably on the Ghost Trail, coming direct from Tombstone. On your way into town, you pass through Ghost Town, a ramshackle stack of row after row of shacks and lean-tos surrounded by lines of tents. Those who can't afford living in the city squat here.

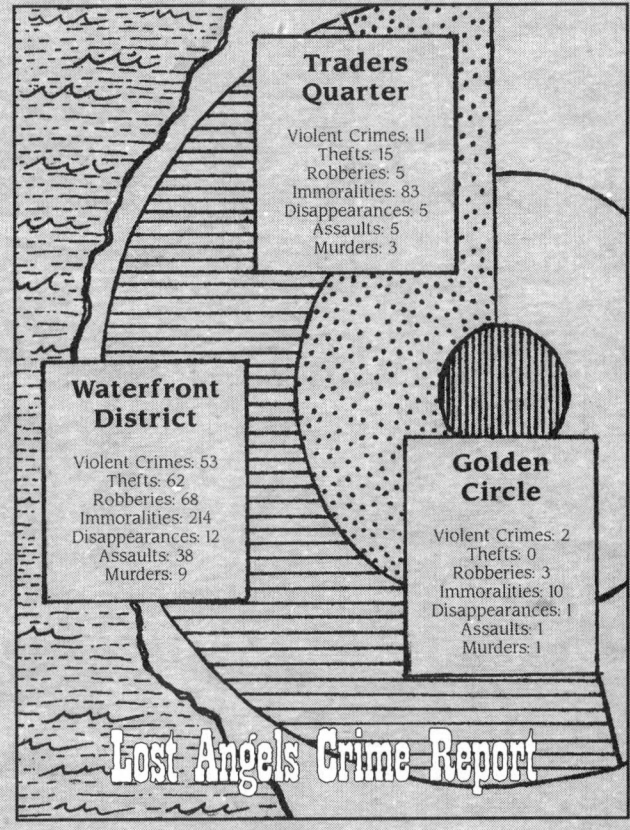

Traders Quarter

Violent Crimes: 11
Thefts: 15
Robberies: 5
Immoralities: 83
Disappearances: 5
Assaults: 5
Murders: 3

Waterfront District

Violent Crimes: 53
Thefts: 62
Robberies: 68
Immoralities: 214
Disappearances: 12
Assaults: 38
Murders: 9

Golden Circle

Violent Crimes: 2
Thefts: 0
Robberies: 3
Immoralities: 10
Disappearances: 1
Assaults: 1
Murders: 1

Lost Angels Crime Report

The Ghost Trail eventually becomes Sixth Avenue, right when you cross over Sixth Circle. That's the town proper. That neighborhood's full of houses and businesses that cater to the throngs outside the city. This is the main registration point. Roads also enter town from the north and south, and there are registration booths at Third and 10th Avenues too.

Most other traffic comes through by means of Prosperity Bay, the city's gateway to the Maze. All visitors coming in this way are required to register at the Customs House at the corner of Third Street and Sixth Circle.

There are some crazies who come in by air—either by balloon, ornithopter, or some other means—but with Grimme's antitechnological bent, no one's been able to construct a proper landing zone. There are lots of open spaces that get used for this purpose though, and the best pilots know them all by heart. The most popular one's just out back of a bar called the Vestibule, right on the outskirts of Ghost Town. Anyone trying to land in the city itself might be in for a rude surprise. Rumor has it that something patrols the skies for Grimme, and several unexplained crashes back that up.

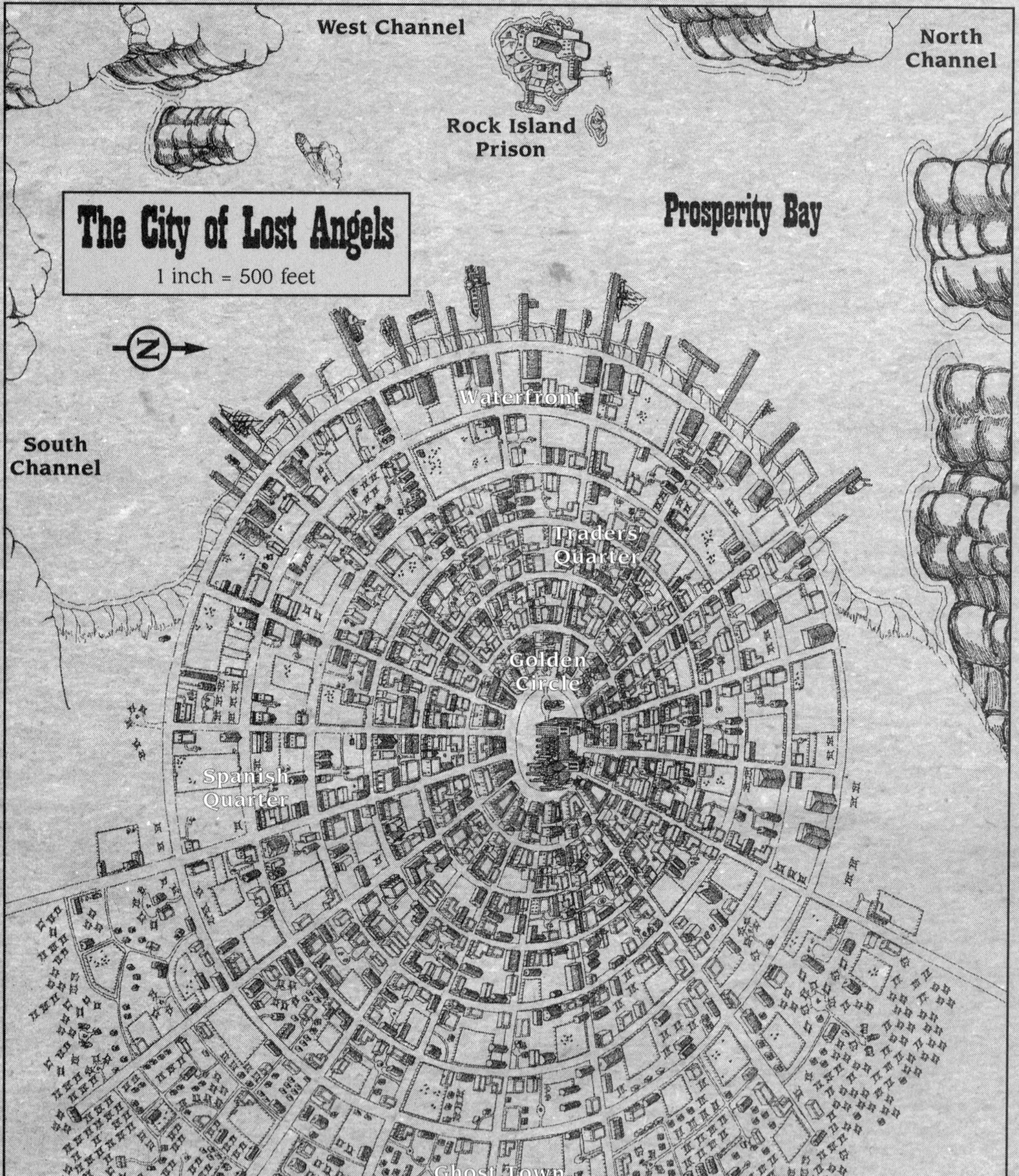

West Channel

North Channel

Rock Island Prison

The City of Lost Angels

1 inch = 500 feet

Prosperity Bay

N

South Channel

Waterfront

Traders' Quarter

Golden Circle

Spanish Quarter

Ghost Town

Tent City

The Districts

Most of Lost Angels is the part of the city you see when you first walk in, but there are four other parts that have identities of their own: the Waterfront, the Spanish Quarter, the Traders' Quarter, and the Golden Circle. I'll cover each of them in some detail here.

The Waterfront

The Maze's morning fog rolls into the city's Waterfront District first, before continuing into the city and eventually dispersing. The smell of sea and sulphur soaks into cloth, salt crystallizes in the corners of glass panes, and the place stinks of dead fish.

A dozen boats, everything from little knife boats up to massive steam-powered warships, sit at the docks at a time. Exotic visitors of Russian, Chinese, Indian, and European descent mill about the district, waiting for boats out of town or for illicit deals to come their way.

The Docks

The Waterfront's docks are the center of activity during the day. Merchants, traders, slavers, foreign laborers, Triad gangs, and dock urchins—kids apparently without parents or any means of support—wander about the place. Most of them pretend to notice what a rotten place they're stuck in, but they don't hesitate for a second to get the Hell out of town the first chance they get.

At night, everyone clears off the docks. Ship crews return to their boats or head deeper into town if they can afford a stay at a flophouse or brothel.

Nobody sleeps out in the open at night. Those too cheap or too stupid to know better are rarely heard from again. I tried putting together a team to investigate this problem once, but I lost them too. As far as I'm concerned, it's Grimme's problem now, and I'm no longer sure which side I'm rooting for.

Warehouses

Just off the docks are row after row of warehouses. Various interests, both within and beyond the city, own these warehouses, which store everything from bolts of exotic fabric to opium (hidden within bolts of exotic fabric) to, on rare occasion, food.

The warehouses are all well guarded. Heavily armed patrols walk beats around most of the places at night—although not all—and they only rarely have any kind of clashes. The only windows in most of these places are 20 feet up, right along the roof's edge. Some warehouses also have skylights, which crews open during the day so they can work inside without lanterns. Either way, cat burglars are in for a challenge.

The Labyrinth Saloon

The Labyrinth Saloon is a popular hangout in the Waterfront, mostly because it opens at sunup, and a sailor who's stuck in town rarely wants to wait to start his drinking. The dark interior of the place is always packed with people either on their way from one port to another, or waiting for a way out of town.

The Labyrinth is so named not only for the Great Maze that rises up just beyond the docks, but because of the way it was built. The Labyrinth's founder—a wealthy Greek merchant named Minos and one of the first immigrants to the city after Grimme founded it—started the business as a simple saloon.

As the city's population grew, Minos wised up and started buying adjacent businesses before land prices went sky-high. He couldn't afford to tear down the old buildings, so instead he opened up the walls between then.

The saloon is now a confusing maze of small rooms and meeting halls, all branching off of the saloon's main hall, which is where you walk into the place. Stairs go to floors that don't connect in any other way except by stairs from other floors. More than one drunk has gotten himself good and lost for a couple days within the Labyrinth.

Back in the Pinkerton days, whenever we were hired to find a person who went missing in the Waterfront, this is where I'd start. That's not just because the place swallows people whole. It's also the unofficial headquarters of the district. If Percy Navwell—the Labyrinth's overeducated bartender—doesn't know about it, it's not happening in the Waterfront.

Because of the Labyrinth's layout, it's a favorite meeting place for traders from throughout the Great Maze. We used to use it for other clandestine meets too. As long as you can actually manage to find the people you're looking for, you can always locate an out-of-way spot for a quiet conversation without any eavesdroppers.

Agency Special Report #187: Lost Angels, 1877

The Water Shortage

Clean water is as much a problem for the City of Lost Angels as food. While the city's location makes it a great port, it's hard to drink the salt water in Prosperity Bay.

Grimme was thinking when he came up with the plans for his city though. The fresh waters that pour from the Spouts—a bunch of waterfalls that spray right out of a cliff face just south of the city—actually come from an underground river. Grimme was smart enough to tap into this source of water, and he had a system of sewers built so that the people could draw on the water easily.

Of course, just because the church has easy access to the water doesn't mean the people do. One of the other ways Grimme keeps a stranglehold on the city is by only giving church members access to the wells that reach into the clean side of the sewers.

Anyone in town can dirty the other side of the sewers. Most places don't have indoor plumbing yet, so that half of the sewers doesn't get used much, but Grimme's ready for that time when it comes.

There are only a few public wells scattered around town, and they're guarded by the Guardian Angels, who carefully restrict how much is pulled each day. Theoretically this ensures that the wells never run dry, but being of a naturally suspicious nature, I'm not so sure I buy that rationalization.

Anyhow, there's usually plenty of water to drink, but its hard to find enough to bathe in. Other folks have tried getting around the restrictions by collecting rainwater, but there's been precious little of that lately.

As for visitors, they're not entitled to any water until they join the church. In the meantime, they're free to purchase the water from a churchgoer, but the prices are incredibly high. Most sailors prefer to get their liquid refreshments in a fermented form, if you know what I mean.

Dr. Neptune's Effervescent Waters

An enterprising scientist going by the name of Dr. Neptune (an obvious alias—where do these jokers come up with these names?) has come up with his own solution to the water shortage, which surprisingly hasn't been shut down by Grimme's enforcers. At the far north end of the Waterfront, Dr. Neptune has set up a massive water extraction and filtration operation that dips directly into Prosperity Bay.

Neptune's process uses simple sea water, which he filters through nets and then cheesecloth to remove large particles (dead fish, boats, tiny crabs, what have you). From there, he pumps the water into massive holding tanks, where it's allowed to sit while even smaller particles sink to the bottom. He then skims off the top of the tank and filters that water through "activated ghost charcoal," which is the remains of ghost rock that has been burned as fuel.

Believe it or not, this crackpot process actually works. I've seen a lot of crazy schemes in my time, but using ghost rock to actually clean water takes the cake.

The water comes out extremely clean and slightly effervescent, bubbling like a fresh beer. It even has a head on it when poured, but this floats into the air pretty darn quick.

Unfortunately, the ghost-rock charcoal has a side-effect on the water. (Doesn't it always?) Besides taking the salt out of the water, it also puts some unknown chemical in. Unfortunately, this mysterious stuff is a really powerful hallucinogenic.

Agency Special Report #187: Lost Angels, 1877

Top Secret   "Read It & Weep!"   Alpha Clearance Only

Despite this effect, most customers just don't care. When you're living in Ghost Town and nearly dying of thirst, seeing a bunch of pink elephants trying to steal your water from you is the least of your problems.

Folks looking for just a bit more fresh water—as well as those who are plain out— scrounge together their pennies to pick up a gallon whenever they can. A gallon of Neptune's water sets you back two bits, in either Confederate or Union coins.

This stuff's not cheap, so most folks carefully ration it out. Typically, responsible people cut the effervescent water with what little well water they can get their hands on. The hallucinogenic effects are weakened by this, but they're still there.

Most folks can handle the cut water just fine, but not everyone falls into that category. The sick and the young are particularly liable to have severe problems with it, about on the par of a fool who tries to drink the stuff straight.

Dr. Neptune doesn't even drink his own water except when he's got company. On these occasions, he uses the water to brew an exotic blend of spiced teas for himself and his guests.

Hardwick's Boarding House

Hardwick's Boarding House isn't the seediest establishment of its kind in Lost Angels, only because other boarding houses are so much worse. This three-story building overlooks Prosperity Bay, and it's got a damned good view of Rock Island Prison. Most of the board house's guests are either transient miners or dock workers, and the view serves as a reminder about where they might end up if they don't keep on the straight and narrow path.

The boarding house, owned by one Sidney Hardwick, charges two bits a day, or $1 for a week's stay. It has 20 rooms, all more or less the same. The top floor is comprised of four good-sized apartments, which Hardwick calls Presidential Suites and for which he charges 50¢ a day. He also leases them long-term for $10 a month.

Hardwick himself is a crotchety old man without any sense of morals, despite the fact he attends services at the cathedral every week. He rents rooms to anyone with cash, no questions asked. Although he stares at his patrons as they come and go, he never reports anything he's ever seen through the Guardian-required peepholes that dot his establishment, despite the fact he uses them constantly.

The Cleaner

Just as Scotland Yard is dealing with Jack the Ripper, the City of Lost Angels is dealing with a "ripper" of its own. They call him or her or it the Cleaner.

The Cleaner kills soiled doves. Pretty darn imaginative, huh? It gets better. He also guts and cleans the victims like a fish. Their organs are never found.

It gets better still. When the body finally floats back into Prosperity Bay, the empty body cavities are always filled with a batch of live fish, with mussels in the eye sockets, and eels wherever they can wriggle into. I'm told they're tasty too.

Naturally, public reaction to finding these corpses—which show up about twice a month—is horror and shock. Still, I hear rumors that some scientists have gone so far as to conduct occult experiments to determine how to replace organs with fish. So far, I haven't heard of any positive results.

Hog didn't get anywhere with this one, and although the Guardian Angels claim to have people on the case, they have no real leads.

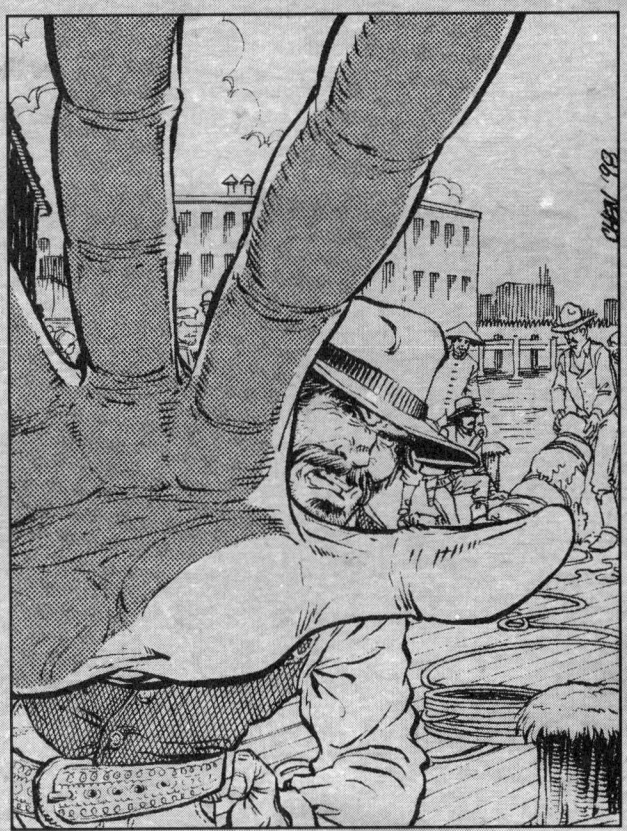

Shipping

Of course, the Waterfront's also where most of the shipping in and out of the Maze happens from. Most people might come in by way of the Ghost Trail, but most food and ghost rock make their way in and out of the city on ships.

Ships of all sizes sail in and out the West Channel on their way to the open waters of the Pacific. Other, often smaller, ships brave the North Channel, making the run back and forth from Lost Angels to Shan Fan.

Every now and then, a ship uses the South Channel, but it's pretty darn rare. The only thing down that way are the sunken ruins of San Diego. Of course, there's another outlet to the sea, but the West Channel is a lot shorter and safer.

With the city now firmly in his control, Grimme charges a stiff fee to every ship that unloads or takes on cargo in his port. Most captains pay this tax grudgingly, but since Grimme's the only game in town, they really don't have much of a choice. The Rockies objected to this at first, but they've quieted down now, for reasons I'll get to later.

Smuggling

Of course, if there's one thing I learned in my days with the Pinkertons, if there's a law, someone somewhere is going to find both a reason and a means to break it. When Grimme started taxing the only port in town, a lot of people set their minds to figuring out a way to not have to pay.

The fact is that only people who trade in goods have to pay the tax, and if the Guardian Angels don't see the goods moving on or off a ship, they don't charge the fees. Most smugglers—like them or not, that's what they are—simply sail into town under the cover of night and unload their goods while no one's looking. This is a risky business for a few reasons.

First, the searchlights on Rock Island sweep the bay regularly, and they often catch incoming ships in their lights. If this happens, you can be sure a flight of Guardian Angels is ready to meet the ship. In any case, navigating the Maze on a dark night is only a half-step shy of insanity.

Of course, people try it all the time, mostly on their way out of town. While it's hard to get into town unnoticed, it's fairly simple to load or unload a ship in the middle of the night and then take off before the Customs Angels (as they're known) are any the wiser.

Once again, outgoing ships are usually spotted from Rock Island, and ships that leave the port under mysterious circumstances are often refused entry if they try to return. Many smugglers are fond of repainting the names on the ship's exterior after every time they leave port.

There's a lot of money to be made in smuggling, but most good captains are smart enough not to try it. Those who get caught can plan on spending their days on the Rock, watching other ships sail by.

Salvagers

As I mentioned before, the Maze is a dangerous place for a ship. The tides come and go with terrifying ferocity, and the place is lousy with Maze dragons and other creatures of the deep. Many ships lie at the bottom of this series of rocky channels.

Of course, one man's misfortune is another's luck. There are lots of salvage operations throughout the Maze, and three of the biggest are located in the City of Lost Angels.

The most notorious of these is called R.T. Chestnutt's Resupply, but Maze Draggers and Amazing Rescue are close seconds. These outfits each hire spotters around the Maze to constantly survey the land, hoping to spot to foundering ship.

When word reaches Lost Angels that a ship is going down, it's a race to see which salvage organization reaches the wreck first, and rumor has it that more than one salvager makes his living by sending the ships to the bottom himself.

One of our first assignments under the Agency was putting an end to one of these operations which was preying on Union ships. The ones that stick to Confederate or Mexican ships, we leave alone.

Piracy

That brings us to the people responsible for sending a good number of those ships to the bottom: pirates.

Captain Blood—or Capitan Sangre, as the mestizos in town proudly call him—currently holds the record for the number of ships either captured or scuttled. Some estimates put the number upward of 80, but even having sailed on Blood's ship myself (you meet all sorts of interesting people in this job), I find this hard to believe.

Many pirates have been given letters of marque by either the Union or the Confederacy or even the Mexicans to sink ships bearing any opposing flags. They use and abuse these as much as possible. I know our government uses these people as well, but with few exceptions, they're ruthless killers who should all be hunted down and drowned.

But that's just my opinion.

In any case, Grimme's got no official policy on the pirates that make life difficult for people wanting to get to and from the City of Lost Angels. To his mind, it's not his problem, since he's got few ships to speak of.

In fact, I'm told he regards the pirates as a kind of de facto naval defense for his city. Anyone armed force that would want to attack Lost Angels from the sea would have to make it through the Maze, the salvagers, Maze dragons, and pirates.

I hear that Grimme might even be handing out his own letters of marque these days. If that's true, these pirates are going to feel free to raid anyone they like. And I'm sure they'll be well fed for their efforts.

The Spanish Quarter

The Spanish Quarter is the most rundown yet vibrant part of Grimme's Celestial City. Its population is almost entirely mestizo, or "indigenous Hispanic" as the Guardian Angels call them when their in one of their rare better moods. The neighborhood is not friendly to the mostly white Guardian Angels. (There are some mestizo Guardians, but they're few and far between.) The mestizos have mastered a facial expression that embodies both resentment of their oppressors and a hunter's regard for its prey.

Most folks in the Spanish Quarter are poor, and it shows. Broken windows go unfixed, paint peels from walls and door jambs, trash accumulates in narrow corridors. Many mestizo men, lacking any training or education, mill along the edge of their barrio in groups of five to eight, hoping for an empty wagon to come along with an offer for a day's wages for menial labor in the warehouses or on a meager farm. Others get by the best they can, but in a city as expensive as LA, this is never easy.

But the barrio is also more alive than any other part of the City of Lost Angels. Shocking colors jump from buildings, and lavishly decorated crucifixes hang on nearly every wall. A statue of Our Lady of Guadalupe used to stand in the middle of the Spanish Quarter, a testimony of the mestizo's public and private faith. After his Edict, Grimme had it torn down, claiming it was a form of idolatry.

Holy day festivals are common in the Spanish Quarter, but even in their revelry the locals also act out their desperation. Many people, especially the elderly, plan their lives around the next holy day, and celebrate the birthdays of even very minor saints with all the enthusiasm they can muster.

The Guardian Angels drift through the Spanish Quarter now and then, mostly looking for moral offenses worth their time and effort. These days, they have a different form of blasphemy to watch out for.

When the Edict came down, nearly all of the almost entirely Catholic mestizos converted over to the Church of Lost Angels. As you might have guessed, most of these folks are pretty serious about their religion, and they joined up with Grimme's cause in name only.

For some reason, the Guardian Angels ignore all the many clues to the fact the mestizos are lying about their conversions. They don't make them take down their shrines to their saints, they don't stop them from celebrating their saints' days and taking part in other festivals like the Days of the Dead, and they otherwise pretty much leave them alone.

I don't know why this is, and since I'm leaving town now, I may never find out.

El Jefe

The most powerful man in a mestizo area, whether in Lost Angels or any of the dozens of other mestizo towns scattered about the Maze and throughout Mexico, is known as the jefe. (For the Spanish-impaired, that's pronounced HAY-fay.) This roughly translates into boss, mayor, big man, and so on. Anyone known as a jefe is both respected and feared by his mestizo neighbors.

The Spanish Quarter's jefe is a big man named Don Xotli Lopez. He's been the Spanish Quarter's benevolent dictator since Reverend Grimme broke ground for Lost Angels. He wasn't one of Grimme's original group, but he settled here soon after hauling what was left of his family and friends out of the incredible mess that was the newly created Great Maze.

Lopez is generally well liked by the mestizos of the Spanish Quarter, despite the many plights they find themselves in. People come to him for simply advice just as often as they ask for actual aid. I've had the pleasure of meeting the man myself, and he exudes a strong confidence in himself and the power he wields both over and for his people.

Lopez uses the City of Lost Angels as his private fortress. From here, he sends his 12 boys, aged 14 to 28, on assignments throughout the southern Maze and inland California. Outside the City of Lost Angels, he is despised by the mestizo people. The appearance of a Lopez boy and his posse of enforcers means a village is expected to give up 10% of its crops, cash, or both to Don Lopez. The boys have been known to occasionally go overboard in their zeal to do their father's bidding.

None of these settlements were ever able to hire the Pinkertons to protect their interests from Lopez's thugs. Now that we're servants of the US government though, I'm looking forward to someday having a chance at taking Don Lopez down. Because we're leaving right now, that's not going to happen for a while, but I've already paid Lopez a visit to let him know that his days are numbered.

Don Xotli Lopez receives the full support of Padre Pablo Humo, as well as that of Father Gutierrez at St. Dominic's Church. (I'll get to them in a second.) Of course, I don't think either of these men were given a choice in the matter.

The fact is that although Lopez is a real son of a bitch, he's also a thorn in Grimme's side. After all, he represents a large group of heretics posing as the faithful.

The Anahuacs

It turns out that while the Catholics are pretending to be members of Grimme's church, they might also have some Trojan horses of their own. From my days in Old Mexico, I knew about the Anahuac (that's AN-a-wak) religion, a "secret" sect of Catholicism in which the mestizos worship the saints canonized by Rome. When I got to Lost Angels, I realized that this faith had followed the mestizos across the border.

The Anahuac religion is a mixture of Catholicism and ancient Aztec faiths, and all in all it seems pretty harmless. Still, the local leader of this movement is Padre Pablo Humo (also known as "Señor Smoke"), a man who's shown some pretty amazing capabilities, if you know what I mean.

Agency Special Report #187: Lost Angels, 1877

The Anahuacs don't have a church of their own, although I understand they sometimes meet in the far-off ruins of Los Angeles from time to time. Most days, though, Humo just wanders the street, administering to his flock at random. The people all know who he is, and they give him the appropriate amount of respect.

Iglesia del Santo Domingo

The Church of Saint Dominic is a small Catholic chapel that was torched by the Guardian Angels soon after the Edict was handed down. It was once the main center of worship for the mestizo Catholics of the Spanish Quarter. Now it stands as a grim reminder (pun intended) of who's really in charge around here.

The Catholic priest of St. Dominic's, Father Juan Gutierrez, is one of the few preachers of any kind to avoid Grimme's 22:18 bounty. His people keep him safely protected from the Guardian Angels, and there are no traitors among them that are willing to sell out a Holy Man, even for a free meal. If someone was to cross that line, his life wouldn't be worth a wooden nickel in the Spanish Quarter.

The 22:18 Bounty

Didn't I mention this before? In the aftermath of his Edict, Grimme decided to literally put a bounty on anyone showing any signs of "witchcraft": magical powers not granted by the miraculous will of Grimme's version of God. This even includes priests of other religions.

The name of the bounty comes from Exodus 22:18, "Thou shalt not suffer a witch to live." Folks around here take it pretty seriously, since the reward is either $500 cash (in the City of Lost Angels' scrip) or a week's worth of hearty meals at the Rectory.

A lot of folks got turned in during the first few weeks after the Edict, and not all of them were witches. In fact, I'd guess that over half of them were entirely innocent folks that someone just wanted to get rid of for one reason or another.

This witch hunt is making the one at Salem look like a bunch of kids playing hide-and-seek. While Grimme supposedly meant for it to help root out mystical types, in fact it means that no one's safe. One more reason to leave.

Agency Special Report #187: Lost Angels, 1877

Top Secret   "Read It & Weep!"   Alpha Clearance Only

Holy Days

Holy days are actively celebrated by the mestizos in the Spanish Quarter, and it seems like they've got one for every day of the week. Do you have any idea how many saint's days there are on the Catholic calendar?

The most celebrated days are Christmas, Easter, and "los Dias de Los Muertos"—the Days of the Dead: November 1 and 2. Of the three, the Day of the Dead is the most important to the mestizo culture, and it stands as a glaring example of that Anahuac subculture I was talking about before. Most Catholics outside these parts have never heard of the Days of the Dead, but here they're more important than Christmas.

The Days of the Dead holiday is a celebration of dead ancestors. Folks dress up like skeletons, drape themselves with rings of flowers, and dance in the streets. It's one hell of a party, and the real question is what's are the people going to do when the Days roll around this year? Are they going to risk tipping their collective hand to Grimme, or are they going to forgo their most sacred holiday?

Isabella's Botanica

This very popular shop in the Spanish Quarter sells "botanicas": exotic herbs, flowers, and plants used in popular Catholic and Anahuac ceremonies. Isabella del Rio is a great beauty who arrived in the City of Lost Angels from her native Mexico about eight years ago. She came to the city in the company of Padre Humo, so you can pretty well guess where her religious loyalties lie.

The Botanica receives most of its shipments from Maze traders. Isabella pays top dollar for all sorts of odd flowers, leaves, and roots, most of which cannot be found in this hemisphere. Most of the time, she's got a good stock of whatever the folks in the Spanish Quarter need, but these days it's hard to keep a steady supply of anything coming into the city.

Still, if you're looking for flowers from a pretty flower of a lady, this is the place to go. Isabella's also well-connected with the rumor mill that runs rampant in the Spanish Quarter, and in the past she's proven willing to part with any vital information—as long as my having it would help her people. She's dedicated to her people, and there's nothing anyone could do to get her to betray them.

The Golden Circle

This is where the other half lives. Okay, actually, it's where the other 5% lives, the rich movers and shakers that get things done in the City of Lost Angels. Of course, it's also the home of Grimme Manor and the Rectory. Since I've covered that ground elsewhere, I'm not going to go over it again here. There's plenty else to talk about.

Dr. Bernard Grimme Memorial Hospital

This large, wedge shaped building is situated at the two o' clock position on the Golden Circle, right next door to Grimme Manor. The place was named for Reverend Grimme's father, a doctor who was killed in the Great Quake, supposedly while trying to rescue injured folks from the big hospital in Los Angeles, whatever the Hell the name of it was.

The hospital's always open, day or night, and it takes in any member of the church, regardless of ability to pay. It's run by the church, and the staff's salaries are paid for out of the church's coffers. Since the Edict, outsiders are not welcome here.

The hospital has a locked and barred ward for unsavables too. It was overwhelmed last year during that outbreak of the faminite plague. It got so bad that the orderlies were simply opening the doors to the place long enough to toss the poor souls into the prison-like ward where they were either torn to shreds or simply got to wait until they died.

These days, things are a lot better here, but I still avoid the place, except in case of emergency. There are lots of other doctors that don't ask for your soul before they treat you.

The Theater of Lost Angels

This concert hall sits at the four o' clock position on the Golden Circle, in a large, wedge-shaped building that went up before even the cathedral. While Grimme was waiting for the cathedral to be finished, he actually used to hold services here in the auditorium, with his altar directly on center stage.

Since then, the place has actually hosted several international touring companies featuring some of the best plays and operas from Europe and Back East. Local productions fill the seats in between the larger engagements, of which there haven't been any since the Edict.

Agency Special Report #187: Lost Angels, 1877

Top Secret   "Read It & Weep!"   Alpha Clearance Only

And, no, despite any rumors to the contrary, there is no "phantom" haunting the theater. I think we've all heard this kind of story a million times before, and it's got no more credence this time than ever before.

City Hall

As I mentioned earlier, this building, which sits near the seven o' clock position on the Golden Circle, now houses Grimme's theocracy. Former Mayor John Miller still maintains an office here, but his position is less than that of a figurehead. Even so, he's a proven friend of the church, and Grimme has rewarded him by making sure he's taken care of.

Judge Scanlon used to run court out of this place too. He's headed for greener pastures these days—possibly up Shan Fan way—but his courtroom still gets use. If he was dead, he'd be spinning in his grave about the fact that the overflow from the Church Courtroom in the Rectory is being handled here, but there's nothing he could do about it anyhow.

The Rockies

Those of you who know about the scene here in Lost Angels are probably wondering about the Greater Maze Rock Miners Association, otherwise known as the Rockies. This association of fundament magnates control nearly 70% of the Maze's commercial shipping, and they concentrate almost exclusively on ghost rock, gold, silver, and other minerals. Their headquarters is at the two o'clock position in the Golden Circle.

The Rockies' council consists of some of the most powerful men in the Maze, barring Grimme himself, and possibly Kang when he hangs his hat in these parts. When the Edict came down, the real question in town was which way the Rockies would go.

Well, they pretty much all signed up, including both Joshua Lumme and Leo "the Bear" Popoff. They knew that their bread was buttered in Lost Angels, and they weren't willing to risk losing it, although that tithing thing really chaffs their collective hindquarters.

Still, it's pretty much business as usual for the Rockies. The fundament goes in and out just like it used to. The only difference is that the ships are always a bit lighter after passing through Lost Angel's port. The Rockies don't seem to mind much. They just pass the price increases along to their customers.

Paul Deauville

The only real Rockies holdout was Paul Deauville. As an ex-seminarian and a still-devout Catholic, he wasn't about to give in to Grimme's demands.

By all accounts, Deauville's taken off for Shan Fan, and he's running his portion of the Rockies from there. Rumor has it that he's the man behind the latest incarnation of the Men of the Grid, but there's no way of proving that.

Popoff's Mansion

Popoff's place is located on Fourth Street, right across from the Rectory. Some folks would fear to constantly live in the shadows of the Guardian Angels, but not Leo. As a matter of fact, more than one Guardian Angel has expressed a bit of dismay about having to sleep in the Bear's shadow.

With Deauville gone, Popoff has shoved aside Lumme to become the nominal head of the entire Rockies organization. Lumme quietly caved in to Leo when he made his power play, and there are no other challengers. Anyhow, he lives in this mansion, and it's a beaut.

The Golden Circle Ghost

If you've been keeping up with that indispensable source of information known as the *Tombstone Epitaph*, you probably saw our "friend" Lacy O'Malley writing about the "Golden Circle Ghost." Well, he's right. Someone or something was haunting the church elders, although Grimme was able to escape from this torture.

You'll notice I said "was." The ghost was laid to rest in a very public exorcism Grimme held in the cathedral itself. This was during a candlelit vigil being held for those afflicted with the ghost's visits. Dozens of witnesses report having seen the apparition make a personal appearance in the heart of the cathedral, right before Grimme banished the thing back to Hell.

Apparently the ghost took Grimme's word for the fact he had God on his side, since there haven't been any further complaints. I admit to being a bit disappointed personally. Some of those folks could use a few more sleepless nights.

Throop College of Technology

This building at the six o' clock position on the Golden Circle was a budding institution of higher learning until the Edict came down. Soon after that, it was shut up tighter than one of those giant clams they pull out of the Maze every so often.

The place was run by Professor Thaddeus S.C. Lowe, one of the leaders in the "new" sciences, specializing in the refinement of ghost rock into even purer and more powerful fuel sources. The college was named for Dr. Everett D. Throop, one of the pioneers in the field of ghost-rock research. Apparently he was Lowe's mentor Back East before he came out here. None of Lowe's crackpot theories have panned out as of yet, but I don't pretend to understand how these things work. You never know what might happen.

Either way, it's not going to happen in Lost Angels. Lowe and his students left town just ahead of a bonfire prepared especially for himself and those who subscribed to his "witchery." I understand they've headed for Salt Lake City. Who knows? Maybe they'll give Hellstromme or Smith & Robards a run for their money. There are rumors that the college is still occupied by a mechanical man left behind by the scientist, but as far as I know, the place stands empty.

The Trader's Quarter

Lost Angels isn't all just churches, sailors, and mestizos. Grimme may have founded the place here because it was the best place he could find in the Maze, but it's earned its title of "Gateway to the Maze" by being the center of the entire region's commerce.

The trader's quarter is where all the business in town takes place. Sure, materials flow on and off the ships moored at the piers in the Waterfront, but money for the good changes hands here.

The Lost Angels Times

The *Lost Angels Times* is the excuse for a newspaper they publish in these parts. Some days I ache to see a proper *New York Times* again, but until they manage to get cross-continental delivery down pat, I'm stuck with the *End Times*, as the locals call this rag.

The paper's publisher is a Brit by the name of Wilbur St. John-Smythe. Old Bert's quite a character, and it shows in his paper. Bert was a follower of Grimme's before the Edict, and afterward he was only too eager to trumpet the reverend's triumphs from the highest rooftops in town.

Honestly, the paper's pro-Grimme bent just about turns my stomach, but there's no other source of news in town, so most people read it anyhow.

The Rail Barons

The Rockies may have a lock on the Golden Circle, but the rail barons' presence can be found all throughout the Traders' Quarter. None of them are so foolish as to actually advertise their presence, but they've all got offices hereabouts. After all, those people need ghost rock for their wars, and even if Grimme's tossed his hat into that ring, Lost Angels is the best place to find boatloads of that superfuel.

Union Blue and Dixie Rails have no official presence here anymore, but shell businesses from both sides make purchases for their respective governments. Bayou Vermillion and Black River actually maintain secret offices here, posing as other businesses. Wasatch has pretty much pulled out of the area—at least as far as I can tell—with little interest in the city. Meanwhile, Iron Dragon has withdrawn almost entirely to Shan Fan.

The Factories

The Traders' Quarter is lousy with factories, many of which belch filth into the hazy Maze sky. It's not quite as bad as Salt Lake City (okay, it's not nearly that bad), but when you walk through this part of the City of Lost Angels, you know you're in a city.

Since LA is geographically cut off from much of the rest of the world, you can find all sorts of different factories here: tanners, smelters, haberdashers, weavers, and so on.

That brings up another point. Allan, you remember how long I spent trying to figure out who my opposite number is in LA? For years, the identity of my Rebel counterpart eluded me, but I finally figured it out. Of course, that kind of information's too sensitive for even this report to handle. Look for a separate letter from me soon. It'll be marked for your eyes only.

And when you find out who it is, you'll eat your hat.

Bloatworms

This kind of thing could only happen in LA. There's this shyster that lives in the Traders' Quarter, a real snake-oil salesman by the name of Buster McGee, and he claims to have come up with the cure for starvation in the Maze.

You'll never guess how he does it.

He actually gets people to swallow this slimy, little slug he calls a bloatworm, kind of the opposite of a tapeworm. Once in your guts, this thing actually expands to fill the stomach, which makes you look and feel like you shouldn't be as hungry as you are.

Then, it allows you to eat just about any kind of organic material you can get down your throat: leather, rope, wood, or whatever. Assuming you can choke this stuff down, the bloatworm then digests the material for you, and it passes on to the host some of the nutrients from the "food."

This thing is damned expensive, since the bloatworms are rare, and owning one could easily save you life in this place. (I've personally missed more meals than I can count, and the first thing I'm doing once I get out of here is hunt me down a king-sized steak!)

McGee also runs a restaurant in which his cooks prepare normally inedible materials in a way that makes them even tasty. Or so I'm told. I've not had the pleasure myself—and I hope to God I never will.

Ghost Town

If Lost Angels is Hell, than Ghost Town is Hell's poorer neighbor. This is a place where no one wants to live, but it keeps growing every day. There is no law in Ghost Town. It falls under Grimme's purview, as proclaimed in detail in his Edict, but the Guardian Angels never go there.

Whether the Guardians are scared to enter Ghost Town or they just don't care, it's impossible to tell. When the Guardians leave town, whether to join Grimme's crusade or on some other church business, they always stick to the Ghost Trail or the northern or southern road.

Honestly, there's a lot in Ghost Town to be afraid of. Rumors of cannibalism run rampant, and with the way people starve in there, I can almost believe it. I actually saw a crowd of people chase a dog down the street once. When the people caught it, they ripped the poor beast apart and scuttled off, presumably to cook the pieces. I even saw one desperate soul chewing on the raw flesh as he dashed off, hoping to get his fill before he was robbed.

The fact is that Ghost Town's a hard place, but that doesn't mean it's entirely unlivable—especially if you're not particular about how you scratch out a living. Even so, there are always worse places. I'm just not always sure where they are.

It's a hard place full of hard people. The locals have a saying about their home: "Ghost Town: where the weak are killed and eaten." They usually follow that up with a flat laugh that tells you the statement isn't quite as funny as they would like.

Chinatown

There's a large contingent of Chinese living in Ghost Town. Many of these were people that were brought out West to work on the railroads, whether by Iron Dragon or any of the other rail barons' companies.

The Chinese are good people, but you wouldn't know it by the sampling that lives in Ghost Town. (By way of fairness, the same goes for any other people represented in Ghost Town.) Even so, the place is filled with a number of restaurants that would likely be excellent if they weren't so damned expensive. Ingredients are hard to come by out here, and quality ingredients are almost unheard of.

Most folks down here would head for Shan Fan if they could, but they're stuck here for various reasons. Perhaps they've made an enemy in that city to the north, or maybe their employer insists on them living here, even in squalor. Or maybe they've simply been caught in the opium dens that riddle this part of Ghost Town. Either way, they're stuck.

Tent City

If you think Ghost Town's bad, Tent City's even worse. A year or so ago, Tent City was nothing more than a few tents clustered around the edges of Ghost Town, but these day's it's exploded into a full-fledged settlement of its own.

With more and more people coming to the Maze in search of ghost rock or other kinds of riches, the population of the area has exploded—even after the Edict. Normally the overflow from Lost Angels would be picked up by Ghost Town, but even that's spilled over into the surrounding area. The people who live here are too poor to even afford one of the rickety shacks clustered tightly together in Ghost Town. These people live underneath the bottom of the barrel.

The Vestibule

So in the middle of all of this chaos, where do you go to wet your whistle? Let me introduce you to the toughest bar in the Weird West. At least that's what it says on the sign right over the bar.

Standing at the outermost edge of Ghost Town, in a cleared field free of the debris found elsewhere in the outskirts of Lost Angels, is a modest saloon called the Vestibule. The company is good, the liquor is hardly watered down at all, and best of all it's entirely free of Grimme's influence.

The Vestibule is a bright light in Ghost Town, standing out starkly against the darkness that extends out of the City of Lost Angels. Here, people of all stripes tell tales of throwing down against all manner of critters lurking in the countryside.

This is also the last stop of most traveling salesmen and delivery services. Smith & Robards' famous delivery pilots are under strict orders to not go deeper into Lost Angels than the fields outside the Vestibule. The locals here can also read up on news from the outside world (albeit weeks old) in papers delivered to the Vestibule by passersby.

In case you hadn't guessed by now, I spend a good deal of time in the Vestibule. It's the closest thing I can find to what I think of as sane civilization in this place. Soon, that's not going to be a problem for me, but if you find yourself in LA, I suggest you stop at the Vestibule on the way in.

You can identify the place by the sign out front. It reads: "Abandon all hope ye that enter by me."

It was put up there by bartender and owner Ike "Ironman" Murray. Ironman tells everyone he got his name from being built like an automaton, although he's a lot meaner. Rumor has it he actually tore apart an automaton with his bare hands in a pit battle in Salt Lake City. That would explain the scars that cover his arms and face.

Ironman's a nonpartisan kind of guy. He doesn't care for anyone in particular—North, South, or otherwise—although it seems he's got an especially dark place in his heart for Grimme and his Guardian Angels. Anyhow, it makes the place a kind of neutral ground for people from all walks of life, as long as they don't walk around in robes. When you see Ironman, give him my regards.

Agency Special Report #187: Lost Angels, 1877

Food

I've covered water, but I've ignored the food supply problems up until now. That's because there's little more to be said. The fact is that there are too many people in the Maze and not enough food to go around.

You've never seen so many skinny people in one place at the same time. Sometimes visitors call this the City of Skeletons. I have to admit, during the Days of the Dead celebrations, it's hard to tell who's in costume.

That's not to say there's no food available, but the demand for what's in supply is so high as to drive the prices through the roof. Still, people got to eat, so they do what they can. Many folks live on a weak stew of grass and tubers for weeks at a time. A steak is a rare treat indeed.

Mining

Of course, there are new rich people being created all the time in the Maze. Those prospectors that hit it rich find it pretty damned easy to run through all their money fast in the City of Lost Angels. Here, the prices don't bleed you dry—they suck every last drop out of you.

There are dozens of active mines within the domain Grimme claimed when he handed down his Edict—anything within 75 miles of the Cathedral of Lost Angels. Lots of these miners only laughed when they heard the new of Grimme's Edict. When they learned they'd have to join the church and give up 20% of their earnings to Grimme, they stopped laughing.

Most of the miners joined up with the church as soon as they could. Otherwise, their claims were subject to being entirely appropriated from them. The bulk of the miners figured that losing 20% to Grimme was better than giving up 100%, so they signed on.

A lot of these miners, though, they're not the joining kind. They busted their humps getting out here and spent their days scratching fundament out of the ground when they could have been living much easier lives elsewhere. Miner are an independent breed, and these folks decided to simply dodge the Guardian Angel patrols as best they could.

Some of them succeed. Others get caught and are sent to the Rock. Many of their friends have joined the Men of the Grid too.

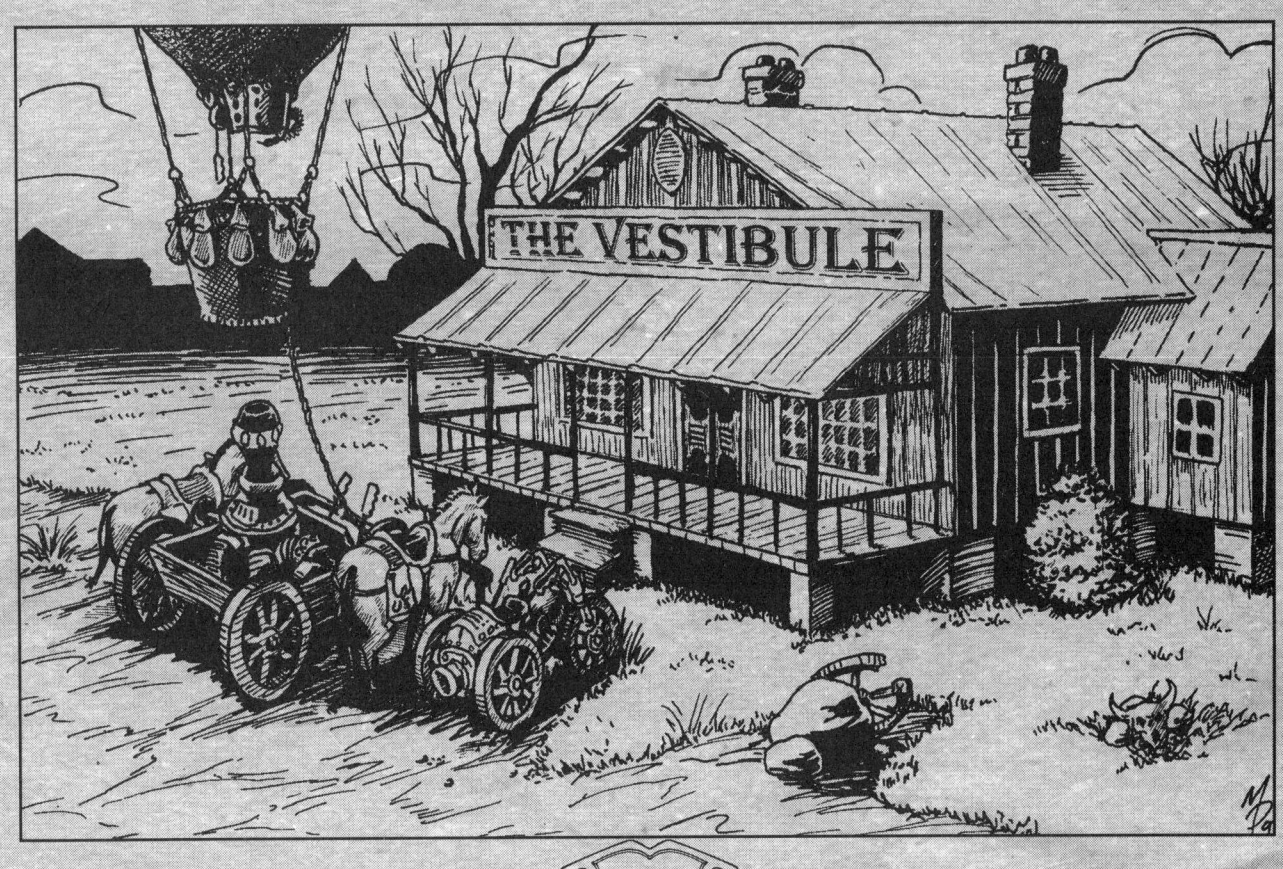

Agency Special Report #187: Lost Angels, 1877

Top Secret   "Read It & Weep!"   Alpha Clearance Only

Chapter Five: The Near Maze

After Grimme the battle of Bloody Sunday, the waters of the Great Maze near the city grew even stranger than ever before. That's like saying your mother-in-law got uglier, Allan. It's impossible to imagine.

The sea waters bubbled up with the stench of sulphur, and the air turned dark and hazy. New, watery creatures slipped up out of the disturbed depths. In short, a nasty place just got a whole lot nastier.

The Near Maze, as the area is called, seems like its always shrouded in fog. All ships approaching from the south and the north can see the haze from up to a mile away. That's supposedly the longest line of sight in the Maze. The fog reaches from the surface of the water to above the tops of the cliffs, enshrouding the small mining towns up there too.

Getting lost in the Near Maze is easier than ever. Without a compass, map, and a lot of skill, travelers take their lives in their hands when they board a boat in Lost Angels. Of course, if they're leaving, they're the lucky ones.

The Rock

No matter how bad things might get in Lost Angels, people always know there's one place that's even worse: Rock Island Prison. Enough's been said about this place before, how it's the most impenetrable prison on the face of this planet. No one's ever broken out. Let me tell you about someone who got in.

I don't know too much about the story, but what little I've been able to dig up points toward an Indian called Stalks-the-Night. Apparently this man had finally had enough of Grimme, and he decided to take the fight directly to the reverend.

Stalks-the-Night waited for Grimme to make one of his regular visits to the Rock, to minister to the faithless there. Then he somehow slipped out into the Rock under cover of night and went to confront the church leader.

I don't know what happened out there—I'd give my right eyetooth to know—but there was one Hell of a light show that night. Beams of light stabbed out from atop the Rock, and the whole place seemed to glow with the energy the island prison was giving off. It all ended with a thunderous crack that rattled the windows in the Vestibule, where I was that evening.

I have no idea what happened to that crazy Indian, but if he really made it out to the Rock that night, he must have been on the losing end of that fight. After all, no one's seen him since—and I know lots of folks who seen Grimme every Sunday.

Jehosephat Valley

With the constant threat of cannibalism in a place as desperate for food as Lost Angels, the Guardians are careful to collect bodies as soon as they crop up. They take them directly out to the local boneyard: Jehosephat Valley.

Jehosephat's only about 10 miles from the northeastern edge of Lost Angels, just off the northern road out of town. It's got a chapel (from the Church of Lost Angels, of course) right out front, at which people can come to grieve for those they've lost.

No one who's not a member of the Guardian Angels is allowed within the gated fence that surrounds the valley. The Guardians claim they're there to keep grave robbers from getting in. Seems to me they're trying even harder to keep something inside from getting out.

I just hope they're doing a good job.

Mission San Xavier del Bac

This is the largest mestizo settlement in the area, outside of the Spanish Quarter in Lost Angels itself. Don Lopez leaves this little town alone. Although it's as mestizo as anything, it's also only 22 miles to the south of Lost Angels. This means that the people here are already paying tithes to the Church of Lost Angels. For that reason, Lopez's sons have little sway here.

There's a small chapel for Grimme's church here, but the Guardian Angels don't come by too often. The mestizos all but openly worship their own faith here, their special blend of Catholicism and their own ancient rites. Shrines to the saints are scattered about the city, and these have somehow managed to escape the Guardians' notice so far.

The Days of the Dead celebrations here are fantastic, beating out even those in Lost Angels. After all, the people here don't have to be watching over their shoulders for the Guardians all the time. If you're into this kind of party, you owe it to yourself to make it down here next November.

Railhead

In the early months of the Great Rail Wars, one thing that allowed some companies to leap ahead of their competitors was the presence of handy towns that provided a base of operations for construction jobs. Some areas were just too desolate for the rail companies to build through, so they didn't. Bayou Vermilion solved this problem by creating Railhead.

Railhead is a mobile town. Built along a rail line running straight out of Tombstone, Bayou Vermilion's Railhead is built atop a half-mile-long strings of flat cars. There's a casino, a dance hall, a hotel, a general store, a trading post, a barber shop, a bank, even small, narrow homes. Everything you might find in any company town is built on a flat car and towed behind a massive ghost-rock powered steam engine.

The engine itself is a wonder of mad science. Two floors tall, it sports five smokestacks. Guards armed with long rifles and Gatling pistols patrol the engine day and night, protecting the enormous engines.

35

In addition to the shops on rails, plenty of support businesses have sprung up around Railhead. Lots of these are in massive tents that can be struck and repitched quickly. Sure they're not as mobile as the rest of Railhead, but many of these aren't actually owned directly by Bayou Vermillion, so at least the workers are getting some choices. Still, each of these places must pay a licensing fee to BV or get run out of the mobile town. After all, it's still their right-of-way.

Railhead moves ahead once a week to keep pace with the workers on the railroad. This usually on Sunday when the town's blue laws prohibit the sale of liquor anyway. The employees and support citizens of Railhead batten down the hatches and wait for the engine to lurch ahead on newly laid rails, then set up shop for another week of backbreaking work.

The mobile company town of Railhead has a perfectly enclosed economy. The town's mayor, Jean St. Cyr, does not allow trade with outsiders unless its done with Bayou Vermilion scrip. Railhead even maintains its own law enforcement: Sheriff Paul Westerling and two deputies hired from among the most competent law dogs the company has found along its rails.

The largest pavilion in the workers' tent camp is owned by Xiao Pi-lung, an opium trader and the elderly patriarch of the mobile Chinatown that follows the train. Xiao's connections to the Shan Fan triads make him a powerful ally for BV, and he provides lots of cheap, opium-addicted labor to Railhead.

Railhead is still a lot closer to Tombstone than Lost Angels. Grimme knows all about the mobile town and its slow grind toward his city, but he's yet to launch a serious attack against the place. It's only a matter of time though.

Petersen Asylum

I've always said that there's worse place to spend your days than on the Rock, but Dr. Sanderson Petersen seems Hell-bent on proving me wrong. His asylum, located atop a high-peaked mesa overlooking the City of Lost Angels, is giving the Rock a run for its money as the worst place to live out your life.

Dr. Petersen set up the place as a means of caring for the people driven insane by the horrors of the Maze—we get a lot of that around here it seems—all in all, a noble cause. Unfortunately, it seems he's not been able to actually cure anyone as of yet. Still he's keeping these lunatics off the streets.

There are actually two ex-Pinkerton operatives on an extended stay at Petersen Asylum after running into something unspeakable out in the Maze. I put them there myself, which was one of the hardest things I've had to do in my life. Still, like I said, it keeps them off the streets.

Ships of the Near Maze

In addition to the stable locations, there are two notable ships worth mentioning. Both of these spend so much time in the Maze, they might as well be declared towns.

The *Evangelist*

This large Maze runner is owned by the Church of Lost Angels. It's captained by Deacon Jonah Blues, an ex-sailor and one of Grimme's most dedicated evangelists. Deacon Blues spends his days roaming from town to town, bringing the word of Grimme to the miners in the Maze.

Most miners hide when they see Blues' ship coming, since they know that if they haven't signed on with the church yet, he's sure to turn them in.

Agency Special Report #187: Lost Angels, 1877

Top Secret   "Read It & Weep!"   Alpha Clearance Only

The *Lucky Lady*

This is a large, Mississippi-style riverboat which houses a floating casino. A couple years back, an enterprising riverman-turned-miner by the name of Claude Reynard decided that scratching a living out a of cliff face was too much like hard work. He sold his stake and then used the money to build a riverboat which he stocked with all sorts of games of chance.

Reynard knew there were all sorts of miners out there with ghost rock just burning holes in their pockets. Unfortunately, to use it they'd have to abandon their claims and come to town. Reynard decided to bring the town to them—or at least the parts guaranteed to strip them of their money faster than a Maze Rat can clean a fish. He's got a reputation for running a fair game, and folks line up for a chance to get aboard his ship. He never drops anchor in Lost Angels, so the Guardians leave him alone.

The Ruins of Los Angeles

Most of Los Angeles fell into the sea during the Great Quake, but that doesn't mean there's nothing here worth knowing about. When things get slow for the salvagers around Lost Angels, you can almost always find their ships wandering around here, looking for treasure in the sunken remains of the city.

La Iglesia de los Muertos

There's one place that didn't get sucked under the waves in the Great Quake: the Church of the Dead. Fun name, right?

This was the center of the Anahuac religion back before the quake, and the priests still come back here every so often on special occasions. I've been there once myself, disguised as one of the faithful, and it's one Hell of a sight. Imagine a Catholic church built in the shape of an Aztec temple, one of those stepped pyramids you might have seen sketches of.

The place is surrounded by skulls on pedestals, which are supposed to keep unbelievers from despoiling the church while the Anahuacs are away. When I went to check the place out, the skulls didn't do a damned thing to me, but on the other hand, the place looked like no one had dared touch it while the Anahuacs were gone. Whether they're mystical guardians or simply scarecrows, the skulls seem to do the job just fine.

Chapter Six: Other Weirdness

By now, you're probably asking yourself why anyone would ever set foot in this city of the damned. You know, I've asked myself that question from time to time, and I didn't always like the answer. These days, I don't care to be here at all, which is why I'm leaving and pulling the rest of my Agency people out with me. It's just not worth it.

Still, other people seem to find good reasons to wind their way out here, and it seems inevitable that the Agency will someday have an undeniable need to be here again—possibly soon. If you're one of the folks that happens to get this assignment (and if you're not, why the Hell are you reading this?), there are some things you're going to need to know about this place.

Now, I'm not talking about who runs what or where to find a decent beer in the Spanish Quarter. (If you ever figure that one out, please let me know.) No, I'm talking about the kind of weirdnesses that you just aren't going to find anywhere else, but it's stuff you need to know about so you don't run afoul of it.

The Land

If it's not enough that there are all sorts of creatures wandering about the place, these days the land seems like its trying to kill you too. It wasn't always like this. Back when I first came to Lost Angels about four years ago, the place was pretty bad, but it wasn't downright terrible the way it is now.

The fruit on the trees out here often turns black before it can be picked—sometimes even before it's ripe. The foliage always seem to be full of burrs and thorns. Some of the plants drip this blackish-red sap that sticks to your fingers and causes most folks to break out in rashes. Even the edges of the blades of grass seem serrated these days.

All in all, not a pleasant place to be.

Patchwork Science

In this starving city, someone's come up with a particularly sick and twisted brand of the "new" science. Its practitioners call it "patchwork science." I think you and I might call it "tampering with the laws of nature."

These lunatics actually take dead tissue and try to stick it full of life. Now, I know lots of us have seen similar things before, but this is something different. Instead of just using one body, they actually stitch together all sorts of different corpses into a whole that's theoretically better than any of the originals.

Anyhow, I've actually met with one or two of these people. Dr. Wilma Meister—who's got a place with a huge laboratory in it, just outside of town—seems to be the leader of these kooks. If we'd been able to get to her before she shared her techniques with the rest of her "sewing circle," we might have been able to stop the spread of this kind of thing.

Unfortunately, it's too late for that. Patchwork beasts are springing up all over the place. I hear rumors that Grimme's even thinking about testing them out as shock troops for his army. When I say "shock troops," I literally mean shocking. A lot of these patchwork nutjobs aren't willing to stick to the forms that Mother Nature came up with, so there are all sorts of different variations that most folks wouldn't come up with in their worst nightmares.

If you happen to see one of these creatures, you're sure to recognize it instantly. They aren't the sort of thing you're liable to miss.

Angels & Demons

There are more things in the Maze than you're ever going to see Back East. Even the widely accepted creatures like Maze dragons aren't found raiding the Atlantic seaboard. Still, ever since Bloody Sunday, things here are pretty weird—even more so than normal. I mean, I see stuff like pirates lining up with the rest of the flock to get their Sunday feast every week.

Nowadays, things are downright strange.

The Army of God

As I mentioned more than a few thousand words ago, Grimme's actually managed to induct fallen angels into his army. Or so he claims.

I know, Allan, I know. It sounds like a bunch of hooey from a mob of Grimme's faithful all more than a little high on sacramental wine, right?

Take my word for it. It's as true as daylight on a sunny day—which we're not getting much of either around these parts.

I've actually seen some of these creatures myself, and they're nothing human. My first guess was that they might be some sort of patchwork creatures, and I guess that's possible. These ones, though, didn't show any of the stitch marks that are the trademark of the patchwork beast.

I've only spotted these creatures from a distance. Grimme's careful not to let them get too close to anyone in town—or anything else that's not going to be dead before it can talk about it. I know that Allan's got people scouring battlefields to see if they can get any reports from survivors of an attack involving these things, but these folks are few and far between. Whether that's due to the fact that these fallen angels don't leave any survivors to talk or it's caused by something more sinister, it's impossible to tell.

Anyhow, most of these things that I've seen actually do have wings. Some of them are feathered, while others are leathery like a bat's. They've also got long claws or talon, and some of them carry flaming swords that light up even the darkest nights. So much for staying inconspicuous, I know. Still, on a dark night, all you see of these "angels" is a flare from the flames on their blades, right before they slice into you. If you're lucky, they sail on overhead, and all you've got is a tale no one's ever going to believe—that and your life.

Even More Weirdness

Even besides Grimme's new troops, there are all sorts of odd things going on in the city and the Near Maze. We've gotten reports of incidents of all kinds, ranging from undead pirates gurgling up from the deep to flaming camels chasing down caravans on the Ghost Trail.

That's right: flaming camels. Sounds like this critter's about 10,000 miles from home, right? But remember that camel corps Lincoln started up way back at the start of the Civil War? A lot of those creatures wandered off into the desert, and you never know what might have happened to them.

There's also that killer wandering around Ghost Town, ripping out people's hearts. The *Tombstone Epitaph* guessed it was Aztecs behind the whole thing, but I'm thinking it's something simpler than that. Of course, since I'm heading out of town and the Guardians refuse to go into Ghost Town on principle, there's little chance of the killings stopping any time soon.

Anyhow, the message here is keep your eyes peeled and your nose to the ground. An open mind doesn't hurt either.

Chapter Seven: The Rebels

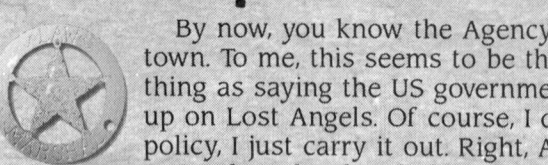

By now, you know the Agency's leaving town. To me, this seems to be the same thing as saying the US government's given up on Lost Angels. Of course, I don't make policy, I just carry it out. Right, Allan?

On the other hand, there's a lot I don't know about the situation, I'm sure. I can hear Allan's voice in my head now. "Don't worry about it, Sam. It's all under control."

Well, I'm not so sure I buy that, but I've got a long history with my boss if not my latest employer. And Allan's never steered me wrong yet. So I'm packing my things here and leaving right after I finish this report, but not without a bit of grumbling. (If I didn't indulge myself in that, Allan might think this report was a forgery.)

Still, just because we're heading out of town with our tails between our legs doesn't mean that the town's been left entirely in the hands of Grimme and his Church of Lost Angels. The fact is that there have been people willing to stand up to the good reverend ever since the city was founded.

Men of the Grid

The first group of people to get in Grimme's face about how he was handling things in the City of Lost Angels were called the Men of the Grid. As I mentioned earlier, these folks made an issue out of the fact that Grimme wanted circular streets instead of straight ones.

The original Men of the Grid were led by a man named Phineas Pascal, and the argument then was about the separation of church and state. (I think you can guess which side of the matter Grimme came down on.)

Grimme's people ran these "Sodomites" out of town more than once in the city's early years. In fact the last time the original Men of the Grid were seen was in 1871, when they were caught trying to actually blow up the Cathedral of Lost Angels.

It seems one of the Men of the Grid had been working at the cathedral as a sculptor, carving the incredible images which cover the building's surface. While working, he'd managed to get himself a set of keys to the place. One night, he and the rest of the Men of the Grid, led by Pascal, stormed the place, disabled the guards, and planted a bomb in the center of the cathedral, right under the altar.

It was a tense standoff for a while. Archangel Gabriel Fannon led the negotiations with the Gridders, but they got nowhere fast. It wasn't long before Grimme himself arrived on the scene. By that time, one Hell of a crowd had gathered to watch the proceedings, and those who secretly supported the terrorists were really enjoying the show.

When Grimme saw Pascal and his cronies sitting on his altar, demanding to be dealt with, he lost his temper, something like Christ going after the moneylenders in the temple, I'm sure he'd say. (If I'm starting to quote scripture back at Grimme, maybe I have been here too damned long.)

Anyhow, Grimme called on his God to strike the unbelievers down, to eradicate them from the holy building they were desecrating. I'll be damned if he didn't get an answer.

This happened before my time, but I've hunted down and talked to some of the eyewitnesses. Apparently, there was a bright flash of light that came from the Heavens, and it tore right through Pascal, turning him into a pile of steaming meat in the blink of an eye. The resulting thunder rattled every window in the cathedral.

Agency Special Report #187: Lost Angels, 1877

Top Secret   "Read It & Weep!"   Alpha Clearance Only

The New Gridders

That was pretty much the end of the Gridders, but they popped up again a couple years back, this time led by Ansel Pascal, Phineas' eldest son. They've maintained an on-again, off-again campaign of terror against Grimme and his church, but so far the leadership has eluded the Guardian Angels.

Since the Edict was handed down, the Gridders have stepped up their attacks. They suddenly seem to have a lot more support and a lot more weapons to help them give force to the manifestos they send to the *End Times*. I don't know for sure where this support's coming from, but I've got my ideas.

The Righteous

There's another group of people that have banded together to fight Grimme and his oppressive theocracy. The Righteous, as they call themselves, are a group comprised entirely of people who the Guardian Angels have been trying to run out of town for refusing to join up with the Church of Lost Angels.

Back before the Edict, there were lots of people who didn't care for Grimme, but they didn't have a bone to pick with him. Even though most of the city signed up with the church rather than leave town, the reverend's new "if you're not with me, you're against me" attitude has made him more true enemies than true friends.

Clergy of all different stripes have joined forces to help hide each other from the Guardian Angels and to strike back at Grimme whenever possible. They meet in different places around Ghost Town—never the same place twice—and plot for the day when they hope to topple Grimme from his celestial throne.

In Closing

Well, Allan—and the rest of you reading my report—I can't say it hasn't been one Hell of a ride here in the City of Lost Angels. I'm not going to miss the place itself, but I'm going to miss being a part of it. The battle between good and evil is going on all across the West, but nowhere more than here does it seem to be more vital. Until next time, adios.

Chapter Two:
The Lost Angels

Well, folks, if that last chapter didn't curl your toes, we've still got more in store for those hero-types out there. Now that you've seen all the different difficulties facing your heroes, we've got some things to help them out as well.

Okay, it's not all going to help, but we wouldn't want you entirely giving up on the City of Lost Angels right away, right?

Abandon All Hope

Welcome back to the City of Lost Angels, the most God-awful address on Earth.

A lot has happened in the city since the publication of *The Great Maze*, a boxed set that concentrated on the shattered California coast and even devoted a whole chapter to the Celestial City. Check out Sam Hellman's report on the subject for all the often-gory details. You won't regret it.

Reverend Grimme, savior of the Great Maze and founder of the City of Lost Angels, has been gathering followers by the hundreds, swelling the city's population near the breaking point. Famine grips the city, driving sane folks to do insane things. The rail barons continue pushing toward the city, bent on overrunning the slack-jawed lunatics who throw themselves in the way of progress. In fact, the Great Rail Wars have heated up so much that Grimme has decided to take a direct hand in things, launching his own grim crusade.

And the people keep coming.

Sometime in the past year, one of Grimme's sermons ended in a blood bath. No two reports of the so-called "Bloody Sunday" incident match (but if you've played through *Devils Tower 2: Heart o' Darkness*, you probably know a good bit about it), but they all make crazy references to monsters, darkness, malevolent shadows, ghosts, you name it.

Since then, the city and its surrounding environs have become palpably unpleasant—even more so than you might think for a boomtown constantly on the edge of starvation. Meanwhile, life is cheaper than ever in the city, as scientists on the frontier of reason crack the code of life itself—at the cost of others' lives.

And the people keep coming.

The city itself seems to send out an almost magnetic pull to folks of all stripes. Heroes from around the world hear the city's cry for help, and they respond. Villains hear Lost Angels' seductive whisper, and they come running. Exceptional people in both white and black hats make their pilgrimage to the City of Lost Angels, and Hell follows in their wake.

And the people keep coming.

How long can Lost Angels keep growing? How long before the End Times arrive, and the wicked city is swept into the sea forever?

The meek might inherit the city, but only because they're too weak to refuse it.

WHAT YOU NEED

To make full use of this book, you should have access to *Deadlands: The Weird West* (of course—if you don't have this book, you're likely in the wrong place, compadre!), *The Quick & the Dead*, *Fire & Brimstone*, and *Ghost Dancers* for all the various new character rules. *The Great Maze* helps put the City of Lost Angels in perspective with the rest of the west coast, but it isn't strictly speaking necessary. To make *Lost Angels* stand alone, we've re-spun some information from *The Great Maze* boxed set, making it all meet up with the newly advanced series of events that have led us to present-day Lost Angels.

You should also bring along a strong stomach and nerves of steel, but we don't sell those. You're on your own there.

THE LOST ANGELS

Most characters in the City of Lost Angels are drawn to the sunny coast by greed, curiosity, or even supernatural influences. Others have been here the whole time, since before the Great Quake.

These are the Lost Angels.

The city's full of all types of people from all walks of life. As the trading center of the Great Maze (and therefore the western coast of North America), hundreds of people pass through Lost Angels every day. Pirates and sailors, rail workers and cowboys, miners and industrialists, preachers and predators, they're all here, and everyone of them is looking to make a mark on the world—or die trying.

One way or the other, Lost Angels is often willing to oblige them.

As the world's biggest port for the exportation of ghost rock, this city is a center of greed. Desperate souls afflicted with a whole different kind of rock fever than you might be hospitalized for flock to the city, hoping to strike it big in the faces of the hazardous cliffs of the Maze. And hundreds more come to fleece the lucky ones of what little they're able to scratch out of the ground.

As the home of Reverend Grimme's relatively new Church of Lost Angels, the city is a kind of Weird Western Mecca, a theological center of a kind rarely found in the New World. These days, his message reaches far beyond the confines of the Maze, and many curious souls make the pilgrimage to his Celestial City.

It takes all kinds.

LOS MESTIZOS

Virtually all the Spanish-speaking Lost Angels, as well as those throughout the southern Maze, are mestizo, folks of mixed Spaniard-Indian descent. The mestizo keep to themselves mostly, practicing an unusual form of Catholicism intermingled with their own traditions.

To play a mestizo, you must take the *mestizo* Edge. Check **New Edges** for more information about this Edge.

Mestizo characters may also read Chapter Three. Everyone else: ¡Alto!

Hispanics of unmixed Spaniard descent are called "criollo." While they normally make up the religious and economic elite of most Spanish-speaking areas, they're ostracized by the mostly mestizo population of Lost Angels. If you want to play a criollo character, all you have to do ruleswise is take Spanish as your character's primary language. Otherwise, you should likely play him like a *tinhorn*. If the character comes directly from España, he should be a *ferner* too.

NEW APTITUDES

While there might be a desperate need for all sorts of skills in the City of Lost Angels, there are a couple new Aptitudes that are mostly particular to the people of Grimme's Celestial City.

FAITH: ANAHUAC

Associated Trait: Spirit

The mestizo folks who live in the Spanish Quarter of the City of Lost Angels have come up with a religion that's a strange mixture of Catholic and Aztec beliefs. While the hero doesn't strictly speaking have to be a mestizo to have this skill, if she's not, she'd better have a darn good reason for how she got involved in this faith. (Also, not all mestizos are Anahuacs.)

There's so much to know about this religion that we've dedicated a whole chapter to it. Turn to Chapter Three if you'd like to know more. Since that's in No Man's Land, though, make sure you get your Marshal's permission before you start flipping through those pages.

FAITH: CHURCH OF LOST ANGELS

Associated Trait: Spirit

Lots of folks living in Lost Angels have converted over to Grimme's frontier brand of Christianity. In fact, these days, it's not just a good idea—it's the law!

As with most religions, not every follower agrees with everything the church stands for, but they still stand with their church against all comers. Of course, lots of folks in Lost Angels are members of Grimme's church in name only. How much your hero buys into what Grimme is selling is shown by his level in this Aptitude.

NEW EDGES

Many of these Edges can only be taken by a citizen of Lost Angels. These folks must take the *Lost Angel* Edge to qualify.

Each Edge description starts with the name of the Edge, with the cost listed to the right of the name.

LOST ANGEL   0

The character is at home in Lost Angels. This Edge enables other Edges and Hindrances that are only available to Lost Angels. You can only take this with the Marshal's okay.

MESTIZO   0

The hero is of "la Raza Mestizo," the semi-indigenous, Spanish-speaking people of the southern Maze and Mexico of mixed Spanish-Indian descent. This Edge allows the character to take any of the Edges and Hindrances that are available only to mestizos.

The majority of Grimme's people don't care much for the "heretics" in the Spanish Quarter. With them, the hero receives all the penalties of being a *ferner*, but he receives no points for it. For this reason, he can't take the standard *ferner* Edge as well, unless he leaves town.

RIGHTEOUS   3

Roll +1 die type higher on the *sinnin'* table when sinnin' in the name of God—when kicking evil's ass, in other words.

Not sure what "evil" entails? That's good! The Marshal should let you know when the hero's *righteousness* is in effect.

If you're already at a d12 die type, add +2 to the final roll. This Edge can only be taken by heroes with the *blessed* Edge.

IRON STOMACH   4

Never let 'em see you sweat (or puke).

After some time in Lost Angels, this hero's seen just about everything Hell can send at the living, and it's left him just a bit jaded. He can disregard any Scart Table result of "weak in the knees" or less. This is for *Lost Angels* only.

LOST ANGELS

CHOSEN ONE — 5

The Powers That Be have decided you're their terrestrial agent. Lucky you.

Your hero may take an advance against future chip earnings. At any time, you may draw random chips from the Fate Pot, for a total number of these "advance" chips up to the character's Grit. Any chips later rewarded by the Marshal must be spent first to pay off this debt, and the hero must spend like-colored chips.

For example, a hero with 3 Grit decides to draw three additional chips in the middle of an important fight. He draws a red and two whites. As soon as the hero receives a red or white chip from the Marshal, it must go immediately into paying back that debt.

The hero is still limited to a total of 10 chips in his personal pot.

There may only be one *chosen one* in a posse. Should two characters with this Edge appear in the same posse, the winner of a Fair (5) *Spirit* contest gets to keep the Edge and the loser is out of luck until she goes her own way. Anyone who goes bust when rolling for the contest loses the Edge permanently.

This can only be taken by a *Lost Angel*.

ARCANE BACKGROUND: ANAHUAC — 3

It looks like Catholicism, it sounds like Catholicism, but this ain't your padre's Catholicism. Mestizo characters with the *faith: Anahuac* Aptitude may take this Edge to join the priesthood of the version of Catholicism practiced in the Spanish Quarter and beyond. Ask your Marshal to let you read Chapter Three for more information.

PATRON SAINT — 1-3

Anahuac worshipers (those with the *faith: Anahuac* Aptitude) usually have a patron saint who watches over him or her. Only they can take this Edge. Get your Marshal's permission to turn to Chapter Three to learn more.

NEW HINDRANCES

Seems you always got to take the good with the bad, so here are some new Hindrances to help balance out your hero.

OUTCAST — 2

This is for *mestizos* only. Some mestizos have forsaken their families and tried to join white society, with mixed results. They are not fully accepted by their mestizo brethren, nor are they accepted by many whites.

Any *outcast* character can suffer from *intolerance* at the hands of mestizo and white characters. Of course, this all depends on the particular situation and how much the people in any given encounter know about the hero and her past.

MARK O' CAIN — 5

Some folks carry with them a mark that's been in the family since the Garden of Eden. Those who bear the *mark o' Cain* are bad seeds, rotten to the core even when they do their best to live above their family heritage.

Bearing the *mark o' Cain* has several effects. First off, anyone who's blessed can sense the mark on your hero, even if he's not a Christian flavor of blessed. Blessed also react at –2 to any social-type roll you make with them.

Second, no blessed powers ever work on the character, for any reason.

Finally, Grimme's people (in particular, the Guardian Angels) seek your character out for possible recruitment. This last part wouldn't be so bad were it not for the induction ceremony, which the Marshal can tell you all about should your hero take the plunge.

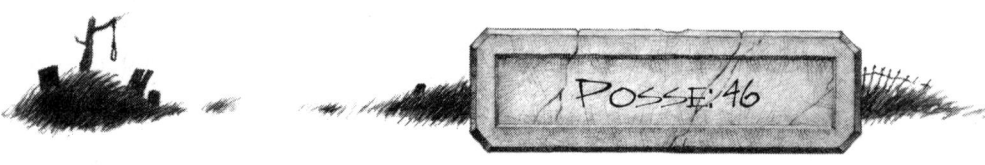

ARCHETYPES

ANAHUAC PRIEST

TRAITS & APTITUDES

Deftness 1d6
Nimbleness 2d10
  Climbin' 1
  Fightin': knife 3
  Sneak 1
Quickness 4d6
Strength 2d6
Vigor 3d6
Cognition 2d6
  Search 2
  Scrutinize 2
Knowledge 3d8
  Area knowledge: Lost Angels 1
  Language: English 1
  Language: Nahuatl 1
  Language: Spanish 2
Mien 4d10
  Tale-Tellin' 2
Smarts 1d8
  Bluff 1
  Streetwise 1
Spirit 2d12
  Faith: Anahuac 5
  Guts 2
Wind: 18
Edges:
  Arcane background:
    Anahuac 3
  Lost Angel 0
  Mestizo 0
  Patron saint 4: San
    Pedro
Hindrances:
  Obligation -5: To
    his church.
  Self-righteous -3
  Stubborn -2
Rituals:
  Ofrenda 1
  Prayer 5
  Singing 1
Favors: Ash mark, benediction,
consecrate, control the dead,
curse, guise, protection,
speak with the dead,
summon the dead.
Gear: Bible, rosary,
hunting knife
(STR+1d6), and $247.

PERSONALITY

¡Hola, compadre! Bienvenidos to the City of Lost Angels and the Spanish Quarter. I sincerely hope you enjoy your stay here.

As a leader of the mestizo community here, I have a sacred obligation to protect my people from the many horrors that have flooded our city. If you are willing to help me in my cause, then I will call you amigo. Otherwise, please get out of my way.

Life under Grimme's edict is hard for my people. I don't expect a gringo like you to understand. Still, I hope you will find time to enjoy all the Spanish Quarter has to offer. If you have need of me, just ask anyone in my part of town about me. Los santos will let me know.

Quote: "There's more to all of this than you want to know."

LOSTON

ARCHETYPES

DEMON HUNTER

TRAITS & APTITUDES

Deftness 2d12
  Shootin': crossbow, shotgun 3
Nimbleness 3d6
  Dodge 2
  Fightin': brawlin' 2
  Horse-ridin' 1
  Sneak 3
Quickness 4d10
Strength 2d6
Vigor 2d6
Cognition 3d8
  Search 2
  Scrutinize 1
  Trackin' 3
Knowledge 3d8
  Area knowledge: Lost Angels 2
  Language: English 2
  Language: Spanish 1
Mien 1d8
  Tale-Tellin' 3
Smarts 1d6
Spirit 2d10
  Faith: Christian 2
  Guts 5
Wind: 16
Edges:
  Lost Angel 0
  Iron stomach 4
Hindrances:
  Curious –3
  Death wish –5
  Superstitious –2
Gear: Crossbow
  (Shots 1, Speed
  2, ROF 1, Range
  Increment 10,
  Damage 3d6),
  20 bolts,
  double-barrel
  scattergun, 20
  shells, bota
  (wineskin) full
  of holy water,
  crucifix, rope of
  garlic, rosary,
  Bible, a horse,
  and $26.

PERSONALITY

Hey, you! Yeah, you! Did you see which way that thing went?

What do you mean, "What thing?" It was 10 feet tall, made of shadows, and had rows of teeth as long as your arm. How the Hell could you miss it?

Damn! I've been tracking that thing for two days, and if I don't stop it soon, more people are going to die.

Ever since Bloody Sunday, this town's been full of all sorts of creatures that would rip your heart out just as soon as say hello. I don't know what Grimme's doing about the "demon railroads," but he ought to take a look in his own backyard!

Hey, you look like you might be handy with a gun. I could use some backup. What do you say?

Quote: "What the Hell was that? Don't just stand there sucking your thumb! Let's get it!"

GUARDIAN ANGEL

TRAITS & APTITUDES

Deftness 2d12
  Shootin': pistol, rifle 3
Nimbleness 2d6
  Dodge 1
  Fightin': brawlin', knife 3
  Sneak 1
Quickness 4d10
Strength 4d6
Vigor 3d6
Cognition 3d8
  Scrutinize 2
  Search 2
  Trackin' 1
Knowledge 2d6
  Area knowledge: Lost Angels 3
  Language: English 2
  Language: Spanish 1
Mien 2d10
  Overawe 2
Smarts 1d6
  Streetwise 2
Spirit 1d8
  Faith: Church of
    Lost Angels 3
  Guts 2
Wind: 20
Edges:
  Eagle eyes 1
  Law man 1
  Lost Angel 0
Hindrances:
  Heroic –3
  Obligation –3: To the
    Guardian Angels.
  Self-righteous –3
Gear: Colt Army, 50 bullets,
Winchester '73, 50 bullets,
knife, Bible, uniform, and
$196.

PERSONALITY

Hold it right there, faithful citizen. Did I hear you speaking badly of the good Reverend Grimme? No? I must just be hearing things. Keep your nose clean, and maybe I won't hear them again.

Despite what some folks might tell you, the Guardian Angels are on your side. We're the only law in town now that Dunston's checked out, and that's just fine with me. He was always getting in the way anyhow.

There's no authority greater than the Church Court, and that's the way it should be. That's what Reverend Grimme tells us every Sunday.

Sure, there are always a few bad apples in every bunch, but by and large, the Guardian Angels are good people. We're here to watch out for you and make sure folks follow the church's teachings. If we all did that, there's no question we'd all get along just fine.

Of course, there are some extra benefits for being a Guardian Angel, not the least of which is getting first crack at those Sunday feasts. After all, if you're going to keep the city safe and the people in line, you've got to keep your strength up.

If you're one of the faithful, and I assume you are, you might think about joining us someday.

Otherwise, I'd advise you sign up with the next caravan taking the Ghost Trail out of town. This is the church's city now, and we're here to make sure it stays that way.

Quote: "Hello, faithful citizen. Are you gonna eat that?"

LOSTON

MAN OF THE GRID

TRAITS & APTITUDES

Deftness 3d8
Shootin': pistol, shotgun 3
Nimbleness 4d10
Dodge 3
Fightin': brawlin' 2
Sneak 4
Quickness 3d6
Strength 2d6
Vigor 4d6
Cognition 2d6
Search 2
Knowledge 2d12
Area knowledge: Lost Angels 4
Demolition 3
Disguise 2
Language: English 2
Language: Spanish 1
Mien 1d6
Persuasion 2
Smarts 2d10
Bluff 3
Streetwise 2
Survival: Maze 2
Spirit 1d8
Guts 3
Wind: 20
Edges:
Light sleeper 1
Lost Angel 0
Iron stomach 4
Hindrances:
Oath –3: Bring down Grimme and his Church of Lost Angels.
Outlaw –3
Stubborn –2
Gear: Double-action Peacemaker, 50 bullets, scattergun, 20 shells, 10 sticks of dynamite, 50 yards of fuse, blasting caps, detonator box, and $130.

PERSONALITY

Damn Grimme and his whole damned church! Folks around here don't know the whole story about him and his so-called "Celestial City." That's what the Men of the Grid are all about.

Sure, at first we were a bunch of cranks going on about having straight streets instead of these silly circles, but it's gone beyond that now. Way beyond.

Ever since Grimme threw down his Edict, things have been different around here. If you're not with the Church of Lost Angels, you can expect the Guardian Angels to knock on your door in the middle of the night. I know many people who have "disappeared" that way. Some were good friends.

You can call us terrorists if you like, but what other choice do we have? The USA and CSA are too busy bickering with each other to do anything against Grimme, and even if they weren't, they've too much to lose in the way of ghost rock if they annoy the "good" reverend.

We're not trying to hurt anyone, but we're going to bring Grimme's city down around his ears!

Quote:
"Careful with that bag. Drop it, and you'll be strumming a harp."

LOSTON

No Man's
Land

CHAPTER THREE: LOS MESTIZOS

There aren't a whole lot of real Spaniards in the city's so-called "Spanish Quarter." (Heck there just aren't that many pureblood European immigrants in the entire Maze, at least when compared to the rest of the population.)

The Hispanic portion of Lost Angels was so named by Grimme's Guardian Angels, nearly all of whom are white and follow, well, whatever religion Grimme is selling. However, there are lots of mestizos, Spanish-Indian half breeds, who speak a strain of Spanish 400 years removed from traditional Castilian Spanish (you know, the kind spoken with the proper lisp and all).

Mestizos have been an integral part of southern California ever since Spanish missionaries and conquistadors long ago marched through Mexico and up the west coast of North America, taking their pleasure with various indigenous tribeswomen all along the way.

The resulting half-breed children of Apache, Yaqui, Aztec, and other tribes learned both the language and religion of their fathers and their mothers, neither of which was particularly compatible with the other. (No, the fathers didn't always stick around to raise their mestizo kids, but there were plenty of Spanish missionaries to bring Catholic ways to the region.) The result was a brand-new society unlike either of the two that spawned it.

LOST MESTIZOS

El Pueblo de los Angeles (destroyed in the Great Quake) was a Catholic mestizo village, in which dark-skinned locals enjoyed the benefits and dangers of living with their light-skinned, European masters (both priests and soldiers). As Americans raced toward the west coast in search of a promised land, the Catholics abandoned el pueblo to the mestizos, who made a life of their own.

The Great Quake killed many mestizo families and scattered many more among the remaining mesas and islands. When the good Reverend Grimme built his celestial city on the edge of the ruins of the California coast, many of the survivors took it as a sign from the heavens. They descended on the new city in droves.

Grimme's plans did not include nursemaiding the locals, whose culture was already deeply infused with their own religion. He couldn't chase them away without tarnishing his savior image, so Grimme let the mestizos into his city as long as they agreed to restrict their settlements to his master plan. Thus the Spanish Quarter was born.

This chapter is for any player with a mestizo hero from Lost Angels or the nearby villages. It's still a part of No Man's Land, so the Marshal has final say on who gets to read this section.

VIVA LA RAZA!

The mestizos of California variously call themselves mestizos, la Raza, pobladores, Chicanos, hispanics, latinos, Californios, and Mexicanos. Each tag has a sociopolitical subtlety that even they can't entirely agree on. However, almost all of them see eye to eye on two vital things that define their lives: family and religion. In the mestizo society, these two things are also tied to one another like a mother to her newborn child.

The most widely practiced religion among the mestizos is Catholicism. However, latino Catholicism (at least as it's practiced in the Maze) is not exactly the Pope's faith. Many elements of Anahuac (Aztec) religion remain, old gods disguised as the white conquerors' saints and angels. In the Catholic chapels at the heart of every mestizo village, one can find rows upon rows of colored candles burning, each color corresponding to a patron saint. The worshipers wear small charms indicating their faith in their personal guardian angels, and their homes feature shrines to departed dead, decorated with paintings, flowers, botanicas, liquor and money.

Extended mestizo families are typically vast by white standards, often resulting from Catholic bans on birth control techniques. Loyalty to one's family is nearly unbreakable to a mestizo. Angry, young men still avenge the wrongful deaths of their great-grandfathers at the hands of the conquistadors or jefes from other families.

Despite each mestizo's tight ties to his community—or perhaps because of it—they are still a fiercely proud and individualistic people. Even within the confines of Grimme's celestial city, they fight tooth and nail to carve out a life of their own.

WITHIN THE CITY

Most of the Maze's mestizo families live in the Spanish Quarter and the adjacent rundown barrio that eventually becomes a part of Ghost Town. A single jefe, Don Xotli Lopez, rules the many families who live in "el Barrio Español."

BEYOND THE CITY

There are many small mestizo villages scattered around the southern Maze. Each is ruled by a jefe, typically a middle-age man with an extended family, friends in the Catholic church, and enough land, money, and guns to do

things his way. Each jefe thereafter is typically the eldest son from the same family in each village. Power is handed down through the generations, just as was done with European nobility.

A mestizo village might be anywhere from two small families to 200 people. Every village has a Catholic presence, typically a small church or, in the case of the larger villages, a mission at one side of the town's square. The larger villages are on wagon or horse trails. Some smaller villages have remained undiscovered since before the Great Quake.

ANAHUAC

Way back when, as Spanish-run missions cropped up along the California coast, the Jesuit padres knew their native flock wasn't practicing traditional Catholicism. Native practices were still vanishing though, and they considered the defeat of paganism the real victory.

What they didn't realize was the native were simply adapting their beliefs to those of their white conquerors. The old spirits took new names as saints, even appearing in native artwork as haloed white folk in robes. Hidden beneath new names and appearances, the native traditions continued unseen.

The most persistent of these faiths also became the best disguised. The Aztecs, the first and largest civilization crushed by the conquistadores, quickly adapted their faith to a form more appealing to the missionaries. But they did not forget their ways, even as pureblood Aztecs were replaced with mestizo children. The whispered and repeated traditions of those people became known as Anahuac, named after the Aztec empire from which the people and their faith had come.

Anahuac is practiced by an elite priesthood within mestizo society. It is most prevalent in the southern reaches of the Great Maze and in Mexico, although Anahuac "cults" can be found interspersed with proper Catholicism as far north as Portland and throughout Arizona.

The Catholic priests who remain in the area continue preaching to their flock, assuming their local traditions are simply new ways to display their faith to God.

French officers and priests in the Maze were the first to recognize the local Catholicism was hiding something dark and dangerous. They had seen such native adaptations before, in Haiti's voudun (voodoo) and Cuba's santería. Anahuac traditions are still called santería by some.

LA IGLESIA DE LOS MUERTOS

The Anahuac priesthood is fairly centralized. While traditions are passed through families, the secrets of the faith are still taught in Lost Angels. On special occasions, the members of the priesthood meet in the ruins of the Old Plaza Church, a place accessible only by traveling through the Maze toward the flooded remains of sunken Los Angeles. These ruins, located on the outskirts of what was once Los Angeles, are called "la Iglesia de los Muertos"— the Church of the Dead.

Anahuacs do not discuss the chapel's name. Some believe it refers to the worship of their dead civilization, while others note that a major part of Anahuac faith is communion with the dead. This relationship is so vital that mestizos celebrate it every year in a festival known as el Dia de los Muertos, or the Day of the Dead.

These days, this celebration takes place on the Catholics' All Saints' and All Souls' Days, November 1 and 2, although it wasn't always that way. This is just another example of how the mestizos have taken on the trappings of another culture while retaining their own traditions. The Day of the Dead has been celebrated by Aztecs and their descendants for over 2,000 years.

The Anahuac priesthood travels to la Iglesia once a year, usually just before the time of this celebration.

THE ANAHUAC FAITH

Players may play Anahuac priests in *Deadlands: The Weird West*. First, the hero must be *mestizo* (see page 45). Second, he must have the new *arcane background: Anahuac*. Finally, he must have at least 1 point in *language: Nahuatl*, the sacred Aztec tongue, and *faith: Anahuac*.

Being an Anahuac priest is a special version of shamanism (see *Ghost Dancers* for more on shamans). The Anahuac perform rituals to earn Appeasement to be spent on favors. These favors are granted by God (as understood by the Anahuacs), often with the help of patron saints (what shamans call guardian spirits).

THE FAVOR

Favors are services performed by God or the saints for the shaman. The form these services can take are based on ancient traditions. Unless generating Appeasement points to store in a patron saint (see page 65 for more on how these work), an Anahuac priest must request a favor before beginning any rituals.

Los Mestizos

The Ritual

Once the priest chooses a favor, he must attract a saint to provide it for him. This is done by means of a ritual. The more powerful the favor requested, the greater the ritual must be.

Each ritual is purchased as an Aptitude and is associated with a particular Trait. The time and difficulty of performing each ritual vary and are listed in the individual descriptions.

Successful rituals provide Appeasement points. The amount of Appeasement a ritual provides is listed in its description. A ritual provides this number of Appeasement points for each success obtained on the ritual roll.

Approval

Once a ritual is completed, the requested favor takes place immediately if the priest has enough Appeasement points. These must be spent immediately on the requested favor. The only exception is made for patron saints.

A priest with a patron saint can perform rituals without requesting a favor, just to store Appeasement in her patron saint. She may only store points equal to the cost of the saint.

It takes a single action to request a favor using only stored Appeasement points. Smart Anahuacs keep enough stored for emergencies.

Annoying the Saints

Although the saints aid those good worshipers who show them proper respect, they have a lot of people to watch over. They can't be spending all their time with the same person.

If an Anahuac consistently disturbs a patron saint for the same favor, the saint may ignore the petition. Every time an Anahuac asks for the same favor in a 24-hour period, add +1 to the Appeasement cost.

Manitous

When an Anahuac goes bust on a ritual roll, a manitou shows up in place of the saint. Draw a card to determine the manitou's *Spirit*. Then roll a contest between the manitou's *Spirit* and the hero's *faith*. If the manitou wins, it inflicts 3d6 damage to the hero's guts, plus 1d6 per raise. Otherwise, it flees back to the Hunting Grounds.

Learning Favors

During character creation, Anahuacs automatically know as many favors as they have levels in their best ritual. They can also add another favor for each point their patron saint is worth. They can pick these favors freely from the ones listed in this book.

Later, the saints don't just hand out favors when you put Bounty Points into purchasing new rituals for your Anahuac, or improving his patron saint. After character creation, if your priest is eligible to learn a new favor, he has to do it one of two special ways.

First, he can find another priest who knows the favor he wants to learn. If your hero is the only Anahuac in the area, he might have to travel a ways to find himself a mentor, possibly deep into Mexico. Finding a teacher can sometimes be difficult, depending on the favor your hero wants to learn. This can (and should) be the basis of entire adventures.

Alternatively, the Anahuac can *speak with the dead* for knowledge of the favor. This means the priest has to already know the *speak with the dead* favor, of course. The hero simply finds himself a dead priest with the knowledge he needs. These long-gone mentors aren't always as clear about how to obtain a favor as they could be. It takes one raise on the ritual roll to glean the knowledge from their cryptic answers.

NON-PRIEST FAVORS

Any follower of the Anahuac faith (anyone with at least 1 level of *faith: Anahuac*) can learn favors with an Appeasement cost of 1. Anything more requires *arcane background: Anahuac*.

SINNIN'

Not only do the Anahuacs have to worry about ticking off their saints, they've got a higher power to think about as well.

Any time an Anahuac priest breaks a rule of her religion, she must make a *Spirit* (not *faith*) roll against a TN from the Sinnin' Table below. Other folks with *faith: Anahuac* only have to worry about violating their religion's tenets when they commit a major or mortal sin.

Failing the roll costs the hero -1 point of *faith*. There may be other penalties as well, although exactly what they may be is entirely up to the Marshal, who should use her judgment on how harsh to be, depending on the severity of the sin and the situation.

SINNIN'

Sin	TN	Examples
Minor	5	Taking the Lord's name in vain, refusing others in need.
Major	9	Theft, refusing others in dire need, telling harmful and deliberate lies, failure to observe holy days or ceremonies.
Mortal	11	Murder, adultery, theft of something of great importance, blasphemy.

THE WAGES O' SIN

An Anahuac who loses all *faith* can no longer request any favors. Also, for an Anahuac priest to buy back his first level of *faith*, he has to pay 3 Bounty Points instead of the usual 1. The saints expect all of their followers to behave, although they are tougher on the ones who are supposed to be leading their flock. (Regular Anahuac worshipers only have to pay the standard 1 point.)

To regain her former status with her patron, the character must spend 5 Bounty Points to regain her first level of *faith*. She also has to complete a quest like those performed by characters seeking to become blessed for the first time.

GROUP RITUALS & CEREMONIES

Anahuacs like to worship in groups, and that means they don't always have to be bothering the saints on their own. There are two ways they can join together to generate a lot of Appeasement points: group rituals and ceremonies.

GROUP RITUALS

In a group ritual, a bunch of Anahuacs get together to perform the same ritual. One of them is named the head priest, and the others follow his lead. Each additional Anahuac priest performing the same ritual raises the leader's die type in the ritual by +1 step, up to +2 steps. For every three non-priest Anahuacs involved, add +1 die to the ritual, up to +3 extra dice.

CEREMONY

A ceremony is simply many simultaneous or sequential rituals. (This is a little different from the way shamans work ceremonies, so pay attention.)

When performing a ceremony, the normal rules about having to immediately spend Appeasement on a favor are lifted—for a while. As long as the ceremony is going on, Appeasement is collected into a single pool and cannot be used. If the ceremony is interrupted, it's considered over, although the participants can try to start over again if they like.

When the ceremony is over, the Anahuac priests involved decide how the points should be divided. They can take up to a day to figure all of this out, during which time the Appeasement sits, unspent and untouchable.

Usually the priests fill their patron spirits up with Appeasement first, then make requests that help the community as a whole. Unspent Appeasement points go away at the end of the day following the ceremony and are lost.

RITUALS

These are the only rituals that earn Appeasement for Anahuac favors. Anahuacs can't perform the standard rituals of Indian shamans listed in *Deadlands: The Weird West* or *Ghost Dancers* unless they're listed here as well. Similarly, shamans can't use these rituals.

Here's how the descriptions of the rituals work:

Speed describes how long it takes to perform the ritual. Most rituals aren't speedy things, so it pays for a smart Anahuac to plan ahead.

TN is the Target Number the Anahuac needs to get on her ritual roll.

Trait is the Trait associated with the ritual. This tells you which dice to use for the ritual roll.

Appeasement is how many Appeasement points the ritual gains for each success on the ritual roll.

Ritual items are things the Anahuac either needs or wants for the ritual. If something is "required," the ritual can't be performed without it. Using anything else in the list gives the Anahuac +1 die for the ritual roll.

HIDING IN THE OPEN

The Anahuac faith would be crushed by the Catholic Church or Grimme himself if either party understood what it preaches. However, most ceremonies are performed in Nahuatl, the ancient language of the Aztecs. Interspersed with the Nahuatl, priests often drop names of various saints and other figures from Christianity. This deception of sorts has kept the Anahuac priests safe for centuries.

Should anyone who speaks Nahuatl listen in on a ritual or ceremony and make a Hard (7) *theology* roll, he immediately realizes that Anahuac is not a Christian faith. What he does with this information is really up to him, but most everyone knows Grimme as been looking for a reason to get the mestizos out of his city.

COMMUNION
Speed: 5 minutes
TN: 5
Trait: Vigor
Appeasement: 2
Ritual Items: Psilocybin 'shroom, peyote button, morning glory (one item required)

While traditional Catholic communion involves eating a wafer that's been transmuted into the flesh of Christ, Anahuac belief puts its believers into direct contact with the saints and angels via botanicas, holy plants that "cleanse the doors of perception," so to speak.

Anahuac communion practices have survived intact since before even their Aztec incarnation. Participants sometimes speak to spirits of their Toltec ancestors. Some impure participants are spiritually attacked by even more ancient "jaguar spirits" they glimpse before they are spiritually consumed.

The physical effects of Anahuac *communion* last about eight hours, regardless of which botanica was used. During this time, all the character's Traits are –2 die types lower than normal in the physical world.

If the character busts on the *Vigor* roll, the jaguar spirits attack him. He takes 3d6 wounds to the *guts* area at the end of his bad trip.

FAST
Speed: Variable
TN: 13–the number of days fasted
Appeasement: 3
Trait: Spirit
Ritual Items: None

Fasting is a long-standing tradition in the Catholic faith, and this has carried over to the Anahuacs as well. It's a sign of respect, as well as a means for the petitioner to put spiritual needs before those of his body, to put aside the things of the flesh for those of the soul.

Each day the priest fasts, he must make a *Vigor* roll versus a TN of 5 plus the number of days he's fasted. Failure means he takes 1d6 Wind. This Wind may only be restored by eating. Even magical healing cannot restore the Wind until the priest eats. That's part of the sacrifice.

At the end of the fasting, the shaman makes the ritual roll. The TN is 13 minus the number of days fasted. (So, for example, if the priest fasts for five days, the TN is 8.) The minimum TN is Foolproof (3), so fasting more than 10 days doesn't really do any good. The saints are interested in seeing their followers get in better touch with their faith, not dead!

OFRENDA

Speed: 4 hours to create, 10 minutes for prayer
TN: 7 (9 for prayer)
Appeasement: 3 (2 for prayer)
Trait: Spirit
Ritual Items: Offerings (required): image, food, flowers, money, liquor

Mestizos revere the dead, regularly offering prayers in remembrance of their dearly departed. The secret Anahuac priesthood is no different, although they know the true names of the ancestors and the dark spirits who watch over them in the Deadlands. This gives them real power.

An ofrenda—a mestizo shrine with offerings—is comprised of an image of the departed soul in question, usually placed in an important part of a house or chapel. The shrine is then heaped with offerings like cempasuichil flowers, colored candles, food, stacks of coins, little cups of liquor, and exotic botanicas. In addition to the Appeasement earned with its creation, an ofrenda earns Appeasement whenever anyone with the *arcane background: Anahuac* Edge prays at it, even if she doesn't know the *prayer* ritual.

Ofrendas are not mobile. They must remain untouched and remain immaculate to allow those that use them to gain Appeasement.

PRAYER

Speed: 1
TN: 9
Appeasement: 1
Trait: Knowledge
Ritual Items: Cross, medallion of patron saint

Whether it's a beast or a Guardian Angel breathing down your neck, it just might be that a prayer's in order. Even if you don't like the answer you get, at least you'll have asked.

Anahuacs like to pray to different patron saints. When they pray, they tend to make promises ("I'll be good—really! Just get me out of this bind!") to their chosen saint, which is why this ritual is identical to the traditional Indian *pledge* ritual.

The petitioner (as the person doing the praying is called) swears to respect and honor the saint and the things or situations that he's the patron of. A prayer to St. Jude, for instance, would likely include promises to fight hard for lost causes—including, possibly, the hero's own plight!

A faithful Anahuac likely lives up to her saint's values daily, so she can call upon her saint without making any extra promises. If she doesn't live by these values, the Marshal should feel free to penalize the wayward worshiper whenever she calls upon the saint in the future.

Keeping a promise to a saint at any later point instantly repairs the relationship between the hero and her patron. Petitioners should be careful not to abuse this, however. The saints aren't stupid after all.

A petitioner should also expand the type and scope of her prayers to the saints. (The saints don't like to be nagged over and over for the same thing. Even they appreciate a little variety.) Each time she repeats the exact same prayer, raise the TN for success by +1.

PAINTING

Speed: Variable
TN: Varies
Appeasement: 2
Trait: Cognition
Ritual Items: Paint (required)

Face and body painting is tied into the seasons, the gods, and their associated colors. Face painting is so common during some mestizo festivals that few people consider it odd, especially when the priest is wearing festive garb.

When the Anahuac priest is requesting a favor for someone else, that person should be the one who gets painted, not the priest.

Painting	Time	TN
Face	10 minutes	11
Body	1 hour	7

SINGING

Speed: Varies
TN: Varies
Appeasement: Varies
Trait: Mien
Ritual Items: Hymnal, musical instruments

There's nothing better than a rousing song to get the saints going for you—and the more voices, the better.

To fit in with their Catholic brethren, most Anahuacs use songs from Christian hymnals ("Nearer My God to Thee" and the like) for this ritual. Most of these are printed in Latin, though, and many people prefer to sing in their native language (usually Spanish or English). The saints don't seem to care much what language the songs are in, as long as they're sung loudly.

Los Mestizos

El Dia De Los Muertos

The Day of the Dead is the single most important festival in the entire Anahuac year. The ancient Aztecs celebrated it long ago as a time for their people to give respect and honor to their dead ancestors and friends.

When the Spanish missionaries came to Mexico, they told their new converts that their pagan holidays were a blasphemy. Still, the natives weren't willing to give up the occasion, so they came up with a compromise. The festival was moved to coincide with the Catholic holy days All Saints Day (November 1) and All Souls Day (November 2).

Despite the fact that the celebration now covers two days, many people still refer to it by its original name. However, just as many mestizos call the occasion "los Dias de los Muertos" or "the Days of the Dead." In fact, some folks have even taken to starting the celebration a bit early, starting at dusk on October 31, Halloween.

During the festival, the people do spend some time in church, but they mostly dance and sing and celebrate life, and respect the power and certainty of death. And they dance and toy with any unlucky dead who might find themselves walking around on that day.

This is a powerful and mystical time for the Anahuacs. On the Days of the Dead, any mestizo with *faith: Anahuac* 1 or more can spend a white chip as if it were 1 Appeasement point, a red chip as if it were 2 Appeasement points, or a blue chip as if it were 3 Appeasement points. These people can also use the *control the dead* favor with no other prerequisite. They don't even need to know the favor!

This is a good day for serious-minded Harrowed to stay in bed. However, even the most decayed walking corpses are happily accepted at face value on these days—at least among the celebrating mestizos.

The more singers involved, the better. See the rules for group rituals on page 57 for how this works. Many Anahuac priests train a church choir for just this reason.

Of course, the petitioner doesn't need a full backup group to belt out a tune. After sundown, the unlit alleys of Ghost Town often ring with mestizos singing the praises of the saints and then asking for the *protection* favor. As long as they keep singing, they feel, the saints pay attention to them and keep them safe, even on the darkest nights.

The length of the song sets the TN for the ritual. The more the petitioner can get out (or even remember under extreme pressure), the easier it is to get the saints' attention. A chorus takes a full round to get out, no matter how many actions a hero might have. (You can only sing so fast before its sounds goofy, even to the saints.) Verses can each take a minute or more to complete.

Musical instruments can play along with the singers, and these can help with the petition. Each musician in the group must make a Fair (5) *performin'* roll with her chosen instrument. For every group of three like instruments (or for a single instrument of a certain kind) that succeeds, add +1 die to the ritual roll, up to +3.

Padre Angel Oliveri Gandarillas leads an Anahuac choir and an Anahuac band in a *singing* ritual. There are 14 people in the choir (not including himself), giving a (14÷3, rounded down to the maximum=) +3 to the ritual. The band consist of four mariachis (guitar players) and a trumpeteer. They each make their rolls, adding another (4÷3, rounded down) +1 for the mariachis and +1 for the trumpeteer. The whole ensemble gets through three whole verses of "Swing Low, Sweet Chariot" (in Spanish, no less!). The Padre gets to add +6 to his roll, so he's automatically going to beat the TN of 5. He rolls and gets (11+6=) 17. This is three successes, so he racks up 3 Appeasement points.

Singing

Song Length	TN
Chorus	9
Full verse	7
Extra verses	5

Favors

The Anahuac saints grant favors to their worshipers just as spirits grant favors to shamans. These favors generally don't have any outward appearance, since they're not spells exactly. In fact, the Anahuac gods try to hide their works in the shape of coincidence and circumstance. How a particular favor plays out is up to your Marshal to decide.

Each favor has the following entries.

Appeasement is how many Appeasement points is costs to ask for the favor. If this cost is paid, the favor is automatically granted.

Duration is how long the favor lasts. If this is "Concentration" it lasts as long as the Anahuac performs only simple actions and is not stunned.

Range is how far away the target of the favor can be. If the entry reads "touch," the Anahuac must actually touch the target, which requires a successful attack in combat. "Self" means the favor can only affect the Anahuac.

Ash Mark

Appeasement: 1
Duration: Until removed
Range: Touch

The ash mark is the rite of Ash Wednesday in which the priest takes the ashes of the palms of the previous Palm Sunday and applies them to the foreheads of his flock.

The rite is typically performed only on Ash Wednesday, after which hundreds of mestizos walk about Lost Angels with grey smudges on their foreheads. This application of the rite isn't supernaturally charged.

For each Appeasement spent, the priest may apply a more powerful version of the ash mark to a single recipient. Each person so marked receives the *protection* favor as described on page 63. The marked person may invoke the favor at any time by making a *faith* roll against the evil critter's *Spirit*. This favor lasts up to 24 hours or until the mark is removed.

Benediction

Appeasement: 1–5
Duration: Until the next sunset
Range: 10 yards

This favor extends the Anahuac gods' protection to several worthy recipients. The priest can affect one character for each level of *faith* he possesses. All characters to be affected must be within range while he invokes the favor. The invoker can affect himself with this favor.

The invoker can only provide a *benediction* to other mestizos. When successfully invoked, it gives each character +1 to all *guts* checks per Appeasement spent, until the next sunset.

In addition, the first wound level done to a character during the duration of the *benediction* is automatically negated. Treat this exactly as if a white Fate Chip had canceled the wound level.

If more than 1 wound level is done by the first attack to injure the character, the protection still only negates 1 wound level. If multiple wounds are inflicted simultaneously—from a large explosion, for example—the player may choose which wound level he wants to be negated by this favor.

A character can only receive the benefits of a single *benediction* at a time. Any others invoked for her benefit during the duration of the first favor cannot affect her.

Consecrate

Appeasement: Varies
Duration: Permanent
Range: Touch

Anahuac priests use this favor to make objects and places holy to God and the saints. The effect of this is to reduce Appeasement costs for favors requested by means of rituals performed with the object in question or in the place so consecrated.

Each successful consecration of an object reduces the cost of any single favor by -1. The consecration may be repeated a number of times equal to the priest's *faith*. No cost may be reduced lower than 1. The *consecrate* favor cannot be the favor reduced in Appeasement cost via *consecrate*. Finally, the Appeasement cost of only one favor may ever be reduced with a particular item or location.

Any character with the *arcane background: Anahuac* Edge may benefit from a consecrated object or location, but only one priest may ever consecrate a particular item or location.

Appeasement	Item/Location Consecrated
1	Small room or building
2	Large building
3	Large, unwieldy object (can't be easily hidden)
4	Small object (can be easily hidden)

Los Mestizos

Control the Dead

Appeasement: Varies
Duration: Varies
Range: 1 yard/*faith* level

When the spirits of the dead are summoned to this world (see *summon the dead* on page 64), priests can use this favor to bind them to tasks for a while.

Recently, the priests have discovered that the trick works on Harrowed as well. Other than the fact that Harrowed (like most people) typically don't much cotton to supernatural control and are generally known for their bad attitudes, this has proven a powerful favor.

The Appeasement cost for this favor varies according to what the priest demands of the dead soul. As soon as the priest is unable to spend any more Appeasement, the soul is freed of its bondage.

Once the Appeasement is spent and the command is made, the priest and the soul make an opposed *Spirit* roll. (If the subject is Harrowed, whichever side had Dominion should make the test against the Anahuac.) If the soul should beat the priest by at least a raise, the favor is reversed: The dead may now command the living!

To determine the soul's *Spirit*, either use the *Spirit* of the deceased (if it's that of a known character) or draw a card as if you were making a new character.

If the priest is controlling a summoned spirit (see *summon the dead*), he must also spend Appeasement on that favor to keep him in this world.

The Appeasement cost is –1 less (down to a minimum of 1) on any major Catholic holiday, such as Christmas, Ash Wednesday, Palm Sunday, Easter, or the Anahuac's patron saint's day.

Curse

Appeasement: 3/5/7
Duration: Permanent
Range: 10 yards/Appeasement

The priest asks for this favor to call down the wrath of God on a deserving soul. Often the means of inflicting the *curse* is using a hand-symbol, spitting on the ground, or giving the victim "the evil eye." When this favor is granted, the poor target has got a world of hurt coming his way, courtesy of the priest's patron saint.

The number of Appeasement points the petitioner has generated determines the power of the *curse*. The nature of the disease or affliction the subject of the *curse* is going to come down with may vary, but the effects are the same as for the *ailin'* Hindrance. Three Appeasement points causes a *minor* ailment, 5 points causes a *chronic* affliction, and 7 Appeasement points inflicts a *fatal* condition on the victim.

The curse may be lifted at any time by the petitioner who caused it. Other Anahuac priests may lift the curse by simply gathering more Appeasement points than were used to place the curse, and then asking the saints to check their righteous anger.

Guise

Appeasement: 2 or more
Duration: 4 hours
Range: Self

This favor allows the priest to don an illusory appearance. The number of Appeasement points spent determines both how much the priest can change his appearance and how difficult it is for someone to see through the disguise with a *scrutinize* roll. A person must have a reason to doubt the *guise* to make this roll, but since the favor only affects looks, this may not be hard.

Control the Dead

Appeasement	Command
1	Answer a question (This can be more intricate than yes or no.)
3	Perform a simple task with a clear goal that can be concluded in one day.
5	Perform a complex or ongoing task with no clear ending, for a duration not exceeding one week.

Guise

Appearance	Appeasement	TN to Spot
Minor changes to facial features	2	7
May change race and sex, and change height and weight by 25%	4	9
May impersonate a specific person and change height and weight by 50%	6	11

LOS MESTIZOS

HUMMINGBIRD

Appeasement: 1 per hummingbird
Duration: 5 rounds
Range: 5 yards

Hummingbirds are one of many Anahuac symbols of death. This favor summons them, either one at a time or a swarm, to harasses and try to kill the target. For each Appeasement spent, one deadly hummingbird buzzes into the vicinity from parts unseen. The hummingbirds swarm the target for five rounds and then quickly buzz away (unless they've been killed).

PROFILE

Corporeal: D:3d6, N:2d6, S:2d4, Q:3d10, V:3d4
Dodge 2d6, fightin': brawlin' 1d6
Mental: C:2d6, K:1d4, M:1d4, Sm:2d6, Sp:1d10
Size: 2
Terror: 5 (once the attack begins)
Special Abilities:
   Damage: Beak (STR+1d4)
   Flit: When flying, a hummingbird increases its *Nimbleness* to 2d12. This also changes the critter's Aptitudes that are based on *Nimbleness (dodge* and *fightin').*
   Fly: Pace 18
   Pierce: The hummingbird can blow clean through a person, given enough speed. If it gets two or more raises on an attack, the hummingbird actually blasts *through* whatever it was attacking. Increase the damage done by +2 wound levels.

POSSESSION

Appeasement: 4/8
Duration: Concentration
Range: 5 yards/Appeasement

This favor allows an Anhuac priest to possess another human being's body. He can either experience another's senses for 4 Appeasement, or attempt to take over the target's body for 8 Appeasement. To fully possess another human, the priest must defeat him in an opposed *Spirit* roll. Once this is done, the victim's body (but not soul) is totally controlled. The possessed can only force another contest if the possessor tries to make her perform some heinous act.

If the target takes damage while inhabited by the priest, the priest must make a *Spirit* roll against the TN of the wound on the Stun Table. A failing priest takes the same wounds himself.

The priest is in a trancelike state for the duration of the favor and can't take any actions. Once the favor takes effect, however, its range is effectively unlimited.

PROTECTION

Appeasement: 1
Duration: 1 round
Range: Self

Sometimes, especially in Lost Angels, you need a little help to keep the powers of darkness away. To use this favor, all the Anahuac needs to do is spend the Appeasement and raise a holy symbol of some kind (usually a cross or crucifix) or otherwise declare the inherent power of the saints (perhaps by rattling off the Lord's Prayer).

A supernaturally evil opponent must then make a *Spirit* total versus the hero's *faith.* Should it lose, the creature cannot touch the character or otherwise cause her direct harm. Whatever it is, it could still push over a bookshelf the blessed happened to be standing under, but it couldn't fire a weapon, cast a hex, or use any special abilities on her until it wins the contest.

Of course, this doesn't do the Anahuac's companions a bit of good unless they've got *protections* of their own. Heroic Anahuacs often find they can help their friends by standing directly between the evil thing and their pals. This can be a really awkward place to be should the favor suddenly fail.

Anahuacs shouldn't rely on this miracle too often, since the winner of the contest is likely to waver back and forth.

SCREAMING SKULL

Appeasement: 1 or more
Duration: Instant
Range: Touch

Skulls are a central symbol of mestizo faith. Little kids paint their faces like skulls for the Day of the Dead festival, and bakers sell "pan de los muertos" (bread of the dead) complete with grinning sugar skulls baked into the crust.

When the harmless death-fetish stuff isn't good enough to scare away non-mestizos, Anahuac priests find the *screaming skull* favor usually does the trick.

Screaming skull temporarily animates a human skull with a tortured manitou which lets off a horrific scream. This God-awful screech causes a TN 7 *guts* check to all but the Anahuac priest. For each additional Appeasement spent, the TN goes up by 1.

This favor requires a human skull of any age, size, or racial origin. The skull need not be clean, but it must be dead and not already animated by another manitou. (For instance, you can't animate a Harrowed's noggin while he's still using it.)

SPEAK WITH THE DEAD

Appeasement: Variable
Duration: Instant
Range: Self

Central to Anahuac belief is communion with the dead, seeking wisdom from dead ancestors and friends.

The number of Appeasement points required for this favor depends on the magnitude of the wisdom requested. Simply asking a spirit a question costs 1 Appeasement point. Asking a spirit to look into the past increases the Appeasement cost by +1 point for every five years back it's asked to peer backward.

Once the question has been asked, the priest must make a Hard (9) *Spirit* roll. On a success, the spirit has an answer, but it's vague. Each raise makes the answer clearer. On a failure, the spirit doesn't provide any useful wisdom to the priest. On a bust, a manitou lies for it instead. It's up to the Marshal to handle the details.

This favor can also be used to contact a specific ancestor whose name and cause of death is known. In this case, the Appeasement cost is 2 for each hour the priest converses with the spirit.

SPOOK

Appeasement: 1-5
Duration: Special
Range: Self

Because of their long association with mysterious and ancient gods, Anahuac priests have learned how to tap into the most unpleasant parts of the human mind. This favor takes those unpleasant parts and shows them to the victim, who scares himself silly with, well, himself.

When the favor is requested, everyone who can see the priest must immediately make an Fair (5) *guts* check. For each Appeasement point after the first spent on the favor, raise the Target Number by +2.

SUMMON THE DEAD

Appeasement: 2
Duration: Varies
Range: 1 mile/*faith* level

Anahuac priests can call out to the dead both in the afterlife—and even those still roaming this world, in the case of the restless dead who walk the Earth. The better the priest knows (or knew) the soul in question, the easier it is for him to call out to her. However, a priest can also call out to a single undead in the area, up to the range of this favor.

When contacting souls in the afterlife, the range is disregarded, as distances are meaningless there. The spirit usually remains for less than an hour.

The priest must make a *Spirit* roll (see the table below for the TN) to successfully contact and draw the soul in question to him. On a bust, the priest instead contacts a very unpleasant and undesirable soul—most likely a Harrowed who doesn't much like being interrupted, or possibly a deceitful manitou.

Souls summoned from the afterlife appear as incorporeal silhouettes of their original forms. Undead summoned in this world may take hours or days to respond to the summoning, but once the priest has made the roll they are unable to ignore the call until they arrive.

SUMMON THE DEAD

Spirit TN	Relationship
11	Stranger
9	Acquaintance
7	Friend
5	Family member

Patron Saints

There are more patron saints in Catholicism than stars in the sky. At least it seems that way sometimes!

When the mestizos were developing their religion, they clothed their gods and spirits in the names and stories of the Roman Catholic saints. Today, most every good Catholic mestizo wears a little charm with his patron saint's image imprinted on it. A lot of other Christians wear these medals as well, but the meaning is entirely different for them than it is for one of the Anahuac faith.

(For those of you who have read *Ghost Dancers*, the rules for Anahuac patron saints are pretty darn close to those for guardian spirits, but they do have their own subtle differences, so read carefully.)

A patron saint is bought as an Edge for 1 to 5 points. This Edge can never get higher than 5 points.

Each point spent on the Edge allows the priest to indefinitely store an equal number of Appeasement points in the patron saint. A character can only have one patron saint. Since a person is given a saint to watch over them from birth, there is no way for a character to switch patron saints later on. Whatever she's got, she's stuck with.

It's also impossible to fall entirely out of favor with a patron saint. Even if the character is a lapsed believer (her *faith: Anahuac* has been reduced to 0), she can still call on her patron saint in times of need. You can take mestizo out of the religion, but you can't take the religion out of the mestizo!

Any mestizo (actually anyone who's a follower of the Anahuac faith, no matter her origins) may have a 1-point patron saint. Only Anahuac priests (those with the *arcane background: Anahuac*) may initially buy a patron saint worth more than 1 point.

Besides acting as reservoirs of Appeasement, patron saints also grant their charges special abilities with the expenditure of Fate Chips. Anyone with a 1-point *patron saint* may spend white chips on abilities, while 3-point *patron saints* allow you to spend red and white chips, and 5-point *patron saints* grant abilities for blue, red, and white chips.

Any mestizo with a patron saint may spend one Legend Chip to increase the Edge by +1 point, to a maximum of 5. This is the only manner in which this Edge can be improved.

Our Lady of Guadalupe

The greatest patron spirit of the mestizos, Our Lady of Guadalupe (also known as Mary the Immaculate Virgin, the mother of Jesus Christ) appeared in a vision before Juan Diego, an Aztec survivor of the Spanish pogroms. Before Our Lady of Guadalupe appeared to this man, the Spanish missionaries had only forced a few hundred Aztecs to convert to Catholicism. Within five years of Juan Diego's retelling of the vision, several million natives had "converted."

The fact is that the Lady's instructions to Señor Diego weren't to lead his people to the Catholic faith. Nope, she told him how to disguise his Aztec faith in Catholic clothing, thus spawning the entire Anahuac religion as it stands today.

Our Lady's original form was Tlacolteutl, goddess of childbirth and carnal sin. She was also the "eater of filth" in that she consumed the sins of humanity (which had to taste pretty lousy!). Outsiders rarely see the true rituals the Anahuac priests hold honoring Our Lady of Guadalupe, which typically involve drunken orgies and other filthy habits.

White: Treat this chip as a red chip for any single use, except for Bounty Points or any other uses of this patron saint.

Red: Treat this chip as a three white chips for any single use, except for Bounty Points or any other uses of this patron saint.

Blue: The hero may completely reroll a bust and may even add other chips to the roll.

San José

This saint is Miquiztli, the Death, patron saint of the dead and dying. San Josè (named for St. Joseph, the husband of Mary) is death incarnate, both the bringer and the guardian of the afterlife. Few mestizo take this saint as their patron, considering him bad luck.

White: Everybody in sight of the mestizo is prohibited from using chips to avoid taking damage for the duration of the scene. It's up to the Marshal to decide when the scene is over.

Red: When a recently killed character (not this one) is about to make his card draw to see if he comes back Harrowed, he gets to draw one more card for each red chip so spent.

Blue: The mestizo may use the *control the dead* favor even if he does not normally know it. The current number of Appeasement points stored in this Edge is used to determine the level of the favor, although no Appeasement points are used.

San Gabriel

This is Ix, the Jaguar King, a strange and ancient god that has ruled since the Olmecs. Saint Gabriel, his patron saint guise, is the Archangel Gabriel, the herald of the End Times.

White: Spend this chip after the Marshal rolls a bust and take back a red chip from the Fate Pot.

Red: Make the Marshal discard a single chip (drawn randomly).

Blue: The hero may use the white-chip benefits of any other single *patron saint* for the rest of the session. Or if you have access to *Ghost Dancers*, the character can use the white-chip benefits of any single *guardian spirit* for the rest of the session instead.

San Pablo

This saint is the god-king Quetzalcoatl, giver of wisdom, knowledge, and life. In his Aztec origin he's a feathered serpent and creator of the Anahuac faith. In his Catholic guise, Paul was one of the great preachers of the early Church.

White: When the mestizo asks somebody a question and spends a white chip, he and the person being questioned have an opposed *Spirit* roll. If the mestizo wins, the other person cannot directly lie in response to the question. Evasion and omission are still possible, although if the person being questioned busted on the *Spirit* roll, he blurts out the truth anyway.

Red: This works like the white-chip effect, except the target is compelled to volunteer the complete truth if the questioner wins the *Spirit* roll.

Blue: Automatically refill your patron saint's Appeasement pool.

San Pedro

Aztecs who worshiped Ollin, god of movement, found a similar story in the imprisonment and escape of San Pedro, first Pope of the Christian church. San Pedro is the patron saint of prisoners and escapees, which makes him popular in Lost Angels.

White: The character doubles his Pace for one round.

Red: The hero can release any single bond, shackle, or lock that is impeding his freedom. He can use the chip against other locks, but this requires a Hard (9) *faith* roll.

Blue: The character becomes invisible, or perhaps is simply not noticed, for one minute, plus one minute for each success on a Hard (9) *faith* roll.

San Juan

Xolotl, the twin of Quetzalcoatl, is said to create the future just as his twin created the past. In the Catholic faith, he's St. John, author of a Gospel as well as the Book of Revelations.

White: When the character would otherwise be surprised, spend this chip to give him a precognitive glimpse of the ambush and eliminate any penalties for being surprised. This ability does not give the hero enough time to warn others in the posse.

Red: The hero may invoke the *speak with the dead* favor with a number of Appeasement equal to the Appeasement currently stored in the *patron saint* Edge. These points are not spent, only used to determine the favor's effect.

Blue: You may select any single die rolled by another player or the Marshal and make her reroll it. This cannot be used on your own rolls.

San Mateo

Ozomatli, the Monkey, was an important part of the Aztec calendar. Cunning and clever, he manipulated humanity's fate. The Monkey's new guise is St. Matthew, patron saint of bankers, merchants, and luck.

White: Raise the hero's *scroungin'*, *persuasion*, *gamblin'* or *filchin'* by +1 for the next hour.

Red: After spending this chip, the hero may recombine his other chips in any way he sees fit. Two whites become one red, and three whites or two whites and a red become one blue.

Blue: Gain the *luck o' the Irish* Edge for the next 24 hours.

San Judas

Tezcatlipoca is considered Quetzalcoatl's greatest enemy, but he is not necessarily evil incarnate. In the guise of San Judas (in the Catholic faith that's St. Jude, not Judas, the betrayer of Christ), he is the patron saint of lawmen and lost causes—which certainly covers a lot of heroes!

White: Roll a die. If it comes up even, this chip counts as two white chips! These must be spent immediately. If it comes up odd, you've just wasted this chip.

Red: Roll a die. If it comes up even, this chip counts as two red chips! These must be spent immediately. If it comes up odd, you've just wasted this chip.

Blue: Roll a die. If it comes up even, this chip counts as two blue chips! These must be spent immediately. If it comes up odd, you've just wasted this chip.

THE MARSHAL'S HANDBOOK

CHAPTER FOUR: THE MARSHAL'S GUIDE TO THE CITY OF LOST ANGELS

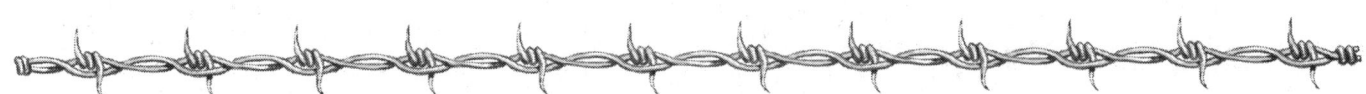

WELCOME, MARSHAL!

It's about time you found your way back to these pages. There might seem to be a whole lot going on in Lost Angels, but trust us, there's even more happening behind the scenes.

But we'll get to all that in a minute. First off, let's cover something that is even more of a concern in the City of Lost Angels than in the rest of the Weird West: fear.

In case you hadn't picked up on this yet, Lost Angels is not a nice place to be. In fact, in the wake of Bloody Sunday and Grimme handing down the Edict, the Fear Level in town has skyrocketed to 5.

This puts Lost Angels only a bit shy of becoming a full-fledged Deadland, the kind of place the Reckoners would find a cozy spot to vacation in. It's a constant battle for the forces of good to prevent the whole thing from slipping over that horrific edge.

In case you've forgotten, no matter what he might say in his sermons, Reverend Grimme isn't actually on the side of the angels—the real ones, that is. In fact, he's the architect of this city of fear.

FEAR

Let's talk about fear.

There are lots of different kinds of fear. You have the mundane fears: fear of falling, fear of failure, fear of speaking in public, fear of commitment, whatever. These may not be the kinds of fears you'd normally associate with a roleplaying game, but even so they have their uses.

Then you have visceral fear like you get in most movies: fear of dead thing, dark places, sudden noises, and scary, gore-dripping monsters. This isn't bad, but how long does the scare stay with you after the movie? Chances are, not very long.

Finally, you have under-your-skin fear that creeps the Hell out of not only the character but the player. That's a mighty fine flavor of fear to cultivate, especially in the City of Lost Angels.

It's at Fear Level 5, for crying out loud!

If Fear Levels were movie ratings, Fear Level 1 would be the Wicked Witch from the *Wizard of Oz*. Kind of scary if you're a kid, right? Otherwise, not too bad.

Fear Level 2 or 3 is more PG-13 or so, which you can get with off-screen violence and maybe a little blood. Fear Level 4 and 5 cover the R-rated stuff that you see in the standard slasher flicks.

By the time you've reached Fear Level 6, your game should have gone beyond the pale of most anything you'll see on film, at least legally. Fear Level 6 is snuff-film scary. We're talking really unpleasant.

Prepared to go on?

These are just our own thoughts on the Fear Levels. If you're not comfortable trying to get so deep under your players' skins (figuratively, of course), feel free to reinterpret the Fear Levels in any way you see fit. It's just a game after all, and everyone has fun in different ways.

CULTIVATING FEAR

At its most basic level, fear is our brain's and body's first response to a threat. It's the "fight or flight" reflex that gets your adrenaline pumping for whatever comes next. Fear prepares us to fight for our lives or run like the wind.

To fully realize the potential of a game set in a Fear Level 5 area, you have to be prepared to get beyond the mechanics of the Scart Table and go straight for the players' jugular. This isn't about rolling dice and telling a player that her hero has just wet herself. It's about actually creeping the player out too.

If you're ready to become the sort of sick bastard that would put your friends through this kind of virtual Hell—for fun, no less—here are some clues for how to poke around in your player's fear centers.

SETTING A MOOD

Establishing a proper atmosphere is the first and most important step to immersing your players into their characters' mood. You've probably read or thought about using different mood-setting tricks like playing background music, dimming the lights, handing out props, and so on. You probably also make sure to put away any kinds of distractions from your gaming sessions, like video game consoles, the remote control for the TV set, comic books, and whatever else doesn't have something to do with the story at hand.

If you aren't doing all that stuff, start right now. At the very least, taking the time to establish a proper atmosphere tells your players you've got something special planned.

IT'S ALL IN THE TIMING

As with comedy (the flip side of terror), the trick to horror is timing. The scariest movies ever made don't actually have that many scares, but good timing gives impact to even infrequent moments of terror.

In fact, as even the Reckoners—the undisputed masters of fear in the *Deadlands* setting—know, less is better. Loading too much scary stuff into your game can desensitize the players to the horrors around them.

When a hero's surrounded by zombies, they're just one big threat, and he just ducks his head and use his Peacemaker to start thumping melons. Being stalked through a graveyard on a moonless night—even by just a single, cunning zombie that plans its attacks carefully—is a lot more creepy.

Pick your scares with care, and build the tale around them. Don't just throw monsters at the heroes like they're in some kind of video game. Build the threat slowly, and make them wait for the payoff.

False starts can also throw off the predictability of the scares. Begin by describing a scary scene, but then defuse it before anything actually happens. Maybe that noise in the next room was just a cat. Or maybe it was the zombie munching on the cat's head. Keep the players guessing.

Also, knock the players off-balance. Calm them down when they think they should be worried. ("Oh, it's just a cat.") Then scare the Hell out of them when they finally relax. ("That's no cat!")

COPPING AN ATTITUDE

A good way to look at the fine art of Marshaling is to not think of it as merely describing a scene, no matter how well you might do it. You get plenty of help with that in our published adventures.

Instead, consider manipulating your players' emotions instead. Heroes can solve riddles and plug the guys in the black hats, but that's really not all that. You have to push their buttons. That's something we can't put in print for you.

Players often joke or quote from favorite movies during a game. If you pay attention, you may find this often happens during a really tense scene. It's a tension-breaker. Instead of laughing along with the joke or joining in with the quote, be impassive about it. Let the tension break eventually, but on your terms.

BUILDING THEMES

After you've gotten external considerations—like atmosphere, timing, and attitude—out of the way, the real question becomes, "What scares people?" What is it that really gets under a person's skin and makes him want to rip it off his body and run screaming into the night? And how can you use that information to help make your game creepier than ever?

Again, keeping in mind that we're trying to bypass the characters and go straight for the players' visceral fear reaction, here are some ideas to explore.

ISOLATION

Isolation is a classic horror theme, but it only works if you establish a baseline of what is considered normal for the story. This baseline should be close to what most folks would consider normal—not most heroes. Lots of heroes are drifters, and it's hard to put fear of isolation into someone who isolates himself.

The more interesting extras the posse knows, the better. Same goes for having the heroes develop reliances on outside groups, such as law enforcement or religious organizations. The players feel that their heroes are usually connected to a living, breathing, and supportive society to make isolation an effective tool. If they're always on their own, they're hardly going to be worried about it later on.

There are many different kinds of isolation to explore in your game. First off, there's being separated from the greater population and society in general, geographically speaking. This happens every time the heroes are stuck in the boonies or locked in a room by themselves, and in the Weird West this is easy enough to do.

There's also standing outside of mainstream belief or thought. The heroes should feel this every time they try to tell doubting townsfolk they're being threatened by the supernatural. Mad scientists should get this sense of isolation a lot too. Whenever they expound on a theory for which some might call them mad, they're separated from society.

Heroes can also be isolated from sources of power or protection. This can include rail barons, law enforcement, families, religion, and so on. It might even come in the form of being removed from the rest of the posse. It can be pretty frightening for even the solidest cowpoke to have to face up against the unknown without his trusted trailmates at his back.

Conspiracies are a special kind of isolation that focus on the persecution of the characters. The fact that the heroes have a kind of knowledge that's actively being kept from the rest of the world sets them apart. Due to circumstances, the heroes might not even willing to tell others of the basis of the conspiracy. Perhaps having such knowledge could put an innocent person's life in danger. Or maybe there's just no way most folks would be willing to believe in the conspiracy.

Grimme's Cult of Lost Angels is a good example of this. If the heroes stumble upon the reality behind the church, they're going to have a hard time convincing any members of the Church of Lost Angels that Grimme's actually committing the horrible crimes the heroes are accusing him of. In fact, the listeners are more likely going to call for the Guardian Angels to haul in these heretics for questioning. To their minds, there's no way their savior could be involved in something as horrific as serving up unbelievers and other rivals for Sunday brunch, and barring hard evidence—and lots of it—there's little chance of these people ever changing their hymn.

LOSS OF CONTROL

A good part of roleplaying is about the empowerment fantasy, of playing characters that are somehow supercompetent compared to the player as well as the fictional population of the game world. You can see this sort of thing in the ultrapowerful hero that's ready to take on the worst that the Weird West can throw at him.

The flipside of this is true horror roleplaying, which can best be characterized as a disempowerment nightmare.

Take away the heroes' toys and magic powers, a little at a time or all at once. They should quickly see how much they've come to rely on these things. Now it's time for them to show the strength of their character instead of their guns (or cards or whatever).

Once you've got the heroes clamoring to get their things back, it's time to play. Give the toys and magic powers back to them in return for services rendered. See how far the characters are willing to go to avoid disempowerment (or restore themselves to their former level of power), and you could quickly find them volunteering for more horrific deeds than you could have ever dreamed up on your own.

THE UNKNOWN

The unknown is terrifying even if all hints indicate the unknown thing in question might be harmless or even beneficial. Hints of an awful, harmful unknown are even better. Keep the players in the dark outside the game, and keep the characters in the dark within the game.

See some of our published adventures for good ways to do this. The one in Chapter Six is a perfect example. At the start of the story, the heroes have absolutely no idea what's going on. It's up to you to reveal it to them slowly and purposefully until they make the leap in logic that carries them to over the threshold of disbelief and straight into what's really been happening.

The main idea here is to give the heroes small glimpses of the overall mystery that they're bravely (or perhaps foolishly) poking their noses into. As they make each realization, they gradually come closer to actually understanding the horrific nature underlying all the clues they've been accumulating during their investigation. When they finally figure out what's really been happening, the shock alone may be enough to set them questioning their choice of career.

Conspiracy-themed horror is most effective when the conspirators manipulate characters into performing foul deeds on behalf of the conspiracy. If Grimme could get the heroes fear of him to cause them to harm innocents or increase the Fear Level in an area outside of his direct realm of influence, nothing would please him more. And just think of the look on the players' faces when they realize their heroes have been had!

Perhaps the most powerful form of isolation is that of the posse members from each other. After all, these are often the people that they depend on for their very lives. Inter-posse paranoia can be very effective, as long as there is true distrust and not simply political backstabbing.

This is easy enough to do in *Deadlands: The Weird West*. The simple inclusion of a Harrowed in a posse can be reason for real distrust. After all, the heroes never know when their buddy's manitou might take over and pull the rug out from under the rest of them.

Remember: You have to give the posse unity and trust before you can hit them with disunity and distrust.

GROSS-OUT

Yes, splatter-type horror has its place, even in *Deadlands: The Weird West*. The trick is to not overuse it. If the heroes are used to standing knee-deep in gore, they're hardly going to be troubled by yet another walkin' dead knocking back their saloon doors.

Remember, you can require a *guts* check for things in the game besides corpses and monsters. If you actually manage to get a player going over something in the game, there's a good chance you should be asking her hero for a *guts* check as well.

Generally speaking, a body is not scary—unless it's walking around and stalking the hero, but that's a whole different story. Intact dead people just lie there like pale versions of their sleeping selves. Sure, when the hero realizes he's got a corpse on his hands instead of a heavy sleeper, he's likely going to be a bit shocked, but that tends to fade pretty quickly.

Mutilation, with or without death, is much more effective, especially if it's of a character with whom a player can relate. There's nothing like a screaming victim spurting red all over a previously tranquil scene to get the blood flowing, so to speak.

MAKE YOUR OWN MONSTERS

We put a lot of effort into coming up with creepy creatures that should be enough to give even the Reckoners nightmares. Once they've been described by statistics and actually shown up in print, though, they're not nearly as frightening as they could be.

Any monsters whose picture the heroes have seen, especially in glorious color, is not scary. Monsters you never see—or only catch glimpses of—are terrifying. Moving shadows, hints of scaly flesh, indications of a presence like puddles of goo or claw marks on the ground are all more frightening than a beast that simply trots up into the light and stands toe to toe with the heroes, waiting to be filled with lead. If you want to use the various beasties that show up in *Deadlands: The Weird West, Rascals, Varmints & Critters, The Quick & the Dead*, or any of the other books, by golly keep those pages out of the players hands.

If you want to take matters a bit further, we recommend coming up with your own creatures. This isn't as hard as it seems. Often all you've got to do is come up with a neat twist on a creature already described in one of our books. Of course, you're welcome to go whole hog too.

THE MECHANICS OF FEAR

Being a game, *Deadlands: The Weird West* mathematically models the effects of fear on the characters. While this is useful for keeping players honest about how their characters would actually react under scary conditions, it's very external—and not very scary.

Things like *guts* checks and Fear Levels are there to help you along as Marshal. Sometimes it's not as easy as you'd like to scare the socks off your players. Maybe the phone keeps ringing or something else happens to interrupt that flow of things you've worked so hard to establish. In times like those, it's time to break out the dice and let them do the work for you.

Also, players tend to be a lot more free with their heroes' lives than the heroes would likely be with their own. The *guts* check ensures that sometimes the heroes can have the reality of their fear enforced upon them, no matter what their players might actually want them to do instead. After all, no one's going to stand up and say, "Billy Joe saw what? My God! I think he's having a heart attack!"

Players rarely willfully let their heroes wet themselves, and sometimes it's hard to tell the players that's happened, even when it obviously should have. That's what the Scart Table's for. It gives the illusion of arbitrary fairness while helping you enforce one of the things that *Deadlands* is all about: fear.

And we're not talking about just the shiver down the spine kind of fear you might even be able to get your players to feel in the middle of a particularly intense session. Nope, we mean liquid fear running down their legs. We mean spinning about and sprinting away in terror. We mean the kind of stuff that could actually stop a heart.

And that's not the kind of stuff you want to do to your friends. Not really. (Hey, if you did scare them that badly, they might never come back to play again.) You want to do it to their heroes. That's where the rules come in.

While fear works more-or-less the same in the City of Lost Angels as anywhere else the Weird West, it crops up a lot more often there than just about anywhere else. After all, it's just a horrific nudge shy of becoming a Deadland, and you've got to reinforce that.

The following sections recap the various mechanics that deal with fear in *Deadlands*. There are even a couple additions to reflect the special badness of Lost Angels.

FEAR LEVELS: A RECAP

So you don't have to go digging around your copy of *Deadlands: The Weird West*, here's a quick recap of what happens at each Fear level. The narrative effects are cumulative.

FEAR LEVEL 1

Shadows seem a little deeper than normal. Ooh, spooky. Apply a -1 penalty to characters' *guts* checks.

FEAR LEVEL 2

Rock outcroppings and other hazards seem more dangerous than before. Hit the characters' *guts* checks with a -2 penalty.

This is the general Fear Level in the Maze, although it can get higher in spots—a lot higher. It's rarely ever lower than this.

FEAR LEVEL 3

The heroes glimpse movements in the corner of their vision. They hear sourceless creaks and moans and things that go bump in the night, and they're otherwise pretty jittery.

Have the heroes take a -3 penalty to their *guts* checks.

FEAR LEVEL 4

The landscape's features wilt with a wasting disease, and the heroes' jitters are replaced with despair. Take -4 from characters' *guts* checks, and you get to draw a Fate Chip whenever One-Eyed Jacks are dealt from the Action Deck, Marshal. This is the baseline Fear Level of the area just surrounding the City of Lost Angels.

FEAR LEVEL 5

Everything in the landscape—trees, watering holes, cattle, cactus—is either sick or dying (or both). Even when the sun is up, it's pale and sickly, unable to entirely pierce the gloom that hangs over the place, even at high noon.

Take -5 from characters' *guts* checks, and take yourself a Fate Chip whenever One-Eyed Jacks (Jacks of Spades and Hearts) or the Suicide King (King of Hearts) are dealt from your Action Deck. This is the baseline Fear Level of the City of Lost Angels and Ghost Town.

This is not a place anyone really wants to be in, but just the same Lost Angels is filled almost to bursting, straining the city's already faltering resources. Funny what greed and religious zealotry can do to people.

FEAR LEVEL 6

The land is transformed into a Deadland. Natural features, like trees and rocks, look like tortured souls. The skies darken with black clouds, ominous thunder rolling over the horizon. The shadows are long and dark and look like they could swallow a man whole and then spit out his bones.

All characters' take -6 to their *guts* checks, and you, Marshal, get to draw a Fate Chip whenever One-Eyed Jacks (Jacks of Spades and Hearts) or the Suicide King (King of Hearts) are dealt from your Action Deck. Also, the fearmonger draws an extra card from the Action Deck every turn. You only get a Fear Level 6 under dire circumstances, all of which involve the presence of the story's fearmonger itself, or temporary increases caused by specific events.

A QUICK CHEAT

A quick way to work Fear Levels is to increase every *guts* check's TN by the Fear Level. This means a TN 7 *guts* check in a Fear Level 5 area (like all of Lost Angels), is treated like (TN 7 + Fear Level 5=) TN 12. This way, all you have to remember is the special Action Deck effects associated with Fear Levels 4 and higher.

TALE-TELLIN'

Normally, spinning yarns about beating back the forces of fear is the heroes' metaphysical weapon against the forces of evil. Unfortunately for the heroes, the City of Lost Angels is Team Evil's locker room, ground zero of the End Times.

Although the heroes might do their darnedest to reassure the locals, townsfolk have become jaded and shell-shocked by the horrors inflicted on them every day. The City of Lost Angels is also a mighty big town—far and away the largest in the entire Great Maze—and it's hard to get the word out to half or more of the population at once.

It's even harder to spread the word about the defeat of evil without Grimme knowing about it. Since the "good" reverend's actually the reason the Fear Level's so high in the first place, he's not about to let a bunch of do-gooders come in and cavalierly knock holes in the wall of fear he's constructed around his city.

In the end, if the heroes can get everything to line up properly, *tale-tellin'* works to lower a Fear Level just like it normally would, but Grimme's constant efforts inevitably push it back up. On a successful *tale tellin'* Aptitude check, the Fear Level drops by –1 as normal.

However, the Fear Level rises back up to 5 within a week. The memories of even a major victory fade quickly in a town as uniquely horrible as Lost Angels, and heroes that were being carried around the Golden Circle by a throng of well-wishers one week can find themselves ignored or—even worse—avoided the next.

The consequences of botching a *tale-tellin'* are particularly keen in the City of Lost Angels. Raising the local Fear Level by +1 instantly transforms part of the City into a temporary Deadland! If this happens, Grimme may call the heroes in for a personal audience. While he supposedly chews them out for their incompetently spreading even more fear throughout an already terrified populace, he's in fact sizing them up, hoping he can manipulate them into even bigger blunders.

If the heroes consistently beat down the Fear Level, they can be sure to attract attention from the Guardian Angels and eventually even Grimme himself. Then they might be called in for an audience of an entirely different kind. If they're not careful, the conversation might come to a conclusion on the Rock, with their names being added to next Sunday's menu.

LOST HEROES

The City of Lost Angels is a mystically charged place, and this has some effects on mystically minded heroes. Most folks don't even notice these things as they go about their daily business, but then heroes aren't ever just "most folks."

The heroes aren't going to know about these different effects when they first wander into town, and you shouldn't just slap them upside the head with what's happening. Drop a few hints here and there. Let them learn about themselves by the reactions they trigger in the people around them. When they finally figure out what's going on, they're going to be in for quite a shock.

NORMAL FOLK

Gunslingers, cowpokes, saloon gals, and all the other heroes of the Weird West who rely on a keen eye and a quick draw to get them through the day (and night) suffer no unusual penalties while in or around Lost Angels. Of course, the Fear Level in town is up to 5, and that should be enough to cause problems for even the most innocent souls.

COMING BACK

Due to all the manitous hovering about the place, just waiting for a chance to cause more mischief, there is a greatly improved chance of a corpse coming back Harrowed while in the city. When a player draws cards to see if his ex-hero is due to shuffle back onto this mortal coil, any face card (Jack through Ace) or Joker indicates the character has returned from the great beyond.

However, it's not quite that simple. There is no cemetery in or even near the City of Lost Angels. Jehosephat Valley (see page 91) serves as the public focal point for mourning rites, although precious few bodies end up there.

Things being how they are in Lost Angels, it takes a special effort to keep the body intact. The Guardian Angels generally handle the disposal of all bodies, meaning they're shipped to the abattoir in the bowels of Rock Island for processing. The butchers who work there know all about the Harrowed, and they've instructed the Angels to destroy the heads of all corpses as soon as they're loaded on the ferry to the Rock and out of sight. Better hope the new Harrowed comes back before that!

SUPERNATURAL TYPES

Characters with *arcane background* Edges have to face several small modifications to the rules when doing their thing in and around the City of Lost Angels. Each different kind has its own cross to bear (so to speak), but there are a few things that affect them all.

STIGMATA

One important side-effect of Grimme's Bloody Sunday ritual is that anyone within the City of Lost Angels (or any part of Grimme's expanded domain) who has an *arcane background* Edge eventually shows outward signs of that Edge. This means that it gets harder and harder for a person with mystical secrets to keep her magical nature private. Eventually her own body starts to give her away. This effect is known as "stigmata" to the local Bible-thumpers.

The stigmata is different for everyone, although the longer a person's been in Lost Angels, the more pronounced it is. Of course, the more obvious it becomes, the less likely someone is going to want to stick around in the city. See **The 22:18 Bounty** for more about why.

The exact marks of the stigmata are related to the Edge itself. Shamans may start looking more like their guardian spirit (see *Ghost Dancers* if you don't know anything about this), while Christian blessed start to exhibit classic stigmata—bleeding from open wounds on the hands, feet, and forehead—especially on holy days. Mad scientists have been known to literally crackle with electricity or exude steam (or ghost-rock fumes). Some hucksters, much to their chagrin, become ruddy, their eyebrows arch and thicken, and soon they start looking for all the world like Old Nick himself.

These are extreme examples. However, once an arcane-influenced hero spends more than a week in town, the stigmata begin to appear. From there they gradually become more pronounced. Most stigmata can be hidden by bandages or bulky clothing, but these measures are only temporary. Eventually, the stigmata become so pronounced that isolation is the only sure way to keep them hidden.

Even though the city has many of these stigmatized people, not everyone reacts well to them. You might even require some extras to make a *guts* check (TN 5 or 7).

If the hero leaves Grimme's area of influence, his stigmata heal in one or two weeks. If he returns, they start all over again.

THE 22:18 BOUNTY

Grimme uses the phenomenon of stigmata to his favor. He's always hated having supernatural types around, since they present the greatest threat to his sovereignty. He knows that a good portion of these souls are the kind of people that could possibly bring down everything he's worked so hard to perpetrate—um, create.

With the handing down of Grimme's Celestial Edict, he's gone past simply decrying arcane-minded people as evil. Now they're servants of the Devil himself, people to be hunted down and strung up—at the very least!

Coincidentally, with the rise of stigmata within the bounds of Grimme's influence, spotting those "evil souls" has just gotten a whole lot easier. Leave it to Grimme to take advantage of that.

To that end, Reverend Grimme has publicly offered a substantial bounty on anyone who exhibits such signs of witchery within the borders of his Celestial City. He calls it the 22:18 bounty, in reference to Exodus 22:18, "Thou shalt not suffer a witch to live."

There is a standing offer of $500 or a week's worth of hearty meals at the Rectory for anyone who reports irrefutable signs of stigmata. Additionally, the Guardian Angels place those reported to show stigmata at the top of their public enemies list, and they hand out money and morsels food to anyone who points them in the right direction.

Between the morality laws and the 22:18 bounty, anyone who doesn't conform to Grimme's strict codes can be expected to be sold out faster than they can say, "Draw, pardner!"

Of course, with people as desperate as they are, more than one person has been falsely accused—and subsequently convicted—of exhibiting stigmata.

Some folks turn people in as a matter of survival. They simply need to feed their families, so they're more than willing to trade a total stranger's life for the promise of meat. (And they're not likely to ask what kind of beast the flesh came from either.)

Others turn in innocents as a matter of revenge. After all, if someone's pushing you around, the easiest way to get back at him is to let the Guardian Angels do that work for you. Some corpses have even been turned in for the bounty. The Angels don't tend to ask too many questions in these cases, even when the reddishness of an accused huckster's skin rubs off on their hands as they cart the carcass away.

HARD DAYS, RESTLESS NIGHTS

As if those magically talented people didn't have a hard enough time during their days, they've got to deal with problems at night as well. Sleep offers no respite for these souls, as the City of Lost Angels reaches out to them even in their dreams.

Characters with any *arcane background* universally suffer from the *night terrors* Hindrance while in or within sight of the City of Lost Angels. If the hero already has this Hindrance, it's doubly bad. He has to beat the Hard (9) *Spirit* roll twice to get a decent night's sleep. When they need that rest the most, they just can't seem to get a break!

Just like with stigmata, you don't need to tell the players what's going on, of course. Just have them make the necessary rolls, then describe the ill effects—if any—to them. Let them figure it out on their own. It's that much creepier that way.

ANAHUAC PRIESTS

The City of Lost Angels is the center of the Anahuac religion in the Weird West, and it's continued to be so, even after Grimme's Edict outlawed all other religions within the boundaries of his city. Since the mestizos make up such a large part of the city's population, Grimme has been reluctant to move against them as a whole for fear of sparking off an open revolt.

In fact, many mestizos have nominally joined the Church of Lost Angels in the wake of the Edict. Of course, in the same way that their Aztec ancestors fooled the Spanish missionaries into thinking they had given up their old gods, the mestizos often pay lip service to Grimme's church while continuing to commune with their saints.

On any Anahuac holy day (like the Days of the Dead) in the City of Lost Angels or any other place over which Grimme holds sway, an Anahuac priest gets to add +1 his *faith* for the duration of the day. This is over and above any other bonuses for the day.

This extra benefit is due to the fact that Grimme's power play (in the form of the Blood Sunday ceremony) attracted the attention of the spirits that play the part of the Anahuac saints. On these days, the saints step up to lend extra help to their followers.

THE BLESSED

All blessed miracles, gifts, and blessings work as normal in the City of Lost Angels. In addition, on any holy days that's a part of the blessed's religion, the blessed can add +1 to his *faith* for the duration of that day. All the excitement from the local flock helps the blessed's relationship with his higher power on those special days.

There is, however, a downside to playing a blessed in this fine town. The blessed are among Grimme's greatest enemies in Lost Angels. He hunts them down with a particular vengeance, paying hundreds of dollars in cash or food for any reports of strange folks exhibiting the stigmata associated with the blessed: haloes, bleeding wounds on the hands and feet, mysterious chime or choir sounds, and so on.

It's twisted for Grimme to persecute people for displaying their holiness in a way that most people can see and understand, but he claims these are the signs of Satan (or, as he would say it, "Say-tun!"). He says anyone outside of his church who claims to be a man (or woman) of God is a liar. Sure, it's nuts, but this is the man parading around with demons, claiming they're the soldiers of God.

HARROWED

Many Harrowed have heard the city's call, but even so, there aren't too many cropping up around these parts. Besides the fact that no one would argue with Grimme that walking dead people should be lynched, few bodies ever hang around long enough for a manitou to get into them. Almost all of them are hauled off by the Guardian Angels and butchered on Rock Island long before that.

Reverend Grimme takes full credit for the lack of Harrowed in the area, although he doesn't reveal the real reason to those outside of his cult. Instead, he tells his worshipers that his holiness keeps the evil dead from snatching them from their beds at night.

Harrowed folks with any brains in their heads (which they've got to have to be Harrowed, right?) steer clear of the Spanish Quarter during the mestizo festivals. It turns out that just about any Anahuac faithful can have her way with a Harrowed on the Days of the Dead. See Chapter Three for all the details.

Other than that, Harrowed don't have any other difficulties in the City of Lost Angels, nor are their lives any easier. All across the Weird West, people are eager to put walking corpses back in their graves. It's just that in Lost Angels they do it at Grimme's request.

Note that because Harrowed don't necessarily have the *arcane background* Edge, they don't suffer from stigmata. Of course, a Harrowed who also happens to have the Edge is affected by the stigmata just as if he were alive.

HUCKSTERS

While in the City of Lost Angels, all hucksters are treated as though they have the *bad karma* Hindrance (see *Hucksters & Hexes*). In short, the huckster receives a backlash whether he draws a Red or Black Joker. The *bad karma* Hindrance is lifted as soon as the character is outside of Grimme's realm of influence.

If a hero's already got *bad karma*, it doesn't get any worse for being in Lost Angels. If the manitous are that mad at you in the first place, stumbling around Grimme's hometown isn't going to make them any more mad.

Other than this unfortunate side-effect of the city—the fact that the manitous seem to be massed around the edges of the city, and they're real mad—hucksters don't suffer any other bonuses or penalties. Having more manitous doesn't mean more power after all.

MAD SCIENTISTS

There is a new form of mad science being explored by researchers in and around the City of Lost Angels: patchwork science, the study of instilling pieced-together corpses with some form of life. This definitely falls under the "things humanity was not meant to know" header, so heroes aren't able to walk this horrific path. It's limited to extras only, characters exclusively in the Marshal's domain. See Chapter Five for all the details on these grisly creators.

Mad scientist inventions and the inventing process are otherwise unchanged in the City of Lost Angels—with one small exception. (Okay, if you're an inventor like Smith & Robards or Dr. Hellstromme, it's not so insignificant.) The Reliability of any weird science device is reduced by −1 when used in the City of Lost Angels.

In addition to all of this, the place is absolutely lousy with gremlins (see the *Deadlands: The Weird West* rulebook) running all over the place. See page 85 for more details about how this affects things in the city.

MARTIAL ARTISTS

With the impending arrival of the rails, the local Chinese population has grown over the past couple years. To date, they have been mostly restricted to the dilapidated outskirts of Lost Angels. They have none of the respect they enjoy in Shan Fan, and most are beholden to one or more of the Rail Barons.

In fact, the Chinese have banded together, and a thriving Chinatown has sprung up inside of Ghost Town. Most Chinese don't spend much time here at all, unless they're haunting one of the many, shabby opium dens the place supports.

In any case, ch'i-based abilities are unchanged in the city and its surrounding environs. Since martial artists don't require the *arcane background* Edge (they have to have *martial arts training* and be *enlightened* instead), they don't show any signs of stigmata. This makes Grimme even more suspicious of any Asians, since he can't tell which of them may be harboring powers that could be used against him.

If you're clueless as to what we're talking about here, run on out and pick up a copy of *The Great Maze*. Inside that boxed set, there's a booklet that details all about martial artists and the fantastic powers they've gained on the road to enlightenment.

GUIDE TO LA

SHAMANS

There are very few Indian shamans in the City of Lost Angels. Hell, there aren't that many Indians around there, period. When the earth fell into the sea, most of them took the hint and headed for (literally) greener pastures.

Most shamans who approach the area experience a powerful vision of the city being completely overrun by the skeletal masau'u and other evil spirits. This is enough to get most of them to leave town on the next stage. Still, some shamans might consider such a vision a challenge.

Rituals, favors, and guardian spirits (see *Ghost Dancers*) all work as normal in the City of Lost Angels. However, entering the Hunting Grounds while within the city is extremely dangerous. Any character who uses the *vision quest* or *portal* favors while in Grimme's domain must beat a Fair (5) *Spirit* roll. A failure calls for a roll the Dementia Table (see *Deadlands: The Weird West*). On a bust, the hero also uses up all the Appeasement he may have earned from rituals or saved with his guardian spirit.

Any shaman with the *lost angel* Edge may only select guardian spirits that favor ghost medicine or war medicine. (Again, see *Ghost Dancers* for all about this.) Other guardian spirits stay far, far away from this part of the world, and they suggest their followers do too.

BLACK MAGICIANS

Hey, this is one group of people who really get a kick out of what Grimme's done with his city. For some strange reason (or possibly not so strange), practitioners of black magic do not suffer from any kind of stigmata. Other than their own flamboyance, they just blend in with the crowd.

This holds doubly true for Grimme and his top worshipers, of course. Their black magic powers appear to be works of God instead. It is this facade which has convinced many of Grimme's worshipers to follow him. After all, a man who can work such miracles must have a direct line to God, right?

In fact, some of Grimme's chosen carry chips from the cathedral's altar with them when they leave town. The dark ceremony he conducted on Bloody Sunday gave these stone chips the ability to disguise the nature of these favored cultists' dark powers too. In this way, Grimme is able to extend his influence even farther throughout the Weird West without tipping his hand.

FEAR IN THE CITY

The buildings of the City of Lost Angels loom ominously over the dark streets. Stray dogs gnaw unidentifiable bones in the gutters, racing away with their prize if anyone lingers over them too long. The wind rarely blows in the City of Lost Angels, leaving what few leaves remain on dying trees to hang motionless as corpses.

The city itself is surprisingly clean, especially as one approaches the Golden Circle. There are no puddles or horse droppings. (It rarely rains, and horses are usually eaten before they get too far.)

Due to the Fear Level, windows and mirrors reflect subtly altered images, different for everyone. Some of these images show how the person might die. Others images show wives and lovers greedily submitting to the lust of the heroes' long-standing enemies—or to shambling heaps of muscle and tentacles. Still others simply show the characters old and washed-out, their lives wasted on meaningless folly. This reflection effect is subtle enough that it doesn't cause *guts* checks—unless you're looking for an excuse, of course. Instead, use it to establish mood or foreshadow events.

THE GREAT QUAKE

The story of Lost Angels really begins with Raven starting the massive earthquake that tossed the California coast into the sea, creating the Great Maze. Out of that disaster came a more sinister horror.

As told in *The Quick & the Dead*, Grimme was a preacher working in Los Angeles when the disaster happened. He tried to lead his followers out of the devastation, but they succumbed to the temptations of starvation before he could succeed. They killed him and ate his flesh.

The being that everyone knows as Grimme is not actually that man. In fact, he's an abomination who took Grimme's form. When "Grimme" returned from the dead, he inducted the followers who had eaten him into a horrific cult. Those who had resisted temptation were killed and eaten, this time with Grimme himself joining the feast.

The new Grimme led his cannibal cultists to the spot where the current-day Lost Angels sits. There they started building the City of Lost Angels, the plans for which came to Grimme in a dream sent to him by the Reckoners themselves.

The cultists were soon joined by other survivors and the vast onslaught of humanity racing to the Maze to capitalize on a newly discovered and extremely valuable mineral: ghost rock. It was then that Grimme founded the Church of Lost Angels as a cover for his real religion: the Cult of Lost Angels.

Regular folks started joining up with Grimme's church, never suspecting the organization's horrific origins. Grimme let anyone into his flock, sinners and the righteous alike. While the righteous swelled his coffers, the sinners were the folks he was more interested in.

GRIMME'S RELIGION

Grimme's church's main purpose is to provide him with a public front for his cult. It's also his main means of recruiting new members into his cult. It's not practical to post bills asking people to join in ritual cannibalism, but all sorts of people are willing to sign up for the Sunday feast Grimme's church holds every week. From there, it's not such a large leap to the cult. After all, whether they know it or not, those folks in the chow line are already developing a taste for human flesh.

Most folks never realize the horrific ways in which they've been staving off starvation. Only those that climb the ladder within the church are ever admitted into the cult, and only then if Grimme's certain of their loyalty. Potential entrants are carefully screened and tested. The final exam consists of knowingly eating a bit of human barbecue in the cult's secret meeting hall on the Rock. If the applicant balks at this, he becomes the entree at the next meal.

Guardian Angels aren't all members of the cult, but anyone higher up than the lowest ranks of the Angels have certainly been inducted into the horrors of how life (and death) really work in Lost Angels.

MOVING UP THE LADDER

You may have noticed that there's a Guardian Angel archetype for the heroes to use in play. There's two reasons for that.

First, the heroes don't know about Grimme's cult, and neither should the players. This archetype should throw them off just a bit.

Second, there's no reason why a hero can't be a member of the Church of Lost Angels. From there it's just a short jump to becoming a low-level Guardian Angel. If they want to join up, let them. You're in for some fun!

The real trick here, of course, is that heroes simply can't move up the ladder in Grimme's church. Sure, they can buy more levels in their *faith: Church of Lost Angels* Aptitudes, but that just means they've really bought into what it is that Grimme's selling—at least during his Sunday sermons. It's got no effect on how much the "good" reverend is willing to reveal to them about the actual mysteries behind his church.

A hero cannot become a blessed member of Grimme's flock for one simple reason: Heroes are here to fight evil, not create it. If a hero actually succumbs to Grimme's lines of reasoning (such as they are) and gets inducted into the Cult of Lost Angels, he is going to inevitably become a cannibal.

If this happens, have a talk with the player about it. The hero has joined the ranks of evil, and so from here on out, he's an extra, entirely under your control, Marshal.

If you like, you can play it out for a while and give the hero a chance to redeem himself, but sooner or later the issue has to be resolved.

WORKING FOR THE OTHER SIDE

Just because a character's fallen from grace doesn't mean that the rest of the heroes (or even the other players) should know that. The fact that they've now unknowingly got a viper at their collective breast—in the shape of a trusted friend—is something you can get a lot of roleplaying mileage out of.

See if you can get the doomed hero's player to work with you on this for a bit. If he's willing, he can play the part of Grimme's spy within his former group of friends. Of course, he's taking his orders directly from you, but that's the price he's going to have to pay for letting his hero slip down the dark path.

If the player doesn't agree, strip him of the hero immediately and swear him to secrecy about how his hero "met his end." Then tell the other heroes that their friend has decided to cut ties with them so that he can more properly perform Grimme's will.

SIN & REDEMPTION

If you think the player just needs a carrot in addition to that honking-big stick, tell him that if he plays the part of the fallen hero well, there's always a chance for redemption. If he wants for his hero to have a chance to return from the darkness, then he's got to play along. There is no middle road.

Of course, if the player goes along with it, it's up to you to come up with a means for the hero to potentially redeem himself. This should vary from hero to hero, depending on the situation, but it should always involve some selfless sacrifice on the hero's part.

If the hero dies in the process of redeeming himself, so much the better. After all, if he's with Grimme, he's no doubt committed some pretty heinous acts, and for that he's got to pay. There are some things that are nearly impossible for a hero to make up for.

This can be a bitter pill for a player to swallow, but if done properly, it can be an excellent send-off for a deserving hero. This is sure to ring truer to the player than simply having his hero taken from him.

SUNDAY, BLOODY SUNDAY

If you want to know more about Bloody Sunday, pick up *Devils Tower 2: Heart o' Darkness*. This adventure details all about what's happened in the Cathedral of Lost Angels on that fateful sabbath.

If you haven't got access to that book, here's a quick recap.

Grimme used a rare ghost-rock diamond called the Heart of Darkness to pull off a ceremony that increased his power. Grimme's got all sorts of black magic powers granted to him by his cult, but the arrangement of the city streets also ensured that as long as he was within the city's borders, his magic has the appearance of coming from God instead of the Reckoners. The ceremony increased the range of this camouflaging effect to 75 miles from the altar in the center of the cathedral.

GRIMME'S CRUSADE

Heady with his newfound power, Grimme decided to take a more aggressive stance against the railroads. This actually is just a means of camouflaging his hunger for taking in more territory in which he can work his foul magic with impunity. The way he plans to do this is by setting up chapels across the Weird West, each containing a chip from the cathedral's altar, which magically extends his influence.

To start things off on the right foot, Grimme launched his crusade by sending a column of his faithful, led by several wings of Avenging Angels., to a town with a fateful name: Helltown.

When Chamberlain's Union Blue forces headed into Helltown, they managed to run off Grimme's crusaders after a vicious battle. The massacre that happened that night, however, had nothing to do with Grimme's people. In fact, it was due to powers within Helltown itself.

What really happened in Helltown? That's one we're holding on to ourselves for just a little while longer.

Grimme was happy to take credit for what happened though, and he's serious about his holy war. Grimme sees a chance to grab power over a lot of land for himself, and he's not about to let it slip through his fingers. No matter where his people go, the story's the same. They walk in innocently enough and establish a chapel. Then they slap down the Edict, telling those that aren't part of the church that they need to get out.

The rail barons are troubled by this, since Grimme's towns always absolutely refuse to sell them the right-of-way through town. This has forced them to take drastic measures, sometimes including razing a town to the ground.

THE FALLEN

It turns out that Grimme's telling part of the truth. He's actually got fallen angels working for him. The only problem is that most people forget that the most famous fallen angel was Lucifer. These "angels" are actually demons!

These demons don't look like standard demons though. They're more like dirty angels, with spiked wings. They come in all sorts of shapes and sizes, although their profiles are often close to each other. Two sample fallen angels are described here. These are supernatural and evil creatures, so the *protection* miracle works against them.

The most powerful of the fallen angels are abominations of the first order, nothing to be taken lightly. The two kinds described here are mere footsoldiers.

Grimme's careful not to tip his hand too much with these allies he's recruited from the darkest part of the Hunting Grounds. They have orders to kill anyone who sees them that's not a member of the Church of Lost Angels.

LARGE FALLEN ANGEL

Corporeal: D:3d6, N:4d8, S:5d10, Q:3d8, V:4d10
Dodge 5d8, fightin': brawlin', sword 6d8
Mental: C:3d6, K:1d4, M:4d8, Sm:1d6, Sp:2d6
Pace: 8
Size: 12

Terror: 9
Special Abilities:
  Damage: Flaming sword (STR+2d8). If the hero catches fire—your call, Marshal—the flames do 1d6 damage every round.
  Fiery Breath: Every other round, the demon can spit flame from its mouth (like a flamethrower that does 3d10 damage).
  Flight: Pace 18

SMALL FALLEN ANGEL

Corporeal: D:2d6, N:4d6, S:4d6, Q:3d6, V:4d6
Dodge 4d6, fightin': brawlin' 4d6, shootin': bow 5d6
Mental: C:1d6, K:1d4, M:4d6, Sm:1d6, Sp:1d6
Pace: 6
Size: 4
Terror: 7
Special Abilities:
  Damage: Bow (STR+1d6, plus venom)
  Venom: The venom from the arrows reduces the victim's *Nimbleness* by -1 die type for the next five minutes. The victim can make a Hard (9) *Vigor* roll to resist this effect. The effects of multiple arrows are cumulative.

THE EDICT

Grimme's manifesto puts everyone who's not in the Church of Lost Angels on notice. He's bound and determined to remake California and the lands around it in his own image. That means he wants everyone to become cannibalistic lunatics, but that's not something you can pick up from reading the Edict.

The Edict is a tool for the Guardian Angels to oppress anyone they like. It's also a warning to the rest of the world. Whether or not anyone actually listens is still to be determined.

DUNSTON CHECKS BACK IN

You can't get rid of a good man that easily. Dunston got out of his office fire unscathed, but he knew when to take a hint. Still, he's wasn't about to let Grimme win. While he left town weeks ago, Dunston snuck right back into Ghost Town on the next dark night. There he met with Ansel Pascal and joined the Men of the Grid.

Dunston's a great addition to the Gridders, since few of the others have any leadership experience. Also, with Dunston's Union connections, he's been able to convince the US government to start supplying the Gridders with weapons, hoping they'll unseat Grimme. For more on Dunston, see Chapter Six.

THE GUARDIAN ANGELS

As we mentioned before, the elite of the Guardian Angels are also high-ranking members in the Cult of Lost Angels. The others honestly think they're doing the right thing, even if it is Grimme's thing. Most Angel flights are equipped with a variety of firearms. Some of the more Biblically inclined members have taken to carrying swords which they refer to as their "swords of righteousness." Many of the cultist Guardians have black-magic powers. Like Grimme, they can use them within 75 miles of the cathedral without revealing their dark secret.

PROFILE

Corporeal: D:2d6, N:2d8, S:2d8, Q:2d6, V:2d6
Fightin': brawlin' 3d8, shootin': pistol, rifle & shotgun 2d6, sneak 2d8
Mental: C:2d8, K:1d6, M:1d8, Sm:2d6, Sp:2d6
Guts 3d6, faith 4d6, overawe 2d8, search 2d8, streetwise 3d6
Pace: 8
Size: 6
Wind: 12
Edges: Law man 1
Hindrances: Self-righteous
Gear: In a wing of five Guardians, two carry pistols, two carry rifles, and one carries a shotgun.

AVENGING ANGELS

Avenging Angels normally only accompany larger patrols in Grimme's army, and they tend to have a specific mission like bringing in someone Grimme has branded an outlaw. They have black-magic powers, which look like powers of good when within Grimme's field of influence.

PROFILE

Corporeal: D:3d8, N:3d6, S:3d6, Q:2d8, V:3d8
Dodge 4d6, fightin': sword 4d6, horse ridin' 3d6, shootin': pistol 4d8, throwin': bolts o' doom 4d8
Mental: C:4d8, K:3d6, M:3d8, Sm:4d8, Sp:3d8
Academia: occult 3d6, faith: Church of Lost Angels 4d8, guts 4d8, leadership 3d8, overawe 4d8, scrutinize 3d8, search 4d8
Pace: 6
Size: 6
Wind: 16
Edges: "The voice" (threatening)
Hindrances: Self-righteous
Black Magic: Bolts o' doom 3, dark protection 3
Gear: Sword, Colt Peacemaker, 1 set of bloody bones, and an altar fragment.

ALTAR FRAGMENTS

The Avenging Angels who work outside of Grimme's home area (within 75 miles of the Cathedral of Lost Angels) all carry a small stone chip (about the size of a bullet) from the altar in Grimme's cathedral. The altar is the focus of the mystical ritual which allows the Reverend and his followers to disguise their black magic while inside the city's rings.

This same ability extends to those who carry a fragment of the altar. This means the Avenging Angels can operate outside the home area without exposing their true nature. *Bolts o' doom* look like heavenly beams, *dark protection* looks like a dim halo, and even bloody ones appear as angelic beings.

THE ANGEL O' DEATH

Garrett Black is a Harrowed so mean he even scares his own manitou sometimes—when he's not making the thing laugh with glee. After his death and return from the grave, his mind snapped, and he's under the delusion that he's actually Death himself.

Black made the mistake of wandering into Lost Angels a few years back, and the Guardian Angels caught him and dragged him before the Church Court for being an "abomination in the eyes of God." Of course, more than one Guardian was lost in the battle to bring Black down.

Once Black was incarcerated on the Rock, Grimme gave him a choice: join the Cult of Lost Angels or suffer in the dungeons forever. Even still thinking of himself as Death, Black was happy to sign on.

The Reverend uses Black to make problems go away—permanently. These are usually people who for one reason or another cannot be dragged in front of the Church Court and shipped off to the Rock. If the heroes ever become a major thorn in Grimme's side, they may receive a visitation from Black too.

Black thoroughly enjoys his role, sometimes too much. His black-hearted soul competes with his manitou to see who's more evil. Some of the things he has done in the course of his duties have almost shocked Grimme himself.

PROFILE

Corporeal: D:3d8, N:3d6, S:2d8, Q:3d10, V:2d6
Fightin': knife 3d6, shootin': pistol 4d8, sneak 5d6, throwin': bolts o' doom 4d6
Mental: C:3d8, K:2d6, M:3d10, Sm:3d6, Sp:3d10
Guts 4d10, overawe 4d10, search 4d8, trackin' 4d8

Edges: "The stare"
Hindrances: Bloodthirsty, degeneration 5, mean as a rattler
Pace: 6
Size: 6
Special Abilities:
    Black Magic: Bolts o' doom 2, cloak o' evil 2, dark protection 2
    Harrowed.
    Harrowed Powers: Charnel breath 3, death mask 2, eulogy 4, marked for death 2
Description: Tall, dark, and deadly.

THE LOST ANGELS

There's a lot going on in Lost Angels that Hellman doesn't know about. Here's the truth.

GREMLINS

Lost Angels is lousy with Gremlins. Something about the place attracts them like flies to a week-old corpse. Every time a gizmo fails its Reliability check, draw a card. If you get a Joker, 1d6 gremlins jump into the device.

The gremlins have a field day with the telegraphs lines running in and out of Grimme's expanded zone of influence. Telegraphs sending for help or relaying bad news are mystically edited or erased from the lines, even to the point that the other end sends confirmation signals. In short, they cannot be relied on at all.

There are no mechanics for this, Marshal. Just have fun with it, and use the gremlins to twist communications in any way that you like.

THE WATERFRONT

The docks of Lost Angels are its connection with the rest of the world. The place bustles with activity from dawn to dusk, closing down only at night—or at least that's how it seems.

THE CLEANER

It seems like every time a few bodies turn up, the papers figure there's some madman behind it. They give him a colorful name, call him a serial killer, and they sell a lot of newsprint.

The fact is that the Cleaner isn't a man. In fact, it's a group of dead men that once sailed on a pirate ship known as the *Scourge of the Seas*. The *Scourge* was one of the most notorious pirate vessels around, and it had letters of marque from both the US and the Confederacy. It was a Mexican ship that finally laid the schooner to rest.

Unfortunately, some of the pirates didn't go to their watery grave so easily. The *Scourge's* captain, one Carl Brutus, busted out of Davy Jones' locker as a Harrowed, and he brought a number of his men along with him as part of his *unholy host*.

Since their resurrection, Captain Brutus and his men have stalked the streets of the Waterfront after dark. Brutus always had a thing for the soiled doves, and the pirates spend their time looking for pretty, young things to bring their captain, who spends his time skulking under the docks. Once they find a likely candidate, they drag her into the water, where Brutus has his way with her. (Sure, that doesn't do a Harrowed a whole lot of good, but Brutus doesn't particularly care about that.) After that, the watery walkin' dead haul the woman's body to the surface, gut it, and fill it with fish as a kind of macabre payment for her services.

Once a daring pirate, death has taught Brutus the lesson of caution, and he rarely ever brings his head above the water's surface these days. He's got his men to do his dirty work for him, and since he doesn't have to breathe, he's happy to spend his days in the deep. Catching them is going to be tough. Finding him will be worse.

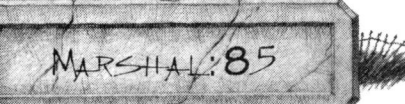

For Brutus' men, use the standard stats for walkin' dead. They all carry large knives that are rusting from their exposure to the salt water.

CAPTAIN BRUTUS

Corporeal: D:3d8, N:2d8, S:3d8, Q:3d10, V:2d6
Fightin': brawlin', knife 3d8, sailin' 4d8, shootin': pistol 4d8, swimmin' 2d8
Mental: C:4d8, K:2d6, M:2d10, Sm:3d8, Sp:3d8
Area knowledge: Great Maze 4d6, guts 4d10, leadership 4d10, overawe 2d10, search 4d8, trade: piracy 4d6,
Edges: Sense o' direction, "the voice"
Hindrances: Cautious
Pace: 8
Size: 6
Special Abilities:
   Harrowed.
   Harrowed Powers: Unholy host 5
Description: A dark, stocky man with many scars. His skin is bloated, white, and puffy.

DR. NEPTUNE

Of course there's something fishy about that water Dr. Neptune's selling. If there wasn't, the Guardian Angels would have slapped down the

mad scientists like a redheaded stepchild. The fact is that filtering water through ghost rock charcoal does remove the salt from it, but it adds a little something special to the mix. It's basically a hallucinogenic drug.

Any character who drinks a glass or more of the water must beat an Onerous (7) *Vigor* check or fall under the water's spell. Common hallucinations include shifting patterns in carpets and wallpaper, sudden appearances of dangerous creatures like snakes and scorpions, and the sudden realization that posse members are actually Harrowed, transsexuals in drag, or Harrowed transsexuals in drag. They might even see themselves and their fellows as fallen angels, come here to weep over the sins of the unrepentant Lost Angels. Use the opportunity to play with the heroes' nightmares here.

Because the effect is entirely subjective, describe it to the player as if it were really happening, not as a die roll result read off the table. It may take them a moment to realize what's going on.

On a bust, roll a result on the Dementia Table in the *Deadlands: The Weird West* rulebook. That's one bad trip. At your discretion, characters that abuse the water can develop a *hankerin'* for it too. Surprisingly, nobody with the *arcane background: shaman* edge is affected by the water. Or if they are, they're already used to being in an altered mental state and can deal with it better.

SLAVE TRADE

At night, when most sane people stay away from the Waterfront, one of the warehouses is used to march out the week's slave offerings from various slavers throughout the Maze. Most of the stock comes from coastal towns and ships sunk at sea, as well as Mexico.

The product hails from all walks of life. The only prerequisite is that the poor souls were unlucky enough to be caught by slavers. Slavery is technically illegal in California, no matter if you believe in claims of either the Union or Confederacy—or even Grimme himself. Still, there are folks who are willing to trade in human flesh in secret, and this is where they do it.

The Guardian Angels can be counted on to buy whatever stock can't be moved in a night. They generally send along an incognito buyer to pick up the unlucky dregs. These people are bound up for a quick trip to the Rock, where they'll spend what's left of their soon-to-be-shortened lives.

THE SPANISH QUARTER

The Spanish Quarter is generally Fear Level 5 like the rest of Lost Angels. During a minor holy day celebration, the Fear Level drops to 4. On a major holy day, such as los Dias de los Muertos or Easter, the Fear Level plummets to 3. Even if you're not mestizo, during these times the Spanish Quarter is the best place in Lost Angels.

EL JEFE

Don Lopez keeps an iron grip on the town, but there's little more to know about him. This man relies on guns, not magic, to maintain the power he's amassed. Well, that's not entirely true. Lopez has Padre Humo in his pocket, and that's often more than enough for him to put down any kind of challenge to his authority.

DON XOTLI LOPEZ

Corporeal: D:4d6, N:2d6, S:2d6, Q:2d6, V:4d6
Fightin': brawlin' 2d6, shootin': pistol 4d6, sneak 2d6
Mental: C:2d10, K:2d8, M:4d12, Sm:3d10, Sp:2d6
Area knowledge: Lost Angels 5d8, guts 4d6, faith: Anahuac 4d6, language: English 2d8, language: Spanish 4d8, persuasion 4d12, scrutinize 4d10, search 2d10, streetwise 5d10
Edges: Dinero 4, Lost Angel, mestizo, renown 3
Hindrances: Obligation -4 (Spanish Quarter), superstitious, vengeful
Pace: 6
Size: 6
Wind: 12
Description: A handsome mestizo with slicked-back, black hair and a wide, white grin.

THE ANAHUACS

Señor Humo is in an interesting position. Both Father Gutierrez and Reverend Grimme tolerate him because he keeps his head low. That's one thing Anahuacs do well. The only other powerful person in town who's in a position to affect him is Don Lopez, and he and el jefe have come to an understanding almost bordering on friendship.

Despite the nature of the city and the religion of which he's the local leader, Humo is a good man doing his best to save the mestizos from the insanity running rampant throughout Lost Angels these days. He cultivates a mysterious demeanor to keep people guessing about him and his abilities. Given a choice, he always tries to resolve any situation diplomatically, but in a pinch he's happy to call upon the saints.

PADRE HUMO

Corporeal: D:4d8, N:3d6, S:2d8, Q:1d8, V:4d6
Fightin': brawlin' 2d6, shootin': pistol 4d6, sneak 2d6
Mental: C:3d10, K:3d6, M:4d8, Sm:2d10, Sp:5d12
Area knowledge: Lost Angels 3d10, guts 5d12, faith: Anahuac 6d12, language: English 2d6, language: Nahuatl 4d6, language: Spanish 4d6, persuasion 4d10, scrutinize 3d10, search 2d10, streetwise 2d10
Edges: Arcane background: Anahuac, Lost Angel, friends in high places 4 (Don Lopez), mestizo, patron saint 5: Our Lady of Guadalupe
Hindrances: Enemy -2 (Guardian Angels), obligation -4 (Anahuacs)
Pace: 6
Size: 6
Wind: 18
Special Abilities:
Rituals: Communion 3, fasting 2, ofrenda 5, prayer 4, singing 4
Favors: Ash mark, benediction, consecrate, control the dead, curse, guise, protection, hummingbird, speak with the dead, summon the dead
Description: A tall, white-haired mestizo who wears colorful clothes. He always bears a mysterious smile on his wrinkled face.

FATHER JUAN GUTIERREZ

The padre's time in Lost Angels has given him stigmata—bleeding from the hands, feet, forehead, and side. It gets worse on holy days, which is when he's busiest. He often keeps a low profile.

Ironically, Father Gutierrez is not a part of the Anahuac cult. Humo and Lopez keep him around as a level of plausible deniability should Grimme ever take a greater interest in their activities. As much as they actually like him, they're more than ready to sacrifice him to Grimme if that would save their own hides.

Having arrived in Lost Angles four years ago from his home in Florida, the padre is oblivious to the cultish underpinnings of the local "Catholic" beliefs, although he's familiar with the local customs. He knows all about Padre Humo and his Anahuac teachings, and he considers himself in a struggle for his people's souls, but he believes the mestizos will side with his God.

The locals jealously protect the padre from the Guardians. He is under the protection of Don Lopez, and even those outside the Spanish Quarter know the meal they'd get for the priest's 22:18 bounty would likely be their last.

PROFILE

Corporeal: D:2d6, N:2d6, S:4d6, Q:3d8, V:4d8
Climbin' 2d6, horse ridin' 3d6, sneak 2d6, swimmin' 3d6

Mental: C:3d6, K:3d8, M:4d10, Sm:4d6, Sp:5d12
Area knowledge: Lost Angels 2d8, guts 4d12, faith: Catholic 6d12, language: English 3d8, language: Latin 3d8, language: Spanish 4d8, persuasion 4d10, professional: theology 4d8, scrutinize 2d6, search 1d6, tale-tellin' 4d10

Edges: Arcane background: blessed, Lost Angel, religious rank 1,

Hindrances: Conscious, enemy -5 (Guardian Angels), obligation -4 (Catholic Church), tinhorn

Pace: 6
Size: 6
Wind: 20
Special Powers:
   Miracles: Benediction, cloak, consecrate item, exorcism, grace, lay on hands, protection

Description: Gutierrez is in his mid-30s, and despite having been out West for a while now, he's still something of a tinhorn. He is tall, dark, and handsome, and he makes many of the mestizo women curse the rules the Catholic Church has on priests keeping themselves celibate.

THE GOLDEN CIRCLE

The Golden Circle is the heart of Grimme's celestial city, and most of the city's power is centered here, both politically and religiously, which are pretty much the same in Lost Angels, especially since Bloody Sunday.

THE CATHEDRAL OF LOST ANGELS

This Gothic cathedral is the centerpiece of Grimme's city. For more details on it, see *The Great Maze* and *Heart o' Darkness*. One detail about this place that you won't find anywhere else is the fact that the cathedral sits right over the central part of the city's water supply. The baptismal font in the front of the cathedral is full of ice-cold water fed into it by a pump that dips down into an underground lake beneath the cathedral's lowest levels.

The lake runs comes from an underground source deep beneath the water, but it lets out into a river that runs directly toward Prosperity Bay. Grimme knows about this place, and he's got it marked as yet another means of entering

or escaping the cathedral in a pinch. The river actually runs underneath the city's sewer system, although there are points at which they can access each other.

GRIMME MEMORIAL HOSPITAL

The fact is that a lot of lives are saved here in GMH, but that's not quite the whole story. Due to the conditions in the City of Lost Angels, the doctors here lose about as many people as they save. During the outbreak of the faminite plague last year, the place was practically a charnel house.

Fresh bodies are regularly hauled out of here by the Mourning Brigade, and they quickly make their way out to the Rock. Sometimes terminally ill patients find their way onto the death cart too, but they're too weak to do anything about it or alert passersby to their plight.

THE THEATER OF LOST ANGELS

What do you know? Sam's right. The place isn't haunted. It's much worse than that. The director of the theater is a man named Sir Oliver Lawrence, a proper Brit who was asked by Grimme himself to set up shop in Lost Angels. Lawrence's acting troupe was renowned across Europe, and it was quite a coup for Grimme to bring them to his "quiet Western town."

The fact is that Sir Lawrence is a twisted man with horrible powers. A student of the black arts, he finally figured out how to get his actors to do exactly what he wanted them to. He entirely wipes their minds and replaces them with the characters whose roles they play on the stage. When they're not on the stage, the actors are nearly drooling idiots, and Sir Lawrence goes to great lengths to keep them locked up, preserving his secret.

Unfortunately, the process of reprogramming his actors makes their performances rather wooden, and Sir Lawrence wasn't willing to gain control at the cost of quality. He's allowed his two leads—Julie Edwards and Conner Bond—to retain their minds and their skills. However, he constantly holds the threat of reprogramming or death over their heads. These two young lovers aren't willing to risk losing each other at their director's hands, so they play along for now, looking for the opportunity to escape.

In the meantime, Sir Lawrence holds auditions so that he can be ready to replace his leads should the need arise.

PROFILE

Corporeal: D:2d6, N:2d6, S:4d6, Q:3d8, V:4d8
Climbin' 2d6, shootin': pistol 3d6, sneak 4d6
Mental: C:3d6, K:3d8, M:4d10, Sm:4d6, Sp:4d8
Guts 4d8, faith: Cult of Lost Angels 3d8,
    performin': actin' 1d10, persuasion 4d10,
    professional: directin' 5d8, scrutinize 4d6,
    search 3d6, tale-tellin' 3d10
Edges: Arcane background: black magic, friends
    in high places 5 (Grimme)
Hindrances: Ferner, high-falutin'
Pace: 6
Size: 6
Wind: 16
Special Abilities:
    Black Magic: Puppet 5 (used to program the
        his actors) and stun 5 (used to keep his
        actors pliant when they're not on stage).
Description: In an effort to compensate for his
    accent and demeanor, Sir Lawrence has taken
    to walking the streets like a well-dressed
    gunslinger, clothed entirely in classic black.
    The illusion that he's from around these parts
    is shattered as soon as he opens his mouth
    and speaks in his clipped Oxford accent,
    something he refuses to disguise.

THE GOLDEN CIRCLE GHOST

For the full story behind this particular
haunting, see *Tales o' Terror: 1877*. For now, let's
just say Grimme took care of the threat to his
friends and leave it at that.

THROOP COLLEGE

The rumors of a mechanical man living under
here are false. There is, however, a patchwork
man who is kept together with metal plates
instead of stitches. This man, known only as
Steel, is the creation of Dr. Adam Primus. (See
page 107 for more about him.)

Primus often sends Steel into Lost Angels by
means of the sewer system. The creature's
objective is to poke around in the ruins of the
college to see if he can find any remnants of
any weird science gizmos that could help the
doctor in his work.

STEEL

Corporeal: D:4d8, N:3d8, S:2d12+2, Q:3d8, V:3d10
Climbin' 2d8, fightin': brawlin', club 3d8, sneak
    4d8
Mental: C:2d6, K:1d6, M:4d10, Sm:2d4, Sp:2d4
Area knowledge: Lost Angels 4d12, guts 3d4,
    search 4d6

  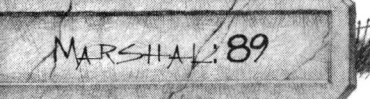

Edges: Brawny, friends in high places 3 (Dr. Primus)

Hindrances: None

Pace: 8

Size: 7

Terror: 9

Special Abilities:

Armor: 3

Undead (Patchwork): Steel is made of four different bodies. They make up his left arm, leg, and torso, his right arm, his right leg, and his head.

Gear: A 12-gauge shotgun with 40 shells.

BLOATWORMS

There's a bit more to Buster McGee's little friends than he knows. The bloatworms do a fine job of making a person feel less hungry, but they also create a craving for human body fluids.

McGee knows all about this little problem, since he's got a bloatworm squirming around in his own guts, but he thinks he's come up with a solution. The food he serves in his restaurant are all marinated in the liquids the bloatworms need. Things like blood may be in short supply, but there are plenty of other fluids that are a lot

more readily available. In fact, the folks that visit the outhouse behind McGee's restaurant are actually helping to contribute to the menu!

Swallowing a bloatworm is easy enough. It only requires a Fair (5) *Vigor* roll to keep the thing down. After that, it's only a matter of moments before the thing takes root in the victim's stomach. From then on, the host can digest any kind of material he can choke down, making it a lot easier to find a meal. It also offers immunity to ingested poisons and the like.

Unfortunately, the host also ends up with a *severe hankering* for other people's bodily fluids.

Getting rid of a bloatworm is a bit trickier. Magics that can heal diseases do the job just fine, but barring that, the victim has to try to starve the damned thing out. Each day the victim goes without food, he and the bloatworm must each make a *Vigor* roll. The TN starts at 5 and goes up +1 each day. A failed roll costs the difference in Wind. This Wind cannot be recovered without eating something.

The bloatworm has a *Vigor* of 3d6 and 12 Wind. Once it reaches 0 Wind, the worm dies. If the victim survives, he'll soon pass the remains.

GHOST TOWN

Sam's pretty much right on the money about Ghost Town. There are few worse places to live. The Fear Level's 5, and there's enough poverty to turn the stomach of the staunchest Guardian.

The rumors of cannibalism are true, and there was even a white wendigo that cropped up here for a week or so. This is one incident you're not going to see in the *Tombstone Epitaph*. Hellman personally investigated the incident, and after he poured hot tallow down the thing's throat, he and his Agents clamped down on the story tighter a giant clam.

Chinatown is a bit of sanity within the Hell that is Ghost Town. The Asians that live here (despite the name of the place, these people come from all over the Far East) have built a subculture in which they take care of each other and their needs. At least, that's how things were working until Bloody Sunday. Nowadays, no one really trusts anyone, and the Chinatown culture is starting to seriously fray at the ends.

Things are even worse in Tent City, where no one really knows her neighbors from one day to the next. Fortunately, most folks don't stay long here, often heading out into the Maze to take a stab at making their fortune. Still, if there's a pit of despair in the area, this is it, especially with all the ex-miners here who finally gave up hope.

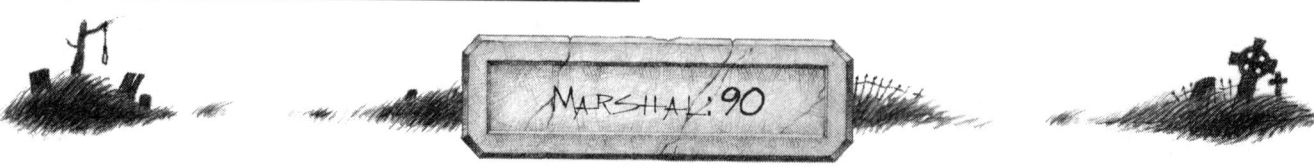

THE ROCK

Hellman's right about Stalks-the-Night going out to the Rock to confront Grimme once and for all, but that's all we can tell you for now. Let's just say that things didn't quite go the way the shaman had hoped, and we'll leave it at that, okay?

For more information on Rock Island Prison, including a full map of the entire complex, be sure to check out *Heart o' Darkness*.

JEHOSEPHAT VALLEY

Talk about a boneyard, Jehosephat Valley's got the biggest crop of human skeletons for miles around. The remains of nearly every person that's ever died in the City of Lost Angels (minus the edible parts, of course) eventually winds up here.

That much death just doesn't go ignored by the Reckoners. That's why there are 20 or more Guardian Angels watching over the place at any given time. A flight of Guardians stands at every one of the cardinal points around the valley, each armed with a 12-pound cannon and a rack of shotguns and ammo.

The Guardians tell people that they're there to keep graverobbers out of the valley, but in fact, they're keeping something far nastier in. From time to time, the stacks of bones have been known to collect themselves into a massive creature of evil. You may have heard of bone fiends and 'gloms (see *Rascals, Varmints & Critters* if you haven't), but this is worse than either. If the heroes go stalking around this massive graveyard at night, they should be prepared to meet the bone 'glom.

The bone 'glom starts out as a single, animated skeleton, but it grows from there, adding skeletons to its bulk until it's one monstrous, clattering collection of bones. It starts out with a single, black skull with just a bit of gray matter still clinging to its insides. From there, it adds whatever bones it can find, and in Jehosephat Valley, there are plenty.

As the bone 'glom adds bones, it gains in Size. It starts out at Size 6, but for every 3 points it adds in Size, it adds another die step to any Traits in its profile that are marked with an asterisk, up to a maximum of d12+4. The bone 'glom can only be destroyed permanently by delivering a maiming wound to its black skull,

which it keeps hidden inside one of its ribcages. Getting at the skull can be a real problem, what with all the other bones surrounding it, so the Guardians have taken to using heavy artillery whenever one of the things arises.

Blasting the thing to Hell is about the only way to effectively stop it, since it can add up to +1 Size worth of bones to its frame in a single action, effectively repairing any damage done. And if there's one thing Jehosephat Valley's got plenty of, it's bones.

Some Guardians have argued for breaking the cemetery up and scattering the place's bones throughout Prosperity Bay, but Grimme prefers the devil he knows. In any case, he sure doesn't want a bone 'glom rising up out of the bay and eating all his faithful. That's his job.

Bone 'Glom

Corporeal: D:2d10, N:2d10, S:4d8*, Q:3d12, V:2d8*
Fightin': brawlin' 4d10
Mental: C:3d10, K:2d8, M:3d8*, Sm:2d8, Sp:4d12
Overawe 5d4*
Pace: 10
Size: 6+
Terror: 9 (2 to 5 bodies)/11 (6 or more bodies)

Special Abilities:
Bone Explosion: If desperate, the creature can fling its body apart. This explosion causes 1d20 damage for every 3 points of Size it has, with a Burst Radius of 10.
Damage: Bite (STR) and claws (STR+1d4)
Undead.
Variable Size: Given spare bones nearby, the creature can add +1 to its Size. This requires a single action.
Weakness: The bone 'glom can only be killed by finding and maiming its black skull.

Petersen Asylum

Dr. Sanderson Petersen is actually a struggling patchwork scientist of a sort. However, he's not interested in working with dead flesh. He's trying to augment the living with muscles and bones taken from other living creatures. (Well, they were living at the time of the amputation.)

Petersen spends his days caring for the insane in his asylum as best he can, which isn't very well. He usually does more harm than good, but since most of the patients have families paying to keep them there on a more-or-less permanent basis, what does he care?

Night, Dr. Petersen takes his scalpel to his next lucky victim and continues his vivisection where he left off. To date, none of his experiments have actually worked. Despite this, Petersen is a part of the Patchwork Circle (see Chapter Five), to which he contributes his findings regularly.

Petersen is the envy of many patchwork scientists, as they assume he has access to the bodies of his patients when they die of whatever it is that's ailing them. If he was to reveal that his subjects were actually alive, he'd find himself kicked out of the circle immediately.

Patchwork Science

There's a lot more to this new branch of weird science that Hellman doesn't know about. In fact, we've devoted an entire chapter to it. See Chapter Five for all the really gory details about patchwork science and why it's not for heroes.

Towns of the Near Maze

Creepy little towns dot the countryside surrounding the City of Lost Angels. The further they get from the Golden Circle, the weaker Grimme's influence. Still, even nearly 100 miles away, the towns live under a pall of evil.

Townsfolk in the southern Maze are isolated by preference. They don't trust outsiders because strangers bring all sorts of awfulness. In the experience of these folks, rarely does a posse wander into town with good intentions.

Isolated from one another as well as the City of Lost Angels, these small towns often grow a brand of religion all their own. Many are mestizo towns where Anahuac rites are played out more openly than normal. Others pick out small aspects of the Bible or other religions tomes and fetishize those aspects into new beliefs. For example, the town of Malkut is run by Jewish kabbalists who name all children numerologically, the better to someday breed a Son of God.

The Fear Level of a typical Creepy Little Town is 4, with an occasional 5 in the case of the most paranoid and dangerous towns.

THE LOST BATTALION

Before the Civil War even began, Abraham Lincoln's War Department tried an experiment in the deserts of the Southwest. Horses had a hard time in the terminally dry conditions, but there was another kind of animal that had proven its ability to prosper in similar climates in the other hemisphere: camels.

So the Union Army Camel Corps, the strangest kind of cavalry the West ever saw (up until the Reckoning, that is), was born. Unfortunately, the experiment was neglected after the start of the Civil war. Still, the camels survived, and some even thrived as the war dragged on Back East.

That didn't last long though. The Great Quake killed camels as well as people, and those animals that did survive were soon after butchered for food. Some of the camels actually fell into a crevasse filled with burning ghost rock. There they were transformed into something horrible: carnivorous beasts that burn with undying flames.

HELL CAMEL

Corporeal: D:1d4, N:2d12, S:2d10, Q:1d8, V:2d10
Fightin': brawlin' 1d12, swimmin' 4d12
Mental: C:2d6, K:1d6, M:3d8, Sm:1d6, Sp:2d8
Guts 2d4, overawe 2d6
Pace: 20
Size: 10
Terror: 9
Special Abilities:
  Burning Pelt: If the Hell camel gets a raise on an attack, it also does 2d6 burning damage. If the victim is wearing anything

flammable, it may ignite. (Your call, Marshal.) If so, the flames do 2d6 damage at the start of each round, until they're put out. The camel's flames can be extinguished normally, but they start up again as soon as possible.
Damage: Bite (STR) and kick (STR).
Undead.

THE HEARTRIPPER

This killer's actually Ernesto Silverio de Acevedo, a Harrowed gunslinger who was killed by a bullet in his heart. Since his return from the dark side of the veil, Ernesto's been wandering around, looking for a good heart to replace his own. To accomplish this, he rips out a victim's heart and sticks it in the hole in his chest. It lays there rotting, and about a week later Ernesto has a hollow feeling that needs filling again.

For more on Ernesto, see *Tales o' Terror: 1877*.

THE MEN OF THE GRID

The Men of the Grid are still being led by Ansel Pascal, the son of the original founder of the organization. Like his father before him, Pascal dreams of bringing Grimme's cathedral down about his ears, but he's careful to never draw the reverend into a direct confrontation.

Ansel's guns are coming from just about every one of the rail barons. He's playing each of them off each other, and he's getting more and more guns and support for his efforts. It's a dangerous game he's involved in though. Since he's declared loyalty to no one but the Gridders themselves, none of the rail barons would lose sleep if he were to suddenly disappear. While he manages to keep harassing Grimme though, he's useful, and he can depend on surviving that long. After that, perhaps he can call on his new friend Hog Dunston's Union connections instead.

THE RIGHTEOUS

This organization is being led by Rockies councilor Paul Deauville, who's barely left town. He's currently living in nearby Carver's Landing, where his men protect him and keep his presence secret. An ex-seminarian, Deauville is still strongly connected with the Roman Catholic Church. In fact, he's even called in a member of the Order of St. George (see *Fire & Brimstone*) to lend a hand. With the collective power of their chosen deities on their side, the Righteous may be the biggest threat to Grimme yet.

PATCHWORK

MARSHAL 94

Chapter Five: Patchwork Science

So-called mad scientists (they prefer the term "masters of the new science") usually end up being fitted for a jacket with wraparound sleeves from long exposure to the voices that whisper the unnatural secrets of "big science" in their straining ears. Others start out mad to begin with, and they go straight from there into the worst parts of Hell itself. (Do not pass "Go." Do not collect $200.)

Some folks attribute this rampant insanity among the new scientists to long hours of exposure to ghost rock, and there's some truth to that theory, but that's not the only kind of cause of the madness that masquerades as reason these days. There are those who, instead of dedicating their minds to steam and steel, have set their minds to the workings of flesh and bone.

These mad doctors knit together the sinews of many different creatures into all-new kinds of "life," if the term can be used that loosely. They imbue motivation into stitched-together cadavers from which the breath has long since left.

This is not a simple undertaking, and it's not one entered lightly.

There are some things that man was not meant to know. How to create life without the help of a good woman (and we're not talking about lab assistants here) is at the top of that list.

Who Sews the Patches?

Well, for one, not heroes. Digging around in graveyards and slapping body parts together from a dozen different donors, not all of which are human, isn't exactly heroic, so that's not something they're allowed to do. (Spending hours in the lab only to have your latest creation rip your head from your shoulders isn't much of a ball either, but that's a whole other story.)

A small cadre of scientists and tinkerers, all of whom have been listening to the voices too long, have discovered a new brand of big science, an assault on the gates of Heaven they call "patchwork science." The acknowledged center of this kind of activity is in the City of Lost Angels, although some lone practitioners of this mystical science can be found scattered throughout the Weird West. There are even a few Back East and in other parts of this spinning world.

For the most part, these patchwork scientists tend to isolate themselves. Most folks look at you like you've grown a second head when you start talking about adding a second head to Spot or Fido. Those that don't decide to just give your house a wide berth are likely to show up on the doorstep with the requisite complement of torches, pitchforks, and nooses. Lynch mobs make poor neighbors.

Still, progress (if piecing together rotting body parts qualifies for that title) marches on, and there always seem to be a few lost souls ready to march to even the most macabre drummer's beat. The various nooks and crannies of the Maze are perfect for these people, since there are so many places that are hard to get to or simply isolated enough that once there's one house on a spot there's no room for any neighbors.

However, just because a patchwork scientist likes her privacy doesn't mean she can totally cut herself off from the rest of the world. At the very least, she needs a ready source of raw materials, and these are most easily found near larger cities.

In the Maze, the biggest and brightest city is Lost Angels, and with all that's going on there these days, you wouldn't think there'd be a lack of bodies to go around.

Okay, the heroes wouldn't think that, and neither would a patchwork scientist looking for a place to build his creepy house on a lonely hill. However, we know better.

Grimme and his Guardian Angels immediately snatch up all of the bodies they can find, supposedly to drag them off for a proper burial. Sometimes they even tell folks they're going to burn the bodies to help make sure no one decides to make lunch out of the uncle he never liked that much anyhow (but thinks would be wonderful with a light wine sauce!).

In fact, these corpses end up in the abattoir in the basement of Rock Island Prison, where the bodies are parsed into unidentifiable chunks of meat. If you've been following, Marshal, you know all about where that meat's headed.

The upshot of all of this is the fact that there are few human bodies to be found in Lost Angels. Finding animal bodies is nearly as difficult, since there are no laws against eating dead animals. In fact, hunters and trappers work hard to bring down just about any kind of wild game in the area, as even the scrawniest creatures fetch fantastic prices in the markets of Lost Angels.

So you're a patchwork scientist, and you've picked up stakes to haul yourself and your plans for world domination—um, peace—all the way to this God-forsaken part of the world. And you eventually realize that you can't find any of the raw materials you really need for your experiments.

What do you think is going to happen?

PARTS IS PARTS

Most patchwork scientists rely on bounties paid to certain undesirables who make their money bringing bodies to them. Lost Angels is full of desperate souls who'd be willing to sell their own mothers down the river (sometimes literally) if she'd been foolish enough to trek out here for the ghost rush herself.

Some of the more ethical patchwork scientists (even those folks who spend their days trying to reanimate dead flesh have some standards!) insist on only purchasing corpses of people that have died of natural causes or in some horrible accident, not of foul play. Of course, distinguishing a corpse that died from a fall and one that had its brains bashed in isn't always easy, especially when confronted with a group of brawny, well-armed thugs eager to take the patchwork scientist's money from him—one way or the other.

In cases like these, ethics are often laid aside. The scientist often tells himself that this is only temporary and that he's working for the greater good of all humanity, but these rationalizations usually ring hollow.

Stepping around ethics is a long, slippery slope, and many patchwork scientists soon find themselves at the bottom.

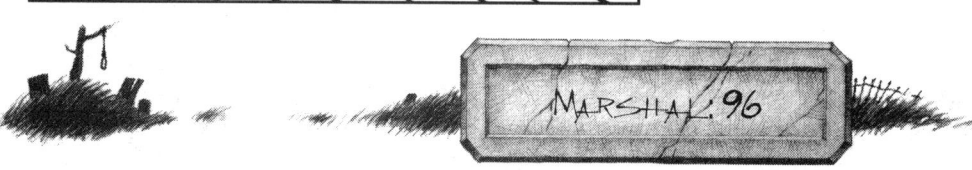

PATCHWORK

To the mind of many patchwork scientists, particularly the less ethical ones, their research requires the researcher to have full access to a wide variety of subjects. Bounties on women are typically half again those of men. Children and infants fetch double the going rate. Besides age and gender, rare specimens from various other races can also fetch a pretty penny.

Healthy bodies can be hard to find. They're in high demand both by other patchwork scientists and Grimme's own horrific larder, and it can take weeks to find just the right cadaver to fit into a scientist's plan.

Diseased specimens are a lot easier to locate and are often available on request, but they're not nearly as good to work with. Plus, there's always the chance for the scientist to actually contract whatever put down his subject. There's no risk of that with a corpse made out of a person by a bullet.

PRACTICE MAKES PERFECT

Even mad reanimators have to start somewhere.

It's not like even the most brilliant minds in the field of patchwork scientist suddenly woke up one ugly morning with the secret of reanimating dead people fully sprung in their minds. Nope, the manitous made them work for it.

Patchwork scientists usually practice their newly developed theories on smaller animals. Since animals are also in short supply in the City, these fringe researchers must breed their own stock.

This is another good reason for a scientist to remove herself from the things of man. Animals of just about any kind are precious food sources in Lost Angels. A patchwork scientist would have to guard his chicken coop with a fully loaded Gatling gun to keep away all of the two-footed foxes that would be prowling around his backyard.

A patchwork scientist's pinnacle achievement is a patchwork person, an entirely new human being comprised of the best parts of other people (and sometimes even augmented with portions of powerful beasts). Patchwork people are exceedingly rare, and those who have been reawakened in this fashion (or seemingly awakened for the first time) are often difficult to control. Just because a mad scientist is able to bring a creature to life doesn't mean he's capable of controlling it. Seems they're like most parents that way.

CREDENTIALS

Making a patchwork creature is a serious undertaking, not something just any mad scientist is capable of. It takes an iron stomach as well as a sharp mind and a keen knowledge of anatomy.

The scientist must, of course, have the *arcane background: mad scientist* edge. Otherwise, the manitous can't whisper into her ear the secrets that she craves. She also needs to have the *medicine: surgery* skill to work on patchwork people.

As mentioned before, most patchwork scientists try out their "pet" theories on animals before moving up to the real thing. For this reason, many have the *medicine: veterinary* skill as well.

The *trade: animal husbandry* skill can come in really handy too. After all, that breeding stock doesn't always get together on its own. As every patchwork scientist knows, sometimes nature needs a helping hand.

Most patchwork scientists also have the *dinero* Edge or some kind of patron (a form of *friends in high places*). Those body parts don't come cheap, you know!

GETTING THE RIGHT EQUIPMENT

First off, the scientist needs to collect the parts he wants to knit together into a cohesive whole. Most often, patchwork scientists hire unsavory types to handle procurement. Common going prices are $100 for a corpse without any specific features, or $50 per specific body part. Additional specifics—race, age, gender—might double these costs.

The body parts are then combined in the name of patchwork science to create new, unheard-of lifeforms. Each body part alters the creature that results from the experiment.

Then the patchwork has to sew all that stuff together, and that requires an extensive collection of different sorts of needles and threads—not to mention a great deal of patience!

Lastly, the "integration process" (the phrase patchwork scientists use for actually getting the various body parts to integrate into a whole creature) requires a large energy source of some kind.

Well-outfitted patchworkers almost always make use of a massive ghost-rock generator that spins a couple large magnets to create an electric charge (about $2,000 from Smith & Robards, Reliability 17).

Collecting lightning via lightning rods ($10 in iron and a blacksmith's time) is a cheaper solution, but this is useless without an electrical storm. Given the climate around Lost Angels, a scientist might be waiting a long time for that essential charge, and what mad scientist is that patient?

BUILDING THE PERFECT BEAST

Patchwork science is big stuff. We're not talking about adding a spring mechanism to a gun here. This is the creation of life where there is none. This kind of work requires some major planning.

We've provided you with a number of examples of patchwork creatures at the end of this chapter, but it doesn't have to end there. The vast variety of beasts that can be constructed is limited only by your own mind. Just think about how many different kinds of animals there are (humans included), and then imagine how many different combinations you can come up with.

THE BREAKTHROUGH

It turns out that the secret behind patchwork creatures is brains!

No, we're not talking about how smart those furiously sewing mad scientists are. We're referring to real gray matter, the kind you find between most creature's ears.

Most first efforts to create a patchwork creature failed miserably. Those that were successful created a walkin' dead that simply didn't have control of any part of his body that hadn't been detached from his brain. A few patchworkers earned themselves some nasty bites from their ungrateful "children," but little else.

It turns out that these early endeavors were shooting in the wrong direction. There was no way to force the separate body parts to integrate with each other. The severed nerves just weren't going to connect up with other nerves they'd never even been introduced to before.

It was Dr. Wilma Meister who finally made the necessary leap of logic. It came to her while she was studying the *Tombstone Epitaph's* report of a battlefield monster the journalist referred to as a "'glom." (See *Rascals, Varmints & Critters* for all about this report and the nature of 'gloms.) In a nutshell, a 'glom is a conglomeration of a number of bodies found on a battlefield.

Meister knew of the walkin' dead. She'd run across more than one in her grisly line of work, and she'd even had a particularly nasty specimen turn up on her operating table. She just couldn't understand how so many of these creatures could bond together into a single entity that acted as one, almost like myriad parts of separate bodies acting as one. The similarities to her own research were not lost on her.

Then it struck her like a bolt of lightning.

Working feverishly, Meister took the brain of a single subject and imbedded pieces of it all throughout her patchwork creature. With the application of a judicious amount of electricity, her creation (a conglomeration of many kinds of cats) finally sprang to life!

It wasn't long until Meister was working her magic on larger and more complicated creatures. She had many more failures than successes, but with every attempt, her base of knowledge grew larger.

THE BASIC THEORY

The general idea behind patchwork science is simple. All a scientist has to do is imbue each separate portion of the patchwork creature's body with a bit of brain that comes from a single source. Once a large jolt of electricity is administered to the body, it may suddenly decide to work together as a whole.

Sometimes this works as planned. Often it doesn't.

WHAT THIS MEANS

All patchwork creatures are *undead*. They aren't affected by Wind damage, disease, or poison. They cannot be stunned. They can only be killed by having their brains destroyed.

As you might have realized by now, Marshal, destroying a patchwork creature's brain isn't as simple as just blowing its head off. Sure, that's a great first step, but in almost every case, that's not going to be enough.

Basically, each separate body part has its own brains. This allows the individual parts to move independently, even if the creature's head is entirely destroyed. To completely kill a patchwork creature, an attacker must maim each body location. Maiming the thing's brain eliminates the threat of any original body parts that weren't detached from the body before its original death. Every other piece has to be maimed separately.

THE BODY PATCHWORK

Let's take a look at a patchwork creature's various parts and what they mean to the whole.

TORSO

Generally, a patchwork creature is mostly made up of one beast or person. It just makes more sense to start with something already put together by nature instead of carefully stitched threads. Unless and until modified, a body includes all limbs, organs, sensors, brain, and humors.

However, the scientist can also create a completely composite creature, in which no part comprises a majority. This is a lot more difficult, but it makes the patchwork creature a lot harder to kill. Plus, there are so many more interesting things you can do with these cobbled-together creatures. You've seen an animated corpse before. We call them walkin' dead!

A composite-built patchwork creature does not require a complete set of organs like an ordinary living being. These things can help the creature in various ways—they weren't put there in the first place for no reason—but they're not strictly speaking necessary.

SENSORS

Most living creatures have the five basic senses, but that's not necessarily true of a patchwork creature. These senses are handled by sensors. If these pieces are missing, they need to be added. Otherwise, the patchwork creature's out of luck.

Just from having skin and flesh, every creature has a sense of touch. The others are bit trickier.

Eyes and ear must be implanted as sets of two for full functionality. A creature with one eye loses depth perception, and one with a single ear can't pick out the direction from which a sound is coming. Tongues and noses work just like you'd expect.

Patchwork creatures receive the sensory abilities of the creature from which the organs came. This may mean sharper distance vision, or night vision, or a keen sense of smell, or hearing beyond the human range.

This can range from the ability to see in the dark by means of a cat's eye, or even the use of a bat's sonar. Of course, there are all sorts of creatures with keener senses than a human being's. An eagle's eyes or a dog's nose would give bonuses of +2 or even higher.

THE PATCHWORK CIRCLE

Unlike some sorts of scientists in other parts of the Weird West, who jealously guard their discoveries from their contemporaries, Meister and the other patchwork scientists working in and around Lost Angels decided to form a loose research circle in which they shared findings with each other in order to accelerate their overall advances. They call themselves—appropriately enough—the Patchwork Circle.

Of course, things like professional envy aren't lightly set aside, even when it's all for the greater good. The exchange of ideas in the circle isn't exactly free and easy, and there is even some measure of espionage and backstabbing among this group of purported fellows. Wheels within wheels spin inside the Circle, and few can keep track of the ever-changing alliances without a scorecard.

Of the members of the Patchwork Circle, Meister is first among equals, the one who first cut the Gordian knot of patchwork science. For this reason, she's accepted as a brilliant mind, although many in the circle think that she doesn't push her experiments far enough.

Of course, they're generally more than happy to do that for her.

One of Meister's most fervent rivals is a man known only as Dr. Adam Primus, who never attends the Circle's meetings himself. This man was actually once a student of Meister, but he left her direct tutelage under a mysterious cloud. Although it's not generally known—except by a few members of the Patchwork Circle—Primus is in fact a patchwork man created by Meister herself!

Neither Meister nor Primus is eager to reveal Primus' origins for fear of the reaction of the others in the Circle. In the meantime, they snipe at each other with an anger their fellows sometimes find unsettling.

MUSCLES

Patchwork scientists can take muscles from larger creatures, like bears, and graft them to smaller creatures, such as dogs or even people. If this is what you want, change the creature's *Strength* to whatever you like, depending on how much of the extra muscle is applied.

NATURAL WEAPONS

Claws, teeth, horns and such are often added to patchwork beings. Adding natural weapons usually gives the creature a *Strength*+2 attack, regardless of which weapon is specifically added. The final patchwork creature can have up to one natural weapon attack for each arm.

ORGANS

While most internal organs aren't important to the health and welfare of a patchwork creature, those that are integrated into the creature are included for specific effects. The most common organs added to a patchwork creature are the heart, lungs, stomach, and brain. These organs have both physical and metaphysical effects when integrated into a patchwork creature.

HEART

A heart grants the creature emotion. Introducing the risk of fear, hatred, or longing normally has too many negative side effects to warrant integrating a heart into a typical patchwork creature, so many times the patchworker even carves the heart out of the torso to prevent complications. Still, complete creatures require all their parts, so some researchers leave the heart in its place.

Just because a creature has emotions doesn't mean that they're mature. A dog's heart can only feel as much as a dog, while even a human's heart can be cold or fickle.

A patchwork creature with a heart imprints itself on the first person it sees upon integration, much like a baby duck might think a dog is its mother. The creature receives the *loyal* Hindrance toward the first person it sees. Usually this is the creator herself.

On most build-to-order jobs, the scientist makes sure the client is the only person in the room when their patchwork companion wakes up from integration. It's usually smart to keep a flamethrower or shotgun around too, in case the imprint doesn't go as planned.

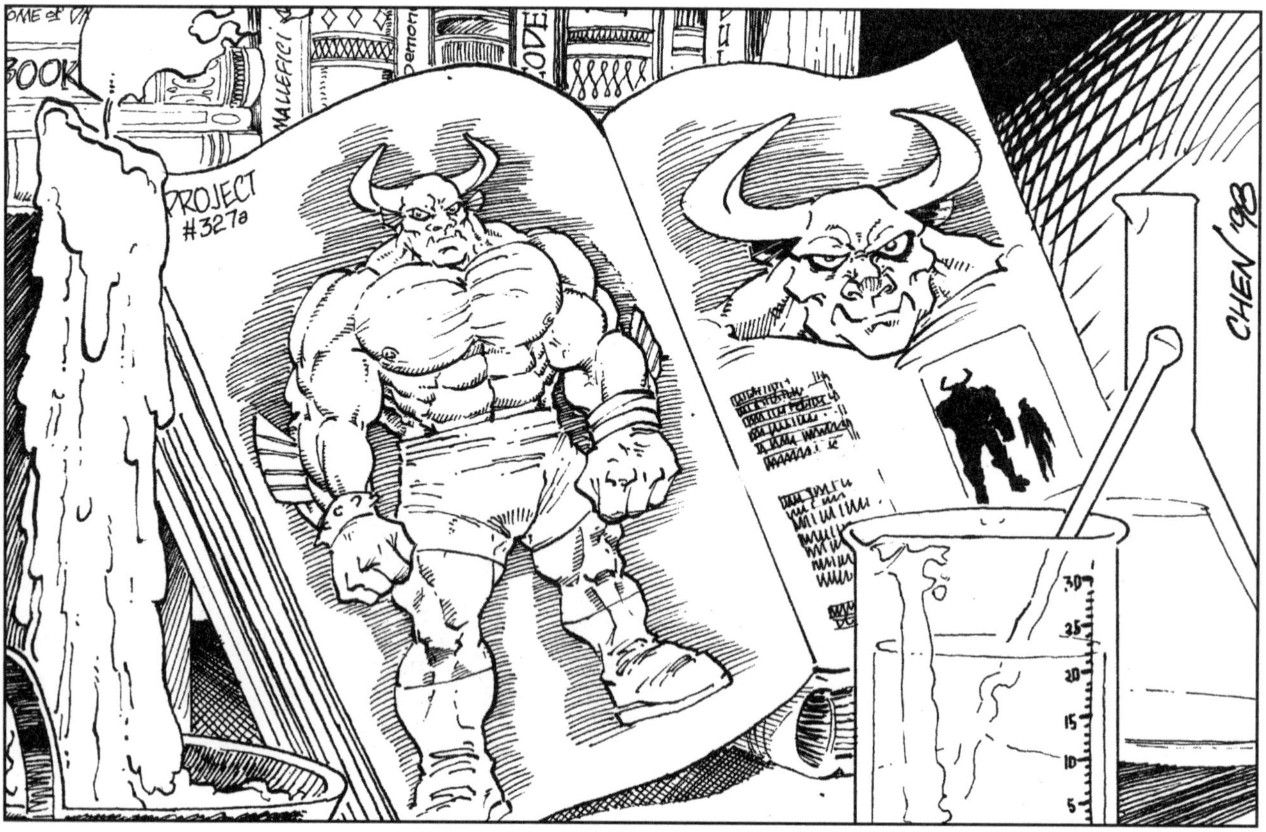

LUNGS

A patchwork creature does not need to breathe—it's dead, after all—but without lungs the creature cannot draw air to talk, bark, meow, or whatever.

Some patchwork scientists have even stuck gills into an occasional creature, despite the fact there's little apparent utility for this. Try telling that to a mad scientist, though, and you might end up as part of his next creation.

STOMACH

Having a stomach means the patchwork creature can eat. This helps with the appearance of humanity in patchwork people. It also allows a patchwork creatures to heal itself, just like a harrowed (as explained in *Book o' the Dead*). In other words, the beast must satisfy a craving for meat.

Any patchwork creature who hasn't eaten at least a pound of meat in the past day can't make a healing roll. The meat doesn't have to be fresh. In fact, it can be long-dead and rotting.

Without a stomach, the creature has no means of absorbing the meat. This means that any wounds it takes are permanent unless stitched back together by a knowledgable patchwork scientist.

BRAIN

The brain is the most vital organ when building a patchwork creature. Each patchwork beast has to have an intact brain of some sort, and pieces of this have to be installed in each separate piece of the creature's body. It's this distribution of gray matter that keeps the beast together.

What the main portion of the brain does for the creature depends on the brain's origins. An animal brain gives the creature the approximate personality of that animal. Dog and wolf brains introduce territorialism, feline brains make the creature a carnivorous hunter, rodent brains make the creature skittish and shy, and so on.

Adding a human brain is a whole other subject. Basically, the creature has the mental Traits of whatever person the brain was taken from. However, the trauma of death and reconstitution (along with the necessary jolt of electricity) has entirely erased the memories once embedded in the brain. In effect, the patchwork person is blank slate, ready to be written upon by the patchwork scientist—or possibly the manitou actually behind the creature's animation.

DISEASED PARTS

The patchwork scientist can integrate diseased parts with varying effects. The patchwork creature may end up a carrier of the disease, or it may simply end up dead on the table, at your whim, Marshal.

Of course, dead beasts aren't all that much fun unless the posse somehow stumbles across the corpses. Finding several corpses stitched together for some unknown reason can be enough to send shivers down the spine of even the most hard-bitten cowpoke.

Assuming the patchwork creature survives, it can then infect others with its disease. To do this, the beast has to come into contact with a potential victim. Once that's been done, the creature makes a *Spirit* roll against the target's *Vigor*. If the beast wins, the target falls ill. Of course, this doesn't happen immediately. The disease has to incubate a bit before it can run its course.

It can be several days before the victim feels sick. By that point, it may be difficult to pinpoint the creature as the source of the illness. The more ordinary-looking the creature is, the less likely the victim is going to be to be able to figure out just what happened.

Dead beasts can infect others with disease too, but you've got to rely on the victim being foolhardy enough to handle the body. Most folks aren't so curious, but you never know.

The specific effects of various diseases are up to you to work out, Marshal. Have fun!

INTEGRATION IS THE KEY

All patchwork creatures start as a collection of dead body parts. Even lunatics who come to a patchwork scientist looking to give themselves new parts have to actually die before they can be integrated with the parts. This fact isn't usually brought up during the negotiations, as it tends to sour the deal.

Integration is the measure of how well the critter can be reanimated after the surgery is complete. Reanimation requires the presence of a manitou. The greater the integration, the more powerful the manitou.

The Integration Table on the following page gives some ideas of how integration works and how rare certain levels of integration are. If you've got a creature of your own that you're just playing around with, feel free to roll on this table. Otherwise, simply pick the result that suits you best and stick to it.

Augmenting Patchwork

In the *City o' Gloom* boxed set, we revealed that Dr. Leonitus P. Gash has puzzled out how to attach mechanical limbs to the body of living creatures. So he's essentially replacing body parts with better ones.

Sound familiar?

Eventually, some enterprising scientist is going to want to take the next step in the inevitable progress of patchwork science: integration of artificial life and steam augmentation. In fact, doing so is likely easier than trying to augment a living, breathing human being. After all, the subject of the augmentation is already dead, so if the scientist botches the job, where's the harm?

However, the secrets of augmentation of living folks aren't all that well-known. In fact, Gash is the only one who's been able to get them to work with any regularity. He owes his success entirely to the mysterious drug X-19, the formula of which is a tightly held secret.

This means that to get augmented a creature has to get to the City o' Gloom one way or another. Alternatively, Gash might decide to take advantage of an invitation from one of the Maze's patchwork scientists to bring his brand of bodywork to Lost Angels.

If a patchwork scientist was to get the idea to send a patchwork person to Gash for augmentation, this would proceed as described under **Augmenting Harrowed** in "A Short Treatise on the Augmentation of the Human Body," a booklet that appears in the *City o' Gloom* boxed set. Gash and his assistants aren't going to react well to seeing a patchwork creature, since such beasts haven't yet been seen beyond the Great Maze. Either way, if Gash can be brought on board, all augmentations to the piecemeal cadaver work as normal.

Integration Table

3d6	Integration Level
3-4	**Patchwork Mishap!** Something's wrong with this one. Draw a card from a fresh deck and consult the Patchwork Mishaps Table on the next page. Have fun with this one, Marshal. You've worked hard for this, and you've earned it.
5-6	**Poorly Integrated:** The patchwork creature falls apart in 1d6 hours.
7-9	**Mostly Integrated:** The patchwork creature falls apart in 1d6 days. This is unexpected and can come at an embarrassing moment.
12-15	**Integrated:** The creature should live indefinitely as long as it eats every day. It resorts to eating itself should it miss a meal, after which it falls apart. Of course, if this thing doesn't have a stomach, it's going to have a real problem!
16-17	**Strongly Integrated.** This creature's as solid as the real thing. Nothing's brining this baby down!
18	**It Lives!** The creature awakens with the spirit of its main brain inhabiting it. If the basic creature started as human, that person's original spirit finds his way back from the Hunting Grounds and takes up residence in his strange new body as a patchworked Harrowed. Otherwise the particular kind of spirit that inhabits the creature is left to your discretion, Marshal.

Patchwork Mishaps

Sometimes when a mad scientist is working on integrating her latest patchwork creation, something goes terribly wrong. When you're dancing around on the very fringes of even the new sorts of science, it's almost impossible to predict every last thing that could go completely wrong.

That's why we've included a Patchwork Mishaps Table for you, Marshal. You don't have to use it if you don't want to. In fact, it's probably better if you come up with your own kinds of trouble for the creatures you concoct, but if you're looking for some inspiration, this is the place to which you should turn.

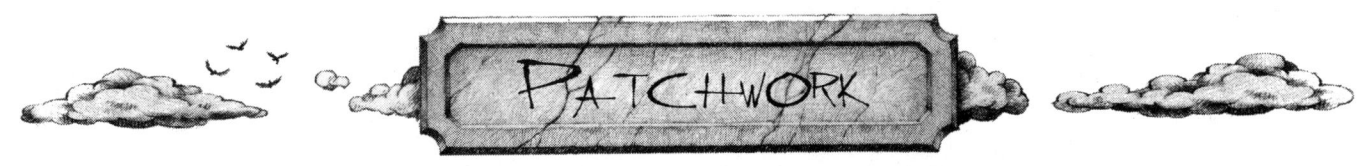

Draw	Mishap
Deuce	**Twice as Bad!** Draw twice on this table. Ignore this result if you get it again.
Three	**Whoops!** The scientist dropped something important during integration, contaminating the final creature. It now has a Reliability of 18 under stressful circumstances. On a malfunction, the critter simply shuts down for 1d6 hours.
Four	**Diseased.** One of the parts carries a terrible disease, which is brought out of stasis by the integration. The creature now has a Reliability of 17 under stressful circumstances. On a malfunction, anyone within about a yard is spattered by goo and must beat a Hard (9) *Vigor* roll or be contaminated with whatever the critter is carrying.
Five	**Sloppy Work.** The stitches start to let go under pressure. The creature has a Reliability of 16 under physical stress. On a malfunction, it loses a random body part.
Six	**Hungry.** Even if it doesn't have a stomach, the creature has an abiding hunger. Every eight hours, it tries to eat anything it can get into its mouth and doesn't do anything else until it's fed.
Seven	**Intelligent.** The creature is possessed of an unnatural intelligence. Increase all its mental Traits by +2 steps.
Eight	**Trippy.** Something about the creature— a pheromone, the mix of its various body parts, or a supernatural power it somehow possesses—induces powerful hallucinations in those around it. These visions might be terrifying, amusing, or precognitive at your discretion, Marshal. Anyone who touches any part of the creature must beat an Onerous (7) *Vigor* roll or experience these visions for 1d4 hours. On a bust, the victim also receives a dementia from the mad scientists' Dementia Table.
Nine	**Beautiful.** The patchworker is smitten with the perfection of his creation. He refuses to sell or discard it. If it's in danger, he must beat a Hard (9) *Spirit* roll to avoid protecting it with his life.
Ten	**Git Off Mah Leg!** The creature has an irresistible urge to mate. Once each day, it humps anything (animate or inanimate) it can get its limbs around, and it does not halt for 1d10 minutes. If anyone tries to stop it, the creature attacks!
Jack	**Oops!** The scientist has stitched together the wrong parts, with unexpected results. Randomly replace one part of the patchwork creature with a different kind of part.
Queen	**Ma-Ma!** The beast emotionally bonds with the mad scientist upon integration, and vice versa. Both the scientist and the creation gain a *loyal* Hindrance toward one another. This overrides the normal imprinting that comes with integrating a heart into the creature.
King	**Loss of Objectivity.** Through a freak series of events, the scientist's soul is yanked from his body and placed in the body of her patchwork creation. She can survive indefinitely as a Harrowed, but only while in her patchwork body. Create the body as normal, but give the creature all the scientist's mental Traits.
Ace	**Abby Normal.** Looks like the lab assistant picked up some bad brains. The thing's mental die types are all d4, and it's got the mind of an untrained (and untrainable) young child.
Joker	**Fearmonger.** The creature awakens, but the Reckoners have instilled it with a particularly nasty spirit. The creature becomes a fearmonger. It does its best to escape the scientist. If successful, it takes up residence near Lost Angels and becomes a new villain.

PUTTING IT TOGETHER

Once the scientist has successfully integrated his patchwork creature, it's time to come up with some numbers to describe the creature in the game.

For patchwork creatures that are essentially modified versions of existing critters, simply use the profiles found in *Deadlands, The Quick & the Dead,* or *Rascals, Varmints & Critters,* and alter them to suit your needs.

For patchwork people or creatures with no discernible "basic" form (that is, patched together with enough bits to give that Darwin fella conniptions), draw 10 cards to determine its Traits and assign them just as if you were creating a hero from scratch.

If a patchwork person is made (mostly) from an existing character, use the original character's Traits, or at least the ones that seem appropriate.

In any case, all patchwork creatures are *undead,* but of a special kind. To be killed, each separate part of the creature must be maimed.

I'M GONNA HEAVE!

Patchwork creatures can cause unenlightened, unscientific types to react badly. The first time any character sees a patchwork creature, he must make a *guts* check. The *guts* check TN starts at 3, plus +1 for each visible part that's been added.

BUYING & SELLING PATCHWORK CREATIONS

Patchwork scientists, ever short on funds, are not above accepting cash in return for their creations. There are many reasons for purchasing such a creature, but most border on madness.

For a nonspecialized creation (just like a regular animal), the markup is typically four times the cost of the parts. This is foul and dangerous work, and the patchworkers have research expenses. They expect to be well-compensated.

For a custom-made patchwork critter, the markup starts at eight times the original cost and goes as high as the market will bear. Patchwork people are a whole different game, but they command even higher prices.

With your permission, Marshal, patchwork creatures may also be bought as a *belongin'* by any character who might be or have had access to a patchwork scientist.

PATCHWORK SCIENTISTS

There are several patchwork scientists plying their trade in or near the City of Lost Angels. Almost all of them are members of the Patchwork Circle, although there are some occasional holdouts. Here are a few of the more notable ones.

DR. WILMA MEISTER

Wilma Meister immigrated to the US from Germany in 1870 with her husband Wilhelm and her boy Henrik. A renowned scientist, Wilhelm wanted to know more about this "new science," and the New World seemed the place to learn it. A physician and a budding scientist in her own right, Wilma supported him every step of the way. His curiosity pushed him and his family ever westward until they finally reached Lost Angels.

Unfortunately, both Wilhelm and Henrik fell ill on the long trek along the Ghost Trail. Soon after their arrival in Grimme's city, they died. Struck with grief, Wilma threw herself into the newly discovered patchwork science, determined to bring her husband and son back to life.

She started out working with cats, and her house just to the north of Lost Angels is filled with patchwork felines of all kinds. She was also the first person to succeed in animating a patchwork person, although this has brought her little of the peace she so desperately seeks.

Wilma is the nominal leader of the Patchwork Circle, although she rarely seems to care.

PROFILE

Corporeal: D:4d10, N:3d6, S:2d6, Q:3d6, V:3d8
Climbin' 1d6, shootin': pistol 1d10, sneak 5d6
Mental: C:5d10, K:4d12, M:3d10, Sm:3d10, Sp:3d12
Academia: occult 4d12, area knowledge: Lost Angels 4d12, guts 5d12, language: English 2d12, language: German 4d12, language: Latin 2d12, medicine: surgery, veterinary 6d12, scroungin' 3d10, scrutinize 3d10, search 2d10
Edges: Arcane background: mad scientist, dinero 4, nerves o' steel
Hindrances: Big britches, curious
Pace: 6
Wind: 20
Gear: Surgeon's equipment and a Colt One-Shot.
Description: Meister is in her mid-50s, with long, gray-streaked, blond hair she wears in a tight bun. She's petite, but she radiates determination. She speaks with a slight German accent.

BROTHER ZEBEDIAH WILSHIRE

Brother Wilshire is a high-ranking member of the Cult of Lost Angels. He's been fully inducted into the worst of the cult's most horrific aspects, and he's discovered that it suits him well.

Wilshire is one of the men that spends his days in the abattoir in the basement of Rock Island Prison, parsing people's bodies into unrecognizable parts so they can be served up as part of Grimme's unholy Sunday brunch. This is not a gentle occupation, which is just fine with Wilshire, since he is hardly a gentle man.

When Wilshire's not busy munching on fresh human flesh, he takes advantage of his access to the corpses of Lost Angels' fallen souls. With Grimme's permission, he slips off with a leg here, a heart there, all for his ambition of building patchwork creatures for Grimme's army.

Wilshire has had some limited success so far. His creations are never the best-integrated, but because they come from so many parts, they're damned hard to put down once and for all.

Wilshire is expanding his research to include the demons and Hellish beasts that Grimme has recently brought in to protect his fair city and act at the vanguard of his burgeoning armed forces. Although he hasn't managed it yet, the mad patchworker's latest ambition is the creation of a patchwork demon. If such a creature could be created, little could stand in its way, and Wilshire would vault to the top of the extremely short list of those in Grimme's favor.

PROFILE

Corporeal: D:4d6, N:3d8, S:4d6, Q:3d6, V:4d8
Climbin' 1d8, fightin': knife 5d8, shootin': pistol 2d6, sneak 3d8
Mental: C:3d8, K:3d10, M:2d8, Sm:4d6, Sp:2d8
Area knowledge: Lost Angels 3d10, faith: Lost Angels 5d8, guts 5d8, language: English 2d10, medicine: surgery 4d10, scroungin' 3d6, scrutinize 2d8, search 1d8
Edges: Arcane background: mad scientist, friends in high places 5: Grimme, nerves o' steel
Hindrances: Big 'un -2, loco -2: constantly mumbles to himself, loyal: Grimme.
Pace: 6
Size: 8
Wind: 16
Gear: Butcher's knife.
Description: Wilshire is a younger man with dark, curly hair and pale blue eyes which dance with madness. He's actually fat from the flesh he snacks on in the abattoir.

DR. ARTHUR CURRY

Dr. Curry lives out in the Maze to the west of Lost Angels. He was once a ship's doctor, and he spent many years sailing the seven seas. He actually did a stint with the US Navy as a ship's surgeon for a while. When the ship he was serving on went down battling a band of pirates on the edge of the Maze, he was one of very few survivors.

The pirates found some use for a surgeon, and they kept him on for about a year. He found his freedom when their ship was attacked by a Maze dragon in 1873, and it foundered on the subaquatic rocks it was pushed up against.

Curry eventually found his way to the City of Lost Angels, where he fell in with the Patchwork Circle. As a surgeon, he was fascinated by the idea of stitching creatures together and creating a new kind of life. However, his tastes ran more to creatures of the sea rather than the land.

Curry spends his days in a secret cove tucked deep within the Maze. There he labors over his greatest ambition: stitching together a marlin and a woman to make the world's first mermaid.

Curry hunts his food (and the beasts that will someday make up his creatures) with a mini-harpoon gun of his own design, which fires mini-harpoons with compressed air. Once fired, it takes three actions to pump the gun up with enough air for another shot.

PROFILE

Corporeal: D:2d6, N:3d8, S:2d6, Q:3d6, V:3d8
Climbin' 3d8, shootin': rifle, harpoon gun 3d6, sneak 4d6, swimmin' 5d8
Mental: C:3d8, K:4d10, M:2d6, Sm:2d10, Sp:3d8
Area knowledge: Maze 3d10, guts 4d8, language: English 2d12, medicine: surgery 4d10, scroungin' 2d10, search 2d8, survival: Maze 3d10
Edges: Arcane background: mad scientist, nerves o' steel, sense o' direction
Hindrances: Curious, stubborn
Pace: 8
Size: 6
Wind: 16
Gear: Surgeon's equipment, Winchester '73, and a mini-harpoon gun of his own design (Shots 1; Speed 2; ROF 1; Range Increment 5; Damage 4d8; Reliability 19).
Description: Curry is tall and lanky, with long, blond hair and a droopy, blond mustache and goatee. He is short with people, preferring the company of creatures of the sea—or his own creation.

PATCHWORK CRITTERS

Here are a few example of patchwork beasts.

PATCHWORK CAT

This is pretty much the standard patchwork creature that every patchworker starts on. Cats run rampant throughout Lost Angels, so parts are never in short supply. Also, they're great at keeping mice out of the pantry.

Patchwork cats come complete with the full range of organs and limbs, so they've got the ability to heal themselves. They usually spend their time chasing after hapless rats, but every now and then they get a little full of themselves and go after bigger game.

PROFILE

Corporeal: D:1d4, N:3d8, S:1d4, Q:3d6, V:2d4
Climbin' 6d8, fightin': brawlin' 4d8, sneak 5d8
Mental: C:1d6, K:2d4, M:2d4, Sm:3d4, Sp:2d4
Overawe 2d4, scrutinize 2d4, search 2d6
Pace: 8
Size: 2
Terror: 7
Special Abilities:
   Undead (Patchwork): The creature can only be killed if each of its parts are maimed. Roll 1d6. That many body parts are separate. It's up to you to figure out which ones they are, Marshal.

THE HAND

Brother Wilshire specializes in creating this particular kind of beast: the disembodied human hand. He takes a small creature like a squirrel and uses its parts to give the hand the sensors it needs to get around. Tiny ears and eyes are inserted under the skin of the wrist, leaving only small slits for the thing to see or hear through. Still, this seems to be enough.

The stump of the hand is invariably sewn up to keep the extra parts from slipping out as the hand walks about on its fingers. Despite its size, a disembodied hand can get around at a fairly good speed in this way. It can climb walls or other surfaces, turn doorknobs, and even fire guns.

The hand's biggest advantage is its size. It can get into places most animals can't reach, much less a whole human being. Also, it's incredibly sneaky.

Wilshire's laboratory is teeming with hands ready to leap to his bidding at a snap of his fingers—the ones on his own hand, that is!

PROFILE

Corporeal: D:1d4, N:3d8, S:1d4, Q:3d6, V:2d4
Climbin' 4d8, fightin': brawlin' 3d8, sneak 5d8
Mental: C:1d4, K:2d4, M:1d4, Sm:1d4, Sp:2d6
Search 3d4
Pace: 8
Size: 1
Terror: 9
Special Abilities:
   Undead (Patchwork): The creature can only be killed if each of its parts are maimed. The hand's only got one part, but any shots trying to hit it are at a -6 due to its small size.

THE PATCHWORK SPIDER

This is another of Brother Wilshire's creations, although it's fairly unique. The center of the beast is a man's chest. A human head is mounted on the back of the chest, right along the thing's spine. Then, eight arms are sewn to the sides of the chest, four on the left and four on the right.

The creature is a grotesque spiderlike construct made mostly of human parts. Wilshire's improved it some by implanting cat's eyes into the head and adding a dog's ears to its face. It works as the lab's guard, and it does a Hell of a job.

PROFILE

Corporeal: D:1d4, N:3d8, S:2d6, Q:3d6, V:2d4
Climbin' 6d8, fightin': brawlin' 4d8, sneak 5d8
Mental: C:1d8, K:2d4, M:2d4, Sm:3d4, Sp:2d4
Overawe 2d4, scrutinize 2d4, search 2d6
Pace: 8
Size: 2
Terror: 9
Special Abilities:
   Cat's Eyes: The beast can see clearly in the dark.
   Damage: The creature can make up to four attacks at once with its front four arms. It needs the others to walk on. It often carries knives from Wilshire's workshop (STR+1d4 each).
   Dog's Ears: The creature has a set of dog's ears, which makes its *Cognition* 4d8 when checking for surprise.
   Undead (Patchwork): The creature can only be killed if each of its parts are maimed. The head, chest, and each arm counts as a separate part, so this one's going to take some work. It has no stomach though, so it can't heal itself.

PATCHWORK

PATCHWORK PEOPLE

DR. ADAM PRIMUS

Dr. Primus was the first-ever patchwork person, constructed by none other than Dr. Wilma Meister herself. Although technically a member of the Patchwork Circle, Dr. Primus never attends the meetings personally, preferring instead to send his assistant Miguelito Lopez in his place.

Miguelito, something of a budding scientist in his own right, is always there to present the doctor's latest findings to the group. He also listens carefully and takes extensive notes so that he can relate any new breakthroughs to his mentor.

Some of the others in the circle figure that Primus isn't interested in attending the meetings because he doesn't want to share his findings with them, despite the fact that Miguelito is stunningly thorough with his reports. Others guess that perhaps the doctor wishes to be treated more as a colleague than a subject of inquiry himself. Others believe he just likes his privacy.

They're all wrong.

The secret that no one but Dr. Primus and Dr. Meister know is that Primus is none other than Dr. Albert Meister himself—Wilma's very own husband!

Wilma's research has always had only one end: the resurrection of her husband and their only son. After years of research and several failed attempts, Wilma was ready to test her theories on her husband's preserved corpse. She was successful all right, but the man who awakened on her table had no idea who he was.

Soon after, Primus left Wilma's care. Despite her protests, there was little she could to do stop him. She continues to hold out hope that she can figure out how to restore a man to life with his memories, but until that time, her son's body lies preserved in a casket beneath her manor.

Meanwhile, Primus spends his days studying himself and those like him. Apparently the loss of his memory has not affected the drive for scientific inquiry he had in his former life.

Primus shows stitches all over his skin, but they're not from his body being joined to other creatures. The disease that ravaged his body also caused his skin to crack and blister, and in death his wife attempted to repair the damage as best she could.

PROFILE

Corporeal: D:4d8, N:3d8, S:2d10, Q:3d8, V:3d6
Climbin' 2d8, fightin': brawlin 3d8, shootin': pistol, rifle 3d8, sneak 1d8

Mental: C:5d8, K:5d12, M:4d8, Sm:3d10, Sp:3d8
Academia: occult 4d12, area knowledge: Lost Angels 4d12, guts 5d12, language: English 2d12, language: German 4d12, language: Latin 3d12, medicine: surgery, veterinary 5d12, scroungin' 3d10, scrutinize 2d10, search 2d10

Edges: Arcane background: mad scientist, brawny, friends in high places 3 (Dr. Meister), dinero 4

Hindrances: Ailin' –1

Pace: 8

Size: 7

Terror: 9

Special Abilities:
> **Harrowed:** As a patchwork man created from a single piece, Primus is basically Harrowed.
> **Harrowed Powers:** Stitchin' 5.

Gear: Surgeon's equipment, a Winchester '73 with 20 rounds, and a double-action Colt Peacemaker with 30 rounds.

Description: Primus is entirely bald. He's quietly reflective but subject to fits of rage.

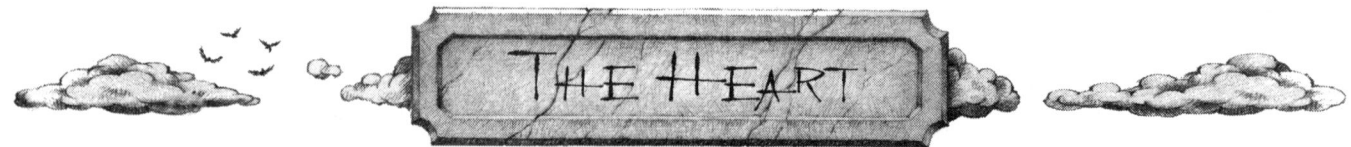

CHAPTER SIX:
THE HEART O' THE MATTER

There are all kinds of bad stuff wandering about in the not-so-fair City of Lost Angels, Marshal, and here's your chance to sling some of it your posse's well-deserved way. Be warned, though. If the heroes aren't careful, they're likely to run afoul of more bad guys than they've got bullets by the end of this twisted tale.

THE STORY SO FAR

Well before the Great Quake of '68 turned most of California into a jumbled-up jigsaw puzzle, Ezequiel Alquezar arrived in the territory, fresh from his hometown in Mexico. Alquezar was a member of a secret cult in Mexico dedicated to rebuilding the power of its member's ancestors in the ancient Aztec empire. He was to serve his order as its ever-prying eyes and ears in southern California, particularly around the important, southerly ports of San Diego and Los Angeles.

Well, if you've been paying any attention at all, you know both those places ceased to exist in the Great Quake. Alquezar, on the other hand, proved a good bit tougher than the California coastline that literally collapsed around him. He eventually made his way to the nearest settlement—the good Reverend Grimme's City of Lost Angels—with the intention of continuing his spying from there.

DELUSIONS OF GRANDEUR

After spending years in a place as twisted as Lost Angels, it begins to wear on a fellow's grip on reality—particularly if it was as tenuous and sweaty-palmed to begin as Alquezar's. About two years or so ago, Alquezar became absolutely convinced that he was the only true follower of the old Aztec ways (even excluding his pals back in his hometown), and he had little trouble convincing a few of the more radical *mestizos* in the Spanish Quarter of the same.

The cult built a small replica of a sacrificial pyramid in a sea cave south of the city. There, Alquezar began practicing the old sacrificial rites, most of which involve removing the heart from a living victim. The cult hoped that this offering to the ancient gods would encourage them to bring about a revolution, returning the cultists to the status and power that the Aztecs held before the arrival of the Spanish conquistadors so long ago.

Anyone who's studied much about Aztec rites notices pretty quickly that those folks didn't go around ripping out hearts every day. They sacrificed humans only on certain festivals. Of course, there's a festival of that type nearly every three weeks or so, but Lost Angels being how it is nowadays, a few extra missing persons doesn't stir up all that much of a buzz.

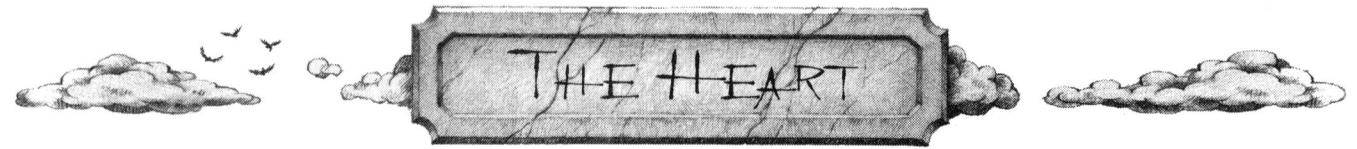
JAGUARS & SERPENTS

Some of the more militant members of the cult took to calling themselves Jaguar Knights, after an ancient Aztec society of warriors that took the jungle cats as their totems. They began practicing with the weapons and tactics of their namesakes as well, in some kind of attempt to appease their ancestors.

Some within the cult have compared what they do to the American Indians' Old Ways movement, with the exception of the fact that North American tribes traditionally draw the line long before ceremonially ripping out folks' still-beating hearts.

Alquezar calls on the Jaguars to assist him when he raids the city for victims. Despite his powers, he's only one man.

The warriors are a powerful ally for the priest, but less than a month ago, fortune smiled on Alquezar. A Maze dragon, drawn by the castoff bodies of the sacrificial victims, entered the cult's sea cave. The sea serpent's neck spines were brightly colored, unlike those of the usual Maze dragon. Alquezar took this abomination to be a sign of favor from the god Quetzalcoatl whose name means "plumed serpent."

According to legend, Quetzalcoatl left on a great journey across the sea long ago. Now, Alquezar believes he has returned and his coming foretells the destruction of the current and last world of human existence by great earthquakes and horrible monsters. (Doesn't sound all that far off from the Reckoning, does it?)

The self-appointed Aztec priest has kept this information from his followers for fear of how they might take the news, but he's doing his best to hedge his bets. He has begun to increase the amount and frequency of his brutal sacrifices in hopes of holding Armageddon at bay. Although he's quite insane—even evil by contemporary standards—Alquezar is convinced of his own righteousness. He judges his actions from an Aztec point of view, and in that world vision, he's nothing less than a hero of his long-oppressed people.

THE CUTTING EDGE

Another player in the story we are about to present is a patchwork scientist by the name of Richard Leeson. Leeson was drawn to Lost Angels because he believed he would be able to more readily find subjects for his experiments in the Maze than in more civilized regions of the country.

While he was right about life being cheap in Lost Angels, he was wrong about death being the same. Grimme's Guardian Angels seem to protect the bodies of the dead with far more fervor than those of the living. He's absolutely right about that too, given the culinary habits of Grimme's faithful!

At any rate, Leeson found himself struggling just as hard to locate "materials" in Lost Angels as he had been in the more comfortable cities Back East. That is until he stumbled onto an unsavory dock rat by the name of Asa Platt.

Platt had a knack for supplying folks with odd commodities, and Leeson's request was no exception. He'd recently found a small tidal pool where bodies seemed to wash up with alarming frequency. The fact those bodies had their hearts cut out didn't matter much to Leeson. He knew he could come up with a substitute ticker from somewhere. After all, that part didn't even need to be human.

Now, where could those bodies have come from?

Neither Leeson nor Alquezar is aware of the other, and it's likely no one else would ever connect the two either—that is, until recently.

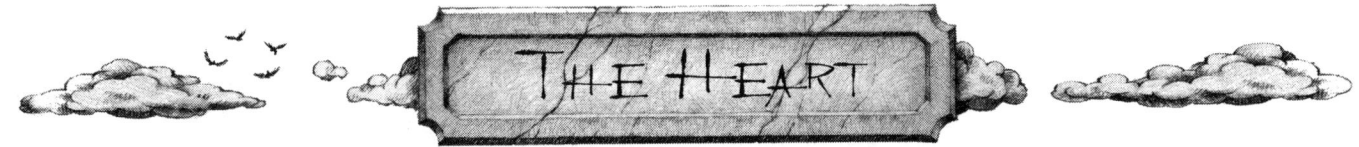

BUTLER SCOTT

Less than two weeks ago, a gunslinger by the name of Butler Scott disappeared in Lost Angels. Shootists are dime a dozen in city, but Scott's disappearance was noted by a couple of very interested parties.

Scott was a newly appointed Guardian Angel, having just completed training in Grimme's new camp to the east of the city. Not too many folks in the city have got the backbone to jump a Guardian Angel, so Grimme's lieutenants are beginning to think Scott was a spy planted by one of the Church's many enemies. Most are sure he's gone to ground, trying to escape the city with information on Grimme and his plans.

The Angels are both right and wrong. Scott was a spy for an outside organization, and he was the only one to have made it through Grimme's new training camp without breaking.

However, Scott never got away. The night before he planned to ride out, Alquezar and his minions kidnapped him for their next sacrifice. Scott's body was found later by Asa Platt and sold to Leeson for "spare parts."

Talk about bad luck! Go through all the trouble of surviving Grimme's training camp just to get sacrificed by Aztec throwbacks and chopped up by some maniacal medical researcher. Just goes to show you, it's always something. Anyway, shortly after Leeson obtained Scott's body, he began work on his final project: a patchwork human built completely from the dead.

About the time the heroes arrive in Lost Angels, Leeson completes his golem. Unfortunately, the creature is driven mad by the process, and it kills its creator and stumbles into Lost Angels.

LOOKING HIGH & LOW

Now, both the Guardian Angels and Scott's original employers are looking for the spy. The people who know who he is don't know where he is, and vice-versa.

In our tale, Scott was employed by Hellstromme Industries. Along with just about every other power in the Weird West, Dr. Hellstromme is extremely interested in Grimme's newfound power, and he's got spies all throughout Lost Angels. (If another power would fit your campaign better, feel free to use that instead. The identity of Scott's employer isn't vital to the adventure.)

Want to guess where the posse comes in?

THE SETUP

Scott's former employers know he survived the camp, and they're *very* interested in getting their hands on his information. The posse is contacted by a representative of Hellstromme Industries (or the group you've chosen instead) with the following offer:

"We need you to go into Lost Angels and find a man by the name of Butler Scott. He has some documents of great importance we need to recover. He was supposed to deliver them to a courier near Yuma, Arizona, a week ago, and we're afraid he has been detained.

"Scott has managed to work his way into Reverend Grimme's Guardian Angels. We've long suspected there was more to the cult than meets the eye, and Scott's report may provide the information we need.

"Scott has worked with us on several occasions in the past, and we trust him implicitly. However, due to the nature of his current job, we can't use our regular agents in the area to contact him, for fear of exposing him if he hasn't already been.

"If you accept the job, we're willing to pay any reasonable expenses plus $250 dollars to each of you when you return with the documents."

The posse is free to bargain for a better rate. After all, their prospective employer suspects this information is very valuable. Have any heroes who haggle make a *persuasion* roll against a Fair (5) TN. The offer is increased by $50 for each success on the highest roll. If anyone goes bust, the offer stands at $250, regardless of what anyone else rolls.

After reaching the agreement, the representative provides the heroes with the following information on Scott. They are told Scott has a tattoo of a rose twined around a dagger on his hand. Scott kept the documents in question on his person at all times.

When approached, Scott should require the heroes to identify themselves. He should use the word "fields" in a sentence, and they must immediately respond with a sentence containing the word "saunter." (Since Scott is dead, this is just window dressing, but have fun with it!)

Finally, at last report he was staying in a place in the Trader's Quarter called Sunset Hotel. Beyond that, the heroes are on their own.

THE HEART

CHAPTER ONE: FOOTSLOGGIN'

Assuming the heroes aren't already in the heart of the Maze, just getting to Lost Angels may be an epic endeavor in itself. Either way, the exact details of the journey are up to you, Marshal.

Feel free to make getting to the town as tough or as easy as best fits into your campaign, but remember that the heroes are going to need to be in decent shape before things get going here. The meat of this adventure actually begins when the posse reaches the city, and if they've already got lots of wounds to lick, they're in for a world of hurt.

MR. SCOTT, I PRESUME?

There are a number of places the posse is likely to visit while looking for Butler Scott. The search provides an excellent vehicle to get the heroes out and roaming about Lost Angels. The most important places are detailed below, but inquisitive cowpokes are liable to stick their noses into any number of unexpected spots in the city.

Luckily, you have a handy guide to the secrets and dangers of Lost Angels in the preceding pages of this book!

THE SUNSET HOTEL

Since this is the only real location their contact gave them, the posse should visit here early in the search.

The Sunset Hotel is located in the Trader's Quarter and is of slightly below-average quality. While it's no dump, most respectable folk are liable to pass it up for a better hotel a few blocks away. Real unsavory characters, on the other hand, are going to be partial to a cheaper price and less questions. In fact, it's exactly the type of place someone who was trying to escape notice might choose to hole up!

The place is owned by Ned Hampton, a middle-aged man with spectacles. Ned isn't one of Grimme's faithful, but he's not foolish enough to be an outspoken opponent either. He's lost more than one customer to the Angels' morality raids, and he's not happy about the lost business.

Unlike many folks in Lost Angels, Ned has somehow found a way to keep a pretty good humor. He politely greets the heroes when they enter and asks how he may be of service. If the posse is interested in staying in the Sunset Hotel, a room costs a whopping $3 a night. Of course, this is one of the places the Angels are watching for Scott or his contacts to turn up—but the heroes don't know that!

If the posse asks about Butler Scott, the desk clerk perks up immediately and says,

"You folks friends or kin? If you are, he's got an outstanding bill with us! I'm holding his stuff here until that bill's paid!"

As long as the heroes are willing to shell out the money for the bill—a whopping $7.50—Ned turns over Scott's belongings to them. Stuffed into a pair of worn saddlebags, the heroes find two work shirts, a pair of pants, a plug of tobacco, a box of .45 pistol rounds, and a single poker chip with the letters "SB" painted on it. (The letters stand for the Shark Bite, a saloon in the Waterfront district, but unless the heroes are Lost Angels natives, it takes a Fair (5) *streetwise* roll to learn that.)

Ned is fairly open about Scott once the heroes pay his bill. He tells the posse:

*"Scott kept pretty much to himself for the couple of days he was here. In fact, I didn't even miss him for a day or so. After the third day without seeing him, I collected up his stuff and put the room back up for rent.
"Course, you're not the first..."*

Ned stops short and glances cautiously around the room. Then he leans in and whispers to the posse:

"'Bout a week ago, a couple of Angels came in asking about Scott. I didn't tell them anything. Hell, I didn't know anything to tell them. But, since I was pretty sure they wouldn't pony up for his bill, I didn't let on I had any of his stuff either!"

Ned shares all the information with the posse he has on the man—which isn't much. He knows nothing more of Scott other than he owed the hotel money, the Angels are looking for him, and he went missing some time ago.

Exactly how long Scott has been missing depends on the time it took the posse to reach Lost Angels. Scott was snatched a week and a half before the posse was hired to look for him, so add the travel time to that.

THE SHARK BITE

The Shark Bite is a single-story saloon and gambling hall in the Waterfront District. The Bite is one of the nicer establishments in the area. In other words, unlike many of the other dives nearby, the heroes don't get the feeling they're taking their lives into their own hands just crossing the threshold.

The Bite is owned by a bald, one-armed man who goes by the name of Jonah. He's gruff and has little to say beyond, "What'll you have?" However, if anyone has the gumption to ask him what happened to his arm, he laughs, points to a pair of enormous shark jaws hanging over the bar, and says, "You should see the other guy!"

Looking around, the posse can see a number of card and dice games going on around the saloon. Many of these are using chips very similar to the one the heroes should have found in Scott's belongings. If asked about the chips, just about anyone in the bar explains Jonah hand-paints them himself. He seems to think it gives the saloon "a touch of class."

No one in the Bite remembers Scott by name. If the heroes ask about a rose and dagger tattoo, they also draw blank looks. However, a disheveled man reeking of alcohol catches up with the heroes as they leave the bar. His name is Hiram Davis, and he overheard the heroes asking about a tattoo. He says:

"You folks looking for a man with a tattoo, eh? Well, I seen him, I did. Course seein' as my memory's dried up I can't quite recall the details..."

As long as the heroes offer him at least the price of a couple of drinks, the beggar motions them over to an alley beside the Bite.

"I was sittin' out here a couple weeks ago when I saw that feller come out.

"I got a good look at his hand 'cause he was a kind soul and willing to show a little compassion to a man down on his luck by givin' me the price of a drink. Anyway, he was walkin' past the alley when the shadow got him! He fought for a little bit—he was a tough customer, he was—but there was others helpin' the shadow. It didn't take too long before they'd trussed him up and dragged him into the darkness.

"Since I seen that, I stay in the middle of the street after dark. I don't want no shadow grabbin' me. I'd advise you do the same!"

What the drunk saw was Alquezar and a couple of Jaguars ambush Scott. Alquezar paints his body black, so Davis didn't get a good look at him. If asked about the "others" with the shadow, he says only that they might have been Indians and they were carrying some kind of swords.

Searching the alley for tracks is futile. Simply too much time has passed for this to do any good.

However, have any hero examining the walls make a Hard (9) *search* roll. If she succeeds, she finds a thin piece of razor-sharp, black rock stuck in one of the walls of the alleyway. A Fair (5) *science: geology* roll identifies it as obsidian. It came from the macautls (see page 126) the Jaguars carry, although the posse can't know that yet.

HAVE YOU SEEN THIS TATTOO?

After visiting the Sunset Hotel and the Shark Bite, the heroes are probably pretty sure Scott has fallen victim to foul play. They're also likely to be fairly stumped about how to find their missing contact. The only clue left to them is Scott's tattoo.

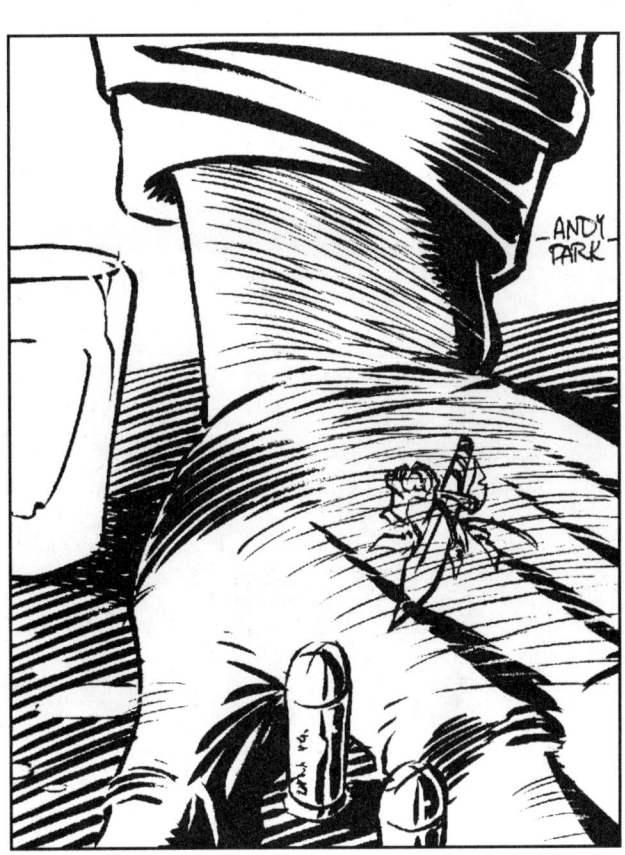

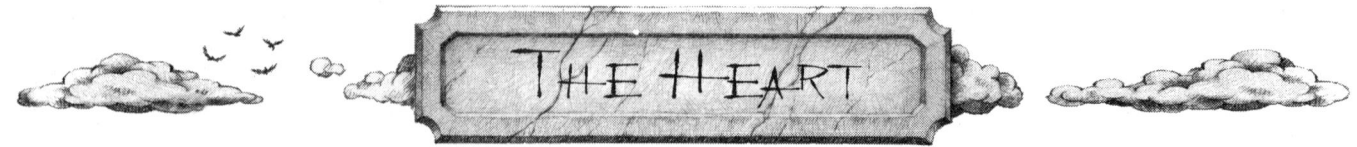

Wandering around the streets asking about the tattoo doesn't meet with too much success—at least initially. In a seaside town like Lost Angels, there are more tattoos than you can shake a bottle of rum at, and most questions about inked skin are met with blank looks or suspicious stares.

Still, there's something to be said for bullheaded persistence. Have the hero or heroes combing the city in the fashion make an Onerous (7) *streetwise* roll. If they succeed, they don't learn anything immediately, but do make a note of it. Later on in Chapter Two, this success just might be important.

Of course, the heroes aren't the only group of investigators looking for Scott, a fact they may have picked up on during their conversation with Ned Hampton back at the Sunset Hotel. Grimme's minions have eyes and ears all throughout the city, and when they're hunting down a suspected spy, they keep their noses close to the ground.

If any hero goes bust on this *streetwise* roll, he's unwittingly drawn the attention of the Angels that are also searching for Scott. See **Stalked by an Angel** (on page 115) for details on this.

The Guardian Angels

If the heroes are foolhardy enough to actually go to the Angels themselves to inquire about Scott, they've opened a whole barrel of worms that they'll be lucky not to get nailed up in right before its tossed into Prosperity Bay. No matter how the heroes might ask about Scott, the Angels claim to know no one fitting the spy's description. However, they immediately tag the heroes as suspicious characters and begin tailing them. See **Stalked by an Angel** on page 115, for just what this means.

The Angels don't put up with a lot of guff in their hometown. If the heroes raise too much of a ruckus here, they might find themselves with a one-way ticket to the Rock!

In fact, the only thing that keeps the Guardian Angels from seizing the heroes right away (they're asking suspicious questions after all) is the hope that the posse might eventually lead them to Scott.

Dunston Returns

The fact that Hog Dunston (see page 83 for the details on Hog) has returned to Lost Angels is an open secret among many of the citizens of Lost Angels, especially those who have joined the church in name only. Finding someone who knows about Hog's current status is only a Fair (5) *streetwise* roll.

Of course, as a Man of the Grid and a Union spy, Hog always keeps his ear pretty close to the ground. If the heroes start poking around, he's bound to hear of it and may even look them up to see what they're all about.

If the heroes manage to find Dunston (or he finds them), he still knows a lot about this town, and he can be pretty darn helpful. If the heroes simply say they're looking for a man, Dunston tells them he'll keep an eye peeled for them.

Should the heroes tell Hog the whole story, he takes special interest in the case. Scott's information could be valuable to the United States government, and Hog becomes determined to lay his hands on it. He's willing to provide as much assistance to the posse as he can without coming into direct conflict with Grimme. Then, when the dust clears, Dunston plans to confiscate the "evidence" and forward it back to President Grant.

Either way, it's important that the heroes make some sort of contact with Dunston or that he at least learns that they're looking for a man with a rose-and-dagger tattoo.

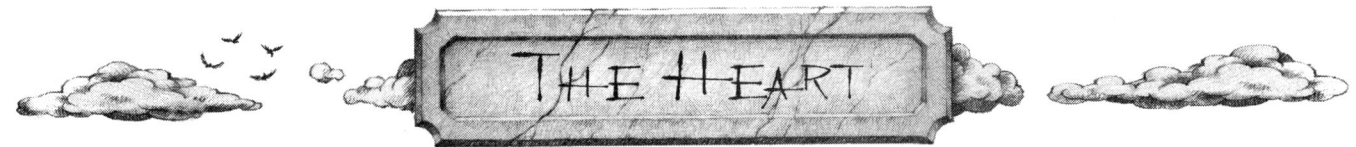

THE HEART

STALKED BY AN ANGEL

Hopefully, the heroes caught on early to the fact that Grimme's followers are just as interested in locating Scott as they are—and they're not likely to be interested in rescuing the missing spy. If the heroes are just clueless, they may find themselves with their own personal Guardian Angels—and we don't mean the good kind! These Angels are more likely to get the heroes into dire trouble than get them out of it.

If the posse draws too much attention to its search, the Angels do take notice. This doesn't take much. After all, informants everywhere are willing to sell out their mothers for favor with Grimme. A group of newcomers means less than nothing to these sorts.

However, like the posse the Angels are interested in finding Scott so they can make sure he's been silenced (if he is in fact a spy). Rather than simply arrest the heroes, the Angels shadow them around Lost Angels, hoping to use them to locate Scott.

Fortunately for the posse, the Guardian Angels aren't particularly stealthy. Although the Angels shadowing them are smart enough to shuck their robes for more standard western clothing, they're still rather clumsy, and they have a hard time concealing their normally extreme arrogance—even in street clothes. Each day have the heroes make a Hard (9) *Cognition* roll. Those that succeed catch a glimpse of a group of five men following them throughout the day.

Once the plainclothes Angels have been spotted, the heroes can try to lose them for a day by getting a raise on a contest of *Smarts* with their stalkers. Should the posse confront the Angels, they play dumb and claim innocence. (The fact they don't just accuse the heroes of a crime should tell them that something's up.) The Angels don't start a fight with the posse, but they do fight back if attacked. If that happens, they try to take at least one posse member alive for questioning.

Keep in mind that starting a fight with Guardian Angels in their city isn't the smartest course of action. If the heroes come to blows with their stalkers in the open—even if they win the brawl—every Angel in the city is going to be on the lookout for them!

As long as the heroes don't force the issue or try to go more than 10 miles from the city, the Angels are content to merely follow them. See Chapter Four for all the gory (sometimes literally) details about the Guardian Angels and the powers behind them.

WHERE DO WE GO FROM HERE?

Give the heroes plenty of time to wander Lost Angels, looking for clues to Scott's whereabouts. Beyond the few locales we've detailed in this adventure, you can find a whole passel of interesting places for the heroes to visit in the earlier parts of this book. Even so, after a couple of days or so, the posse is liable to have exhausted all its leads and ideas for finding Scott.

Hopefully, by the time the heroes are sitting around scratching their heads, they've made some kind of contact with Dunston. Of course, they might also have picked up a tail in the form of the Guardian Angels. Either way, if the heroes haven't found Dunston, he's tumbled to them, and that's enough for them to be able to move on to Chapter Two.

TROUBLESHOOTING

If the heroes didn't meet with one of the three contacts mentioned, it's going to take a little creativity on your part to provide the link to Chapter Two. (It's nothing you can't handle. Honest!) A good solution is to have one of Hellstromme's other agents in the area tip the heroes off to the capture they learn of in Chapter Two.

A really clever posse may already be putting together some sort of Aztec connection by this time. If they're actually that perceptive, that's fine. Chapter Two should throw them a curveball. Let them pursue the line as long as it amuses you and then have their contact drop word of the capture.

On the off-chance the posse gets captured by the Angels, well, they've got an all-expense paid tour of the Rock coming. You can either allow ample escape attempts prior to their arrival on the island, or refer to the adventure *Devils Tower 2: Heart o' Darkness* for the complete lowdown on Rock Island Prison. Trust us, it's not a nice place!

BOUNTY

Getting Scott's belongings: 1 white chip each.
Finding the obsidian shard: 1 white chip.
Not drawing the Angels' attention: 1 red chip each.
Ally: As long as the posse was square with Dunston, he helps them as he can.
Enemy: If the posse draws the notice of the Angels, they've got an enemy to contend with down the road.

CHAPTER TWO: PARTS IS PARTS

After the heroes have had a little time to puzzle over their next step, they receive word that a fellow with a rose-and-dagger tattoo has turned up Ghost Town. He's being held by the Men of the Grid in an anonymous shack there.

This information comes to the heroes by means of Dunston himself. He sends his old deputy Hiram Davis to give them a message. He knows that they're looking for a man with this mark, and he wants them to positively identify him. For that, he needs them to meet him at the Vestibule (see page 32) that evening.

THE MEET

When the heroes get to the Vestibule, Dunston and Davis are nowhere to be found. Ironman, the owner and bartender, recognizes them, though, by the description Dunston gave him earlier in the day. When they order a drink or ask him a question, he hands them an envelope. In it, there's a note from Dunston asking them to meet him out back.

Dunston is waiting for the heroes around the back of the building. He asks them if they think anyone's been following them. If the Guardians have been on their tail, he curses, but he seems determined to follow through with his plan anyhow.

Dunston asks the heroes to follow him into Ghost Town, where their man is being held. He leads them all through the area, taking many seemingly random twists and turns, often doubling back on his trail. Eventually he stops at the rickety door to an old shack and knocks once. Davis opens the door, nods at Dunston and the heroes, and lets them in.

If the heroes ask why the man they're looking for is being held, Dunston tells them he'd tried to murder someone!

The prisoner was apparently sleeping in a barn on the north edge of Lost Angels. When a stable hand entered the barn, the man lurched out of a stall and attacked him for apparently no reason. The victim had never seen his attacker before, and he nearly wet himself when the assailant leaped at him from out of nowhere.

Luckily, the stable hand had been reporting to work with a number of his fellows. The prisoner was enormously strong, and it took four men to subdue him. The stable hands were all loyal members of the Men of the Grid, and they figured the man had attacked them for that reason alone. Unwilling to bring the Guardian Angels into the matter, they immediately turned the man over to Dunston so he could decide what to do with him.

Once everyone's inside the shanty, Davis turns up a lantern and reveals a man tied to a chair in one corner of the room. The man is very badly scarred, with enormous stitch marks visible in a number of places on his face. His lips don't close completely, and his enlarged and black right eye is surrounded by a large stitching scar and is a different color than the other (which is blue). His hair is unkempt and missing in patches across his uneven scalp.

Immediately upon the posse's arrival, the prisoner becomes agitated and begins straining at his bonds. The rickety chair creaks, and even the ropes seem ready to snap.

Play up the impending escape for a moment. Just when things are about to come to a head, though, the prisoner throws back his head and howls in pain. His eyes stare pleadingly at the heroes for a moment, and then he suddenly literally comes apart at the seams. The pieces of his corpse collapse in a heap on the floor.

Dunston hesitates for a moment, suspecting a trick. He orders Davis to cover him. Then he moves cautiously to examine the prisoner. The man is quite dead.

Hey! That's Not Your Hand!

Dunston allows the posse to look over the corpse. The man's hand is indeed tattooed with a rose and dagger like Scott's. However, this man isn't Scott! Well, actually, part of him is, but we'll get to that in a minute.

It takes only a cursory examination of the self-dismembered corpse to realize that the man really did come apart. Apparently the stitching "scars" all over his body were actually holding him together! Gaining this knowledge calls for an Onerous (7) *guts* check from anyone in the room with the body.

Anyone getting close to the body catches a strong odor of formaldehyde wafting off the various body pieces. The stench of death is long gone here. A Fair (5) *medicine* roll or an Onerous (7) *Cognition* roll tells an examiner that the corpse was originally composed of parts from a number of different bodies.

Astute heroes can likely make this realization by simply asking the right questions. Make them roleplay this out though. It's important for the heroes to make this cognitive leap. Otherwise, they might think that they've found Scott's body and simply give up! There's a lot more to this adventure, and we don't want them getting off the hook that easily.

The various pieces' different skin tones, bone sizes, and so on all points to a variety of "donors" having made up the man's body. Furthermore, some of the individual parts don't even appear human! The creature's large eye may have come from a dog or other such animal.

If the posse requests to further study the corpse and succeeds on a Hard (9) *persuasion* roll, Dunston allows an impromptu autopsy. Once they're done, he plans on leaving the body in another part of Ghost Town. The Mourning Brigade will find it around dawn.

Either way, an Onerous (7) *medicine* roll reveals that the man's heart was replaced by one from a large mammal such as a horse. A Hard (9) *medicine* roll tells the examiner the parts were all removed after the original "donors" had already died, and they'd likely been pickled in formaldehyde before being stitched together. Nothing else can be determined about the patchwork man. If you haven't already, see Chapter Five for more on patchwork science.

Empty His Pockets

If the posse asks to see the patchwork man's belongings, Dunston obliges. Even if they don't, the ex-marshal shows the items to the heroes. It's pretty important they get a look at the items, since this is where they find their next lead.

All the man had on him at the time of capture was a bloody kitchen knife stuck into his waistband, a couple of seashells (he picked this up while wandering toward town), and a pocket watch that plays a snippet of Bach's Brandenburg Concerto No. 3 when opened. The watch has an inscription inside the cover that says simply "R. Leeson."

The patchwork man was fascinated by the musical watch and took it from the doctor after killing him.

Dr. Leeson, I Presume?

The quickest way to determine the identity and location of the owner of the watch is to succeed at a Hard (9) *streetwise* or *area knowledge: Lost Angels* roll. This takes from one to four hours of talking to storekeepers or saloon owners. At the end of this time, the heroes have learned of two individuals named Leeson with a first name beginning with the letter "R."

One of the two is Roberta Leeson, a seamstress on the Third Circle. While the stitching on the patchwork man may make the posse a little suspicious, this 62-year-old spinster is completely innocent. The other is Dr. Richard Leeson, who owns a small spread of land along the highlands on the coast north of Lost Angels.

The posse can also gather this information from the deeds in the town records, although it's a little tougher. First, a bribe of at least $15 must be paid to the theocratic clerk in City Hall to gain access to the records. Then, it takes an Onerous (7) *Knowledge* roll and six hours of combing deeds and documents to uncover the names.

If all else fails, Dunston and his contacts in the Gridders identify the owner after a day or so of investigating. Given the heroes' vested interest, the Dunston invites them along when he and his friends head to Leeson's home. They want to know what Leeson has to do with attacks on the Men of the Grid (which is nothing, but they don't know that). This means that the heroes are going to have to work around a few Gridders, but the extra firepower might come in handy in this situation.

Castle Leeson

It's actually more of a one-story frame house, but Leeson chose as remote a locale for the home as he could. Located atop a cliff overlooking the crashing surf of the Maze below, the nearest neighbor is easily a half mile or more away. The only approach to the house is along a trail that hugs the cliff face a good 40 feet above the waves.

The house itself is fairly nondescript, except for a large lightning rod protruding from the north wall of the building. A small porch runs around the other three walls of the house, and the front door is closed and locked. A quick search reveals the back door is broken open. It allows entrance to a small, L-shaped hall. A Fair (5) *Cognition* roll tells the heroes the door was broken from the inside.

Foyer/Sitting Room: A small couch, an armchair, and an end table are the only furnishings in this room. An oil lamp, its wick burned out, sits atop the table.

Study: A desk and a chair are in the center of this room, and the walls are lined with bookshelves. A cursory examination of the books reveals the majority deal with biology, chemistry, and medical science. The desk itself contains pens, ink, paper, and the like. A Fair (5) *search* roll turns up a pair of keys in one of the desk drawers. It's to the laboratory and the caverns below.

A calendar sits atop the desk. Anyone examining it finds a number of dates marked with "A. Platt." The most recent was about two weeks ago. The next date so marked is tomorrow night!

Bedroom: The door to this room stands ajar—mainly because a bloody hand is caught between it and the jamb! The hand belongs to the corpse of a middle-aged man who's been dead a couple of days. He was killed by deep and vicious stab wounds. An Onerous (7) *medicine* roll reveals that the wounds could have been made by the knife found on the patchwork man. Further search of the man turns up no identification, but the heroes do find a broken watch chain dangling from his vest pocket, as well as $45.

The rest of the room contains typical bedroom furnishings: a bed, closet, chest, and nightstand. On the nightstand is a well-read copy of Mary Shelley's *Frankenstein*.

Dining Room: This room is sparsely furnished. Only a small table and four chairs are in here. From the dust on the table, it doesn't appear Leeson ate here often.

The Heart

Kitchen: A small stove, a work table, and a couple of cabinets are in this room. The cabinets contain various foodstuffs, although much of it appears to have molded—most even before Leeson died. He was a mad scientist and a bachelor, after all!

Any hero who searches the foodstuffs and makes a Hard (9) *search* roll finds a roll of 20 $20 Union bills in the flour bin. This is where Leeson hid the last of his "research funds."

A knife-holder on the table has a conspicuous empty space from which the patchwork man took his weapon. A flight of rickety wooden stairs leads into the cellar from this room.

Cellar: This room has a dirt floor and walls. It's filled with boxes and crates of all shapes and sizes, but a moment's search finds all of them empty. An Onerous (7) *Smarts* check tells a hero there are more empty crates than furnishings in the house above! Most of Leeson's equipment was shipped in these containers.

A hero who makes Incredible (11) *Cognition* roll finds a concealed door in the west wall of the cellar. If the posse specifically looks for such a door, the roll is an Onerous (7) *search* instead. The key found in the study easily opens it, as does an Onerous (7) *lockpickin'* roll. The door

and lock can each withstand 50 points of damage from those heroes preferring a less-subtle approach.

Any hero who takes a moment to listen at the door before opening it can make an Onerous (7) *Cognition* roll. (Modifiers for hearing apply.) If she succeeds, she hears the sound of a few dogs snuffling at the door. There is no chance to hear this without actively stopping and attempting to do so!

Good Doggie!

Behind the door waits Leeson's most successful project: Cerberus, a patchwork dog. Cerberus was normally kept chained in the laboratory, but when the patchwork man escaped, he also freed the dog. Cerberus attacked him—only Leeson could control it, and he's dead—so the patchwork man trapped it behind the door.

The abomination has gone a couple of days without eating, and it's now *very* hungry! It immediately attacks when the door is opened. If no one heard the snuffling behind the door before opening it, the posse must roll for surprise against an Incredible (11) TN.

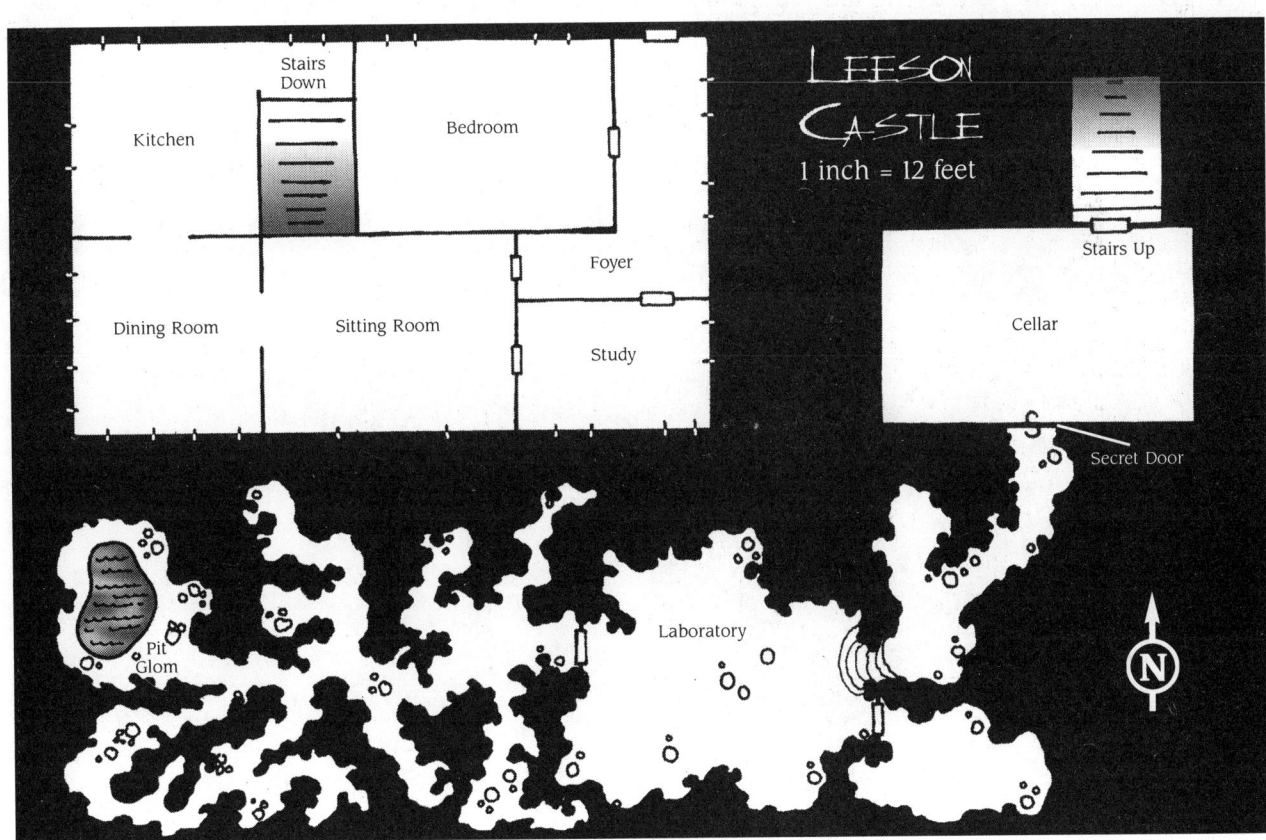

Leeson Castle
1 inch = 12 feet

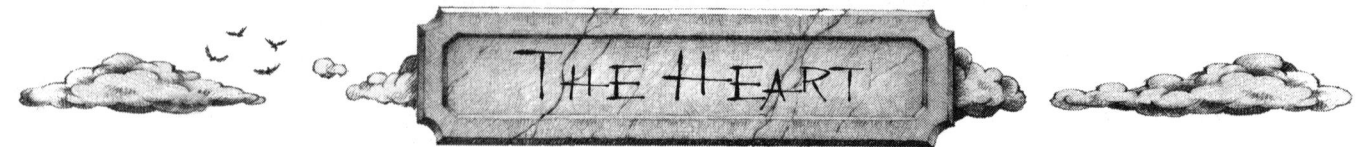

CERBERUS

Like the mythological guardian of Hades, Cerberus has three heads. Leeson grafted a pair of Doberman heads onto a full-grown wolfhound. He also augmented the animal's already powerful frame with muscles from a brown bear. Finally, he replaced many of the abomination's teeth with those from a crocodile.

Large patches of muscles are visible on the animal, as Leeson was unable to cover the added muscle adequately. He also had to completely remove the creature's lips after he discovered the new teeth tended to tear through the flesh.

The three heads snarl, growl, and bark at posse members independent of each other. All told, this is one very unattractive pooch!

PROFILE

Corporeal: D:1d4, N:3d8, Q:3d10, S:3d10, V:2d12
Fightin': brawlin' 4d8, sneak 3d8
Mental: C:3d4, K:2d6, M:2d10, Sm:3d6, Sp:2d6
Guts 4d6, overawe 4d10, scrutinize 3d4, search 3d4, trackin' 6d4
Pace: 8
Size: 6
Terror: 9

Special Abilities:
Damage: Bite (STR+1d8). Each head can bite on each action. Usually all bites are directed at a single target, although if surrounded, Cerberus may attack multiple targets.
Knockdown: In addition to its bites, Cerberus can attempt to knock a human-sized target off its feet. This is a contest of *Strength*. If Cerberus gets a raise on its victim, the victim is on his back and suffers a –4 to all *fightin'* rolls. Additionally, the dog gets a +2 to its attacks against a prone target.
Three Heads Are Better than One: Unless the attacker targets a specific head, any head shot hits a random head.
Undead (Patchwork): The creature can only be killed if each of its parts are maimed. In this case, this means that all three heads must be maimed, as well as its guts (where the bear muscles were added).

THE LABORATORY

A short passageway leads into Leeson's secret laboratory. The area is unlit (better hope the posse's got a light!) and in a shambles. Part of the destruction was wrought by the patchwork man's escape, and the rest was by Cerberus. Broken beakers and bottles lie about the floor, and several work tables are overturned. Surgical tools are scattered about the room.

Two doors lead from the room. One has been burst asunder. It opens into a small cell with straw on the floor. This was the patchwork man's pen. The second is locked and can be opened with the key from the study or a Fair (5) *lockpickin'* roll. The lock to this door can also be broken open with 30 points of damage from a gun or the like.

On a counter along one wall, various limbs and a torso are suspended by hooks and cable. Tubes running to each appear to be circulating formaldehyde through the body parts. (This is why Cerberus didn't eat them.) The torso belonged to a man, and an Onerous (7) *medicine* roll tells a hero for certain the hands on the patchwork man came from this body. The posse has found the remains of Butler Scott.

The cause of Scott's death is obvious. There is a gaping hole in his chest where his heart should be! A Hard (9) *medicine* roll reveals that the wound was caused by a very sharp, but large and primitive instrument. Any hero gutsy enough to dig around in the dead man's empty chest finds a small, sharp piece of obsidian if he succeeds on an Onerous (7) *search* roll.

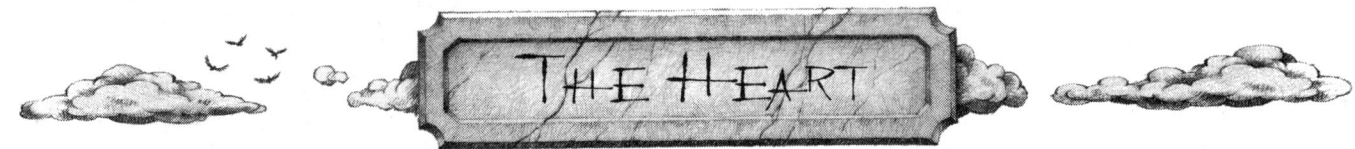
Leeson doesn't have any personal belongings for any of his "subjects." Scott's, in particular, are in the treasury of the Aztec temple complex.

Have any hero searching the rest of the room make a Fair (5) *search* roll. If she's successful, she discovers a small ledger underneath one of the overturned tables. It's badly damaged by spilled formaldehyde and other liquids, but it appears to be a record of Leeson's experiments.

Leeson's Journal

Most of the book is illegible, and only a few pages can be read. Even these short passages are disgusting enough to force a Fair (5) *guts* check. A hero who manages to keep her lunch down finds a reference near the end to the difficulty Leeson had obtaining "materials" for his experiments.

The city graveyard is particularly well-guarded by Grimme's followers, so the obvious source of supply was denied him. Then Leeson made contact with a one-legged man named Asa Platt, who began providing bodies for him. Leeson made appointments to meet with Platt at a deserted warehouse in the Waterfront District on a regular basis. There is also a smudged and crudely drawn map to the warehouse.

What's Behind Door #2?

The locked door opens into a small natural cave complex. Leeson stumbled onto the caves while excavating his laboratory. He used a small pit he discovered back near the rear of the caverns as a dumping ground for his leftover parts. After he began hearing strange sounds in the pit, Leeson added the locked door and began dumping the remains over the side of the cliff into the Maze instead.

The caverns are empty except for the pit of remains in the back. Anyone who makes a Fair (5) *Cognition* roll finds an obvious trail leading directly to and from the pit. Shining a light into the pit is a bad idea because it provokes the critter inside to scuttle up the walls and attack. There's nothing in the pit but the abomination.

The Pit 'Glom

The body parts have melded together into a small, but especially disgusting form of 'glom. (See *Rascals, Varmints & Critters* for more on the original variety.) This abomination incorporates not only human bodies, but also those of animals and even an abomination or two. Arms, legs, heads, and other unidentifiable parts stick out from the central mass of torsos and viscera.

Unlike normal 'gloms, the pit 'glom can't add complete bodies to its mass—only severed parts like Leeson's leftovers. However, this bizarre mishmash of components has made it stronger and tougher than its size would indicate.

Profile

Corporeal: D:2d6, N:2d8, Q:2d10, S:2d12+2, V:2d12+2
Fightin': brawlin', club 6d8, sneak 4d8
Mental: C:2d10, K:1d6, M:1d12, Sm:1d6, Sp:1d8
Overawe 5d12
Pace: 8
Size: 10
Terror: 11
Special Abilities:
   Damage: Claw (STR+1d6)
   Damage Resistance: This creature is very difficult to seriously damage. The core brain for the creature is buried so deeply, a stray shot has no chance of penetrating to it. For this reason, it takes a total of 10 wounds to the guts to drop this critter.
   Multiple Attacks: The monster can make up to three *fightin'* attacks on each of its actions. However, only two of these can be directed at a single opponent.
   Undead.

Troubleshooting

There aren't too many places for the posse to get sidetracked in this chapter. Dunston is the prime candidate for keeping the plot from derailing badly. If the heroes don't find Leeson, Dunston and his friends lead them to the scientist's laboratory. Again, should the heroes miss the clues to Asa Platt and the meet (see Chapter Three), the Gridders uncover them and casually bring them to the posse's attention.

If you don't feel like using the Gridders, you can always rely on the posses' employer. Hellstromme's got dozens of people in the city. While they aren't going to expose themselves too much for fear of discovery by Grimme's thugs, they can nudge the posse in the right direction if the heroes lose the trail.

Bounty

Finding Leeson's identity without Dunston's help: 1 white chip each.
Defeating Cerberus: 1 white chip each.
Defeating the pit 'glom: 1 red chip each.
Discovering Platt's name and the upcoming rendezvous: 1 blue chip.

CHAPTER THREE: CULTURE SHOCK

The heroes are on the verge of discovering the fate of Butler Scott and the whereabouts of his journal. Their only link, however, is the name of Leeson's ghoulish supplier. Fortunately, they have a day to recover from the horrific encounters at Leeson's laboratory and plan their strategy.

THE MEET

The warehouse where Platt and Leeson scheduled their meetings is perfect for conducting business away from prying eyes. None of the few other businesses in the area are open after dark, and the warehouse itself is unlocked. (It's owned by Hellstromme Industries coincidentally, although this has nothing to do with the plot. It's just one of life's little ironies.)

Platt arrives around midnight. He draws a rickety, old handcart behind him, and there's a crumpled form lying under a sheet in the back.

Even if the heroes have been working with Dunston, he asks them to try to capture Platt. He's called in plenty of favors from the Gridders for this escapade already, and he's not willing to risk their lives for this. He also hints it might be a good way to repay him for all the assistance he's provided the posse so far.

The heroes can approach the meet in several ways.

Ambushing the body snatcher is one route. Platt has been supplying corpses for a couple of months now and has gotten a little complacent, so getting the drop on him isn't that difficult. As long as no one goes bust on a *sneak* roll, the man doesn't notice the heroes until they spring the trap. Platt's a weasel and a coward, not a fighter, so if he doesn't have a clear escape route, the man surrenders to any show of force.

The heroes can also try to bluff their way into his confidence. If the heroes have a convincing story, roll a contest of *persuasion* or *bluff* versus Platt's *scrutinize*.

As long as only one or two cowpokes are visible when he arrives, Platt's willing to do business. If there are more than that, he tries to drive nonchalantly past the warehouse.

The posse may decide to simply tail Platt. Unfortunately, this doesn't accomplish much. The wharf rat takes his wagon down to the docks and dumps the body into the water. Then he heads to a seedy bar in the Waterfront and proceeds to drink himself into a stupor.

TALKING TO PLATT

Once the posse confronts Platt, he's initially reluctant to admit anything. A quick look on the back of his wagon turns up a fairly fresh corpse of a woman. Once this has been exposed, his resistance is short-lived. Any mention of turning him over to the Guardians gets him to blab.

Platt immediately blames Leeson for any wrongdoing, claiming he thought the man was a legitimate medical researcher. Platt is actually innocent of any crime (in this matter) other than body-snatching. The posse should quickly realize he's much too lily-livered to actual attack anyone to create the cadavers himself.

Anyone examining the corpse in the back of the wagon finds it is almost naked and has a wound in her chest similar to that found in Scott's torso. There are a few strands of seaweed in her hair, and the smell of saltwater is pretty strong around the corpse.

If he's asked where he gets the corpses, Platt readily confesses to finding them in a small cave to the south of Lost Angels. The cave, which he calls "the blowhole," is somehow connected to the waters of the Maze, and occasionally bodies wash up into it with the tide. He also confirms that all the bodies have similar chest wounds. Platt has no idea how they happened.

Platt's not thrilled about revealing his source, but he knows the jig is up on his ghoulish business. If asked, he agrees to take the heroes to the cave—provided they go now. Regardless of any assurances, he's pretty sure the heroes intend to turn him over to the authorities eventually, and he plans to leave town tonight!

If the heroes don't agree to leave now, they can threaten or bribe Platt to wait however they want, but short of being locked up, nothing keeps the man around until daylight.

ASA PLATT

Corporeal: D:2d8, N:3d6, Q:2d6, S:2d6, V:3d6
Dodge 4d6, sneak 5d6
Mental: C:2d6, K:2d6, M:2d4, Sm:2d8, Sp:3d4
Guts 2d4, scrutinize 2d6, search 4d6, streetwise 5d6
Edges: Eagle eyes
Hindrances: Habit (chewing tobacco) 1, yeller
Pace: 6
Wind: 10
Gear: A wagon, a lantern, a bottle of cheap whiskey, and $25 dollars in mixed Union and Confederate currency.
Description: A weedy man with stringy black hair and a habit of mumbling his words.

Thar She Blows!

About a quarter mile south of Lost Angels, just about where the ground begins to rise toward the cliffs lining the South Channel of the Maze, lies Platt's small tidal cave. If Platt guides the posse there, the journey takes only about 20 minutes or so.

If the posse is looking for the cave with directions but without the benefit of a guide, it's a little tougher. After every 20 minutes searching, allow the heroes to each make a Hard (9) *search* roll. Once a cowpoke succeeds, he finds a small, sheltered cave heading down and back into the rocks of the coast.

The cave is about three feet wide and between five and seven feet high and extends out of sight. A good two to three feet of water cover most of the floor, even during low tide. At high tide, the cave is completely submerged. In fact, water often shoots forcibly out of it when the tide rolls in, hence Platt's name for it: "the blowhole." When low tide occurs is up to you, Marshal, but we recommend making it as inconvenient for the posse as possible!

Under no circumstances, short of being prodded at gunpoint, does Platt enter the cave. Dunston and his Gridders go along only if he knows about the nature of Scott's report. Otherwise, he tells the posse that, since its obvious by now that there's no danger of the Gridders being exposed, it's no longer any of his concern.

The rocks under the water are uneven and jagged, and any hero walking down the cave must make a Fair (5) *Nimbleness* roll or plant a foot wrong and take 1d6+3 damage to a leg. If the character goes bust on this roll, the damage is 2d6+3.

After 10 minutes of fighting and crawling through the sea cave, the posse reaches the edge of the Aztec Cavern map (see page 125). The posse finds the badly decayed remains of four other victims washed up on the sandy areas of the passage.

Each of the waterlogged corpses has the same gory wound to its chest, and many have been worked over by hungry animals. (There's not a whole lot of meat to be found in these parts—even for the local fauna.)

A Fair (5) *medicine* roll reveals to the successful hero that a really big critter—along the lines of a massive shark or worse—made off with a fair portion of one of the bodies. This, of course, was the work of the Maze dragon known to Alquezar as Quetzalcoatl.

Out of the Hole & Into the Fire

A little over a hundred or so feet beyond the sandy areas of this passage, the blowhole opens onto a ledge in a massive cave. The ledge sits at water level during low tide. To the left of where the heroes enter the cave, a cliff rises 25 feet to a plateau.

The face of the cliff is very rough, and it's covered with ample foot- and handholds, so climbing the wall only requires a Foolproof (3) *climbin'* roll. Failing this roll means the cowpoke fumbles around for a couple of minutes and has to start over.

Going bust on the roll, however, drops the hero into the drink below! While the fall does 1d6+5 damage to the hero, at least the crashing of the surf masks the sound of the hero's splash from anyone who might be listening. Keeping afloat in the rough waves is an Onerous (7) *swimmin'* roll however!

Once the heroes have reached the clifftop, they are faced with an unexpected sight: a cave dominated by a miniature stepped pyramid, complete with an Aztec priest and a cadre of warriors!

PYRAMID O' DOOM

Fear Level 5

Alquezar has made the cavern as close a reconstruction of an Aztec temple as he can. Other than the obvious fact that it is underground, he's done a fairly good job. The entire chamber is well lit by enormous bonfires and torches around the cavern.

The Pyramid: The pyramid itself is 30 feet tall and steep walled. Steps ascend it on each of its four sides. However, these steps are very steep and narrow. Any hero attempting to run up the stairs must make a Fair (5) *Nimbleness* roll each round he's on the steps or tumble to the bottom, taking 2d6+10 damage from the fall.

The top of the pyramid has a large altar set near the edge of the plateau closest to the cave opening. Here, Alquezar performs his sacrifices before hurling the body down the steps and into the waters of the Maze.

Skull Mounds: At the base of the pyramid sits a scattered pile of picked-over skulls from early victims of the cult. Some of these are displayed on a rack, while others are stacked beneath. Dried skin is evident on a few of the skulls.

Sacrificial Poles: Occasionally, Alquezar has victims hung from these eight-foot poles. The sacrifices hang there until either they die from thirst or "Quetzalcoatl" stops by for a quick snack. Currently, there is only one living victim here, a sailor from Shan Fan captured in Lost Angels' Waterfront District.

Holding Pens: These are stout cells made by placing thick, wooden posts in the mouth of several natural caverns. Future sacrifices are kept here until needed by the cult. There are presently two victims awaiting their end. Both were recently captured in the city. Their identity isn't important. They can be sailors from the Waterfront district, gunslingers down on their luck, or you can use them for links to other, later adventures, Marshal.

Treasure Chamber: This room contains the clothes and personal effects of well over a hundred victims. Given the nature of most of the cult's victims, there really isn't much treasure to be had. A determined search takes a good two hours and turns up $133 Confederate, $128 Union, three derringers, two Peacemakers, an .44 Army pistol, 98 rounds of various calibers, two Bowie knives, and more boots and hats than a cowpoke can shake a feathered serpent at. Also, a Hard (9) *search* roll locates a sheaf of papers sewn into the lining of a jacket: Scott's report!

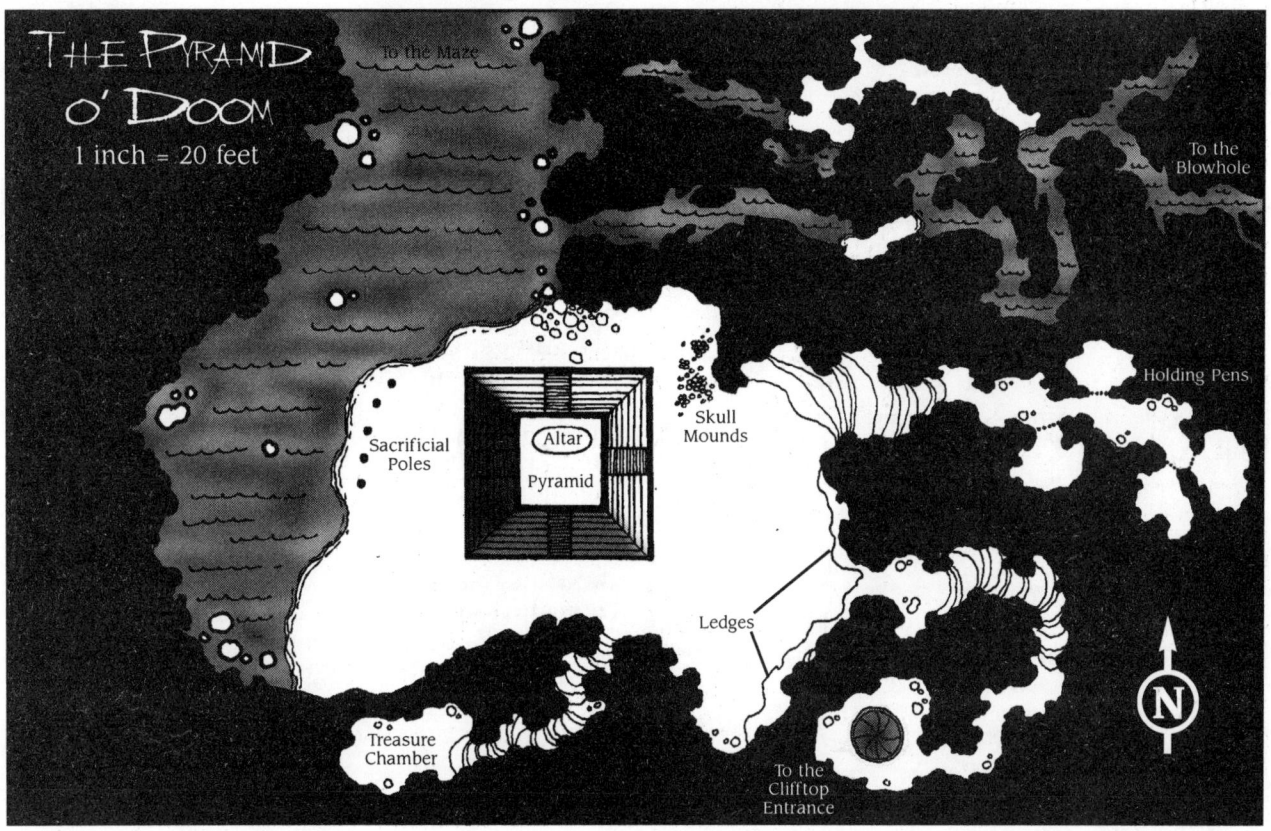

THE PYRAMID o' DOOM
1 inch = 20 feet

To the Maze

To the Blowhole

Holding Pens

Sacrificial Poles

Skull Mounds

Altar

Pyramid

Ledges

Treasure Chamber

To the Clifftop Entrance

N

NOT SO FAST!

Okay, we did give you the rundown on the chamber first, but the posse isn't going to get much of a chance to explore straight off. Alquezar, thanks to his *forewarnin'* spell (he's not only psychotic, he's paranoid to boot!), was warned of the heroes' approach, and he's got an ambush waiting for them.

Alquezar himself is hidden atop the pyramid, and he has Jaguar Knights scattered around the chamber. Some are over the side of the cliff near the sacrificial poles, a couple are in the holding pens, and so on.

The cave is peppered with hiding places, so feel free to have the pesky warriors pop up just about anywhere. The heroes are likely to be distracted by their first look at the temple anyway.

Once the posse moves up to about area of the skull mounds or begins to climb the pyramid, the Aztecs attack. Remember to have the heroes roll for surprise, but since they're probably on edge by now, the TN for the *Cognition* roll is only Fair (5). (They'd have to be pretty clueless to not be expecting something to happen when they poke around an Aztec temple.)

There are four Jaguar Knights scattered about the cave and temple, plus two for each posse member in the chamber (including Dunston and any Gridders who might be along too). Alquezar starts the combat with his *dark protection* already in place and hurls *bolts o' doom* at the posse from the top of the pyramid. He uses his *stun* spell (poison darts) against anyone who attempts to climb the steps.

At first, the Aztecs try to take the heroes captive rather than kill them. (They can use the sacrifices!) However, once the battle begins to turn against them, all bets are off.

Four rounds after the battle begins, the Aztecs get a bit of "divine" intervention. The Maze dragon Alquezar has come to worship as an avatar of Quetzalcoatl arrives. The abomination rears from the waves and attacks the hero closest to the cliff edge. Its great size allows it to reach nearly everywhere in the cavern. This is a fantastic time for a *guts* check!

After the Maze dragon enters the cavern, the fight is to the finish. The only way it ends is if the heroes defeat the Aztecs or somehow escape the chamber. Even if they do get away, Alquezar and his followers begin a fanatical hunt for the posse that can end only in death.

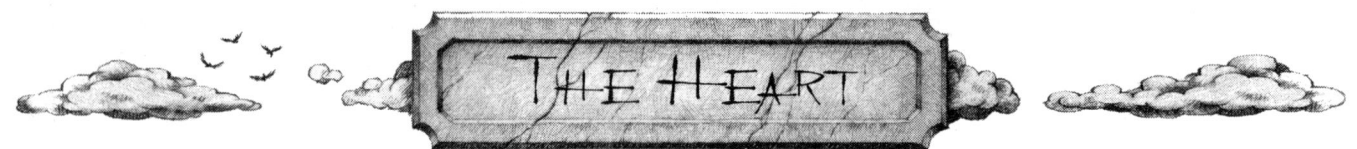

The Heart

Alquezar

Once a member of a secret Mexican cult, Alquezar has been warped by the influence of Lost Angels. He now believes himself to be the last true follower of the Aztec beliefs and that only his sacrifices forestall the end of the world.

Alquezar follows many of the more horrific practices of ancient Aztec priests. He paints all exposed skin on his body black. He never washes the blood of his victims from his hair. He even ties small bones or bits of flesh into his snarled locks. His temples are constantly bloody from auto-sacrificial wounds.

On feast days, Alquezar flays a victim alive and wears her skin inside-out like a cloak for as long as 20 days. Other times, he wears a black and green cloak to denote his status as a priest.

Alquezar has a strange pendant around his neck. It resembles his obsidian knife, but it has jagged saw-teeth instead of a surgical edge like his sacrificial blade. Actually, it's a key to a part of a temple belonging to his old Mexican cult down south, although he never intends to return. This key may prove useful to the heroes should they become embroiled in events in the upcoming *South o' the Border*.

Profile

Corporeal: D:2d6, N:2d8, Q:3d8, S:3d6, V:4d10
Fightin': knife 6d8, sneak 5d8, throwin': bolts o' doom 4d6
Mental: C:4d8, K:1d8, M:2d10, Sm:3d8, Sp:2d12
Academia: Aztec history 5d8, faith: black magic 5d12, guts 3d12, overawe 4d10, scrutinize 2d8
Pace: 8
Wind: 22
Terror: 5 (His appearance is pretty unsettling!)
Special Abilities:
    Damage: Obsidian knife (STR+1d6).
    Black Magic Spells: *Bolts o' doom* 2 (burning hearts from the altar fire; only usable from pyramid), *cloak o' evil* 4 (heat waves blur his form; usable only on pyramid), *forewarnin'* 2 (reading entrails), *pact* 5 (with the Maze dragon he worships), *stun* 3 (poison darts with maximum range of 5 yards).
Gear: His cloak, his necklace key, and that's it.
Description: He's covered with blood and black paint, and he's got bits of bone tied into his long, dark, natty hair. He snarls when he talks.

Jaguar Knights

These are cultists are each armed with a macautl: a wooden sword imbedded with wicked pieces of obsidian. They wear a light armor made from a hardened cloth boiled in brine.

When possible, the Jaguar Knights seek to take enemies captive for later sacrifice. They target an opponent's legs or arms with their attacks, attempting to disable them or weaken them from blood loss and fatigue (Wind).

Jaguar Knights try to fight in pairs. Each trains extensively with a partner, and they are skilled in combat teamwork.

Profile

Corporeal: D:1d8, N:3d8, Q:2d10, S:2d8, V:3d10
Dodge 2d8, fightin': brawlin', sword 5d8, sneak 4d8
Mental: C:3d8, K:2d6, M:1d8, Sm:3d6, Sp:3d6
Guts 4d6, scrutinize 2d8, search 3d8
Pace: 8
Wind: 16
Special Abilities:
    Teamwork: As long as a Jaguar Knight is with his partner, he gets a +2 bonus to all *fightin'* rolls. Also, anyone attacking him in hand-to-hand combat receives a −2 to any *fightin'* roll.
Gear: A macautl (STR+2d6), a suit of brine-boiled cloth (Armor −4), and $10 each.

"Quetzalcoatl"

According to legend, the god Quetzalcoatl—often depicted as a feathered serpent—left the Aztec empire on an ocean voyage, promising to return one day. When the Spanish first landed in Aztec part of the New World, the Aztecs thought the Spanish leader was actually Quetzalcoatl, a fact which left them vulnerable to attack.

The brightly colored neck spines on this Maze dragon have convinced Alquezar the critter is an avatar of the god Quetzalcoatl. He believes the abomination is a sign of the gods' approval for his endeavor, and thanks to the black-magic spell *pact* that he's worked with the monstrous creature, it has become a powerful ally to the murderous priest.

If Alquezar is killed, the *pact* is ended, and the Maze dragon is free to leave whenever it likes.

Profile

Corporeal: D:1d4, N:2d10, Q:1d10, S:5d12+4, V:2d12+4
Fightin': brawlin' 4d10, sneak 5d10, swimmin' 5d10
Mental: C:2d10, K:1d4, M:1d12, Sm:1d6, Sp:1d4
Size: 24 (50 yards long)
Terror: 11
Special Abilities:
  Armor: 1
  Damage: Teeth (STR+2d12).
  Swallow: The dragon's mouth is large enough to swallow an unlucky cowpoke in a single gulp. With two raises on an attack, it gobbles down a man-sized target (Size 7 or less). The victim takes 4d6 points of damage to the guts every round from the crushing gullet and acidic bile. The only way out is to cut a hole (by doing 20 points of damage with a shotgun or a cutting weapon) and crawl through it.

Aftermath

Assuming the heroes defeat Alquezar and his allies, they have plenty of time to search the temple afterward, and they should be able to find Scott's papers. They can also find a passage at the back of the chamber that leads to a winding stairway that exits into a small, hidden cave high on a rocky hill south of Lost Angels.

If the heroes were successful in crushing Alquezar and his cult, it counts as defeating a fearmonger. The heroes have earned a point of Grit for their trouble. Although they've beaten the cultists on their home ground, they may yet face more conflicts, depending on how careful they were in their investigation.

If Dunston is onto Scott's mission, he and some Gridders confront the posse at this point and attempts to confiscate the documents. He isn't willing get into a gun battle with the heroes over it—after all, he is a good guy, and he's not really sure how important the papers are—but unless the heroes can come to some kind of an agreement with Dunston, bad blood is sure to develop here between them and the Gridders.

Should the heroes have somehow tipped the Angels off to their investigation, they've got a special welcoming party waiting just outside of town. Five Guardian Angels attempt to take the posse into custody, and they are loaded up and ready for a blazing gun battle. If the heroes surrender to the Angels or are taken alive, they're in for a long stay on Rock Island. Even if they defeat the Angels, they'd best take the old Heel-Toe Express out of the city if they leave any of their attackers alive.

In addition to all of this, the heroes may have taken the key from Alquezar. This could eventually lead them south of the border as noted earlier. Or the key's owners may come looking for their missing friend and their lost property.

Finally, even though Alquezar is dead, a number of cultists are still around. These folks may be more than just a little angry at the heroes for killing their spiritual leader, and they might come looking for some payback!

Troubleshooting

If the posse loses Platt before he has a chance to spill his guts on the blowhole, Dunston and his Gridder friends can pick up the weasel. If he has a chance to get away before he shows the heroes the cave entrance, the posse can find it as described above.

If the Aztecs prove too much for the posse and the heroes manage to escape, Dunston raids the cave the next day, his curiosity getting the better of him. By this time, the Aztecs have run off, although the goods are still in the treasure chamber—including Scott's papers. If this happens, the posse has picked up a new enemy in Alquezar.

Bounty

Getting the location of the blowhole from Platt: 1 white chip.
Recovering Scott's documents: 1 red chip.
Defeating Alquezar and the Jaguars: 1 red chip each.
Killing the Maze dragon: 1 blue chip each.

Don't Get Caught In The Same Old Web

Pinnacle Entertainment Group invites you to check out our Weird Website™ devoted to Deadlands™: The Weird West™, Deadlands: The Great Rail Wars™, and Deadlands: Hell on Earth™. We've crammed the site with sticky strands of tasty tidbits sure to please that ornery imagination, and we update the site regularly. So come on by and visit for a spell, or two, or three...

www.peginc.com

THE **WEIRD WEST** ™

ORIGINS AWARD WINNER — The Year's Best Games

HELL ON EARTH
The Wasted West Roleplaying Game ™

THE GREAT **RAIL WARS**
MINIATURES BATTLE GAME ™

ORIGINS AWARD WINNER — The Year's Best Games

™